COROMANDEL
SEA CHANGE

by the same author

COROMANDEL
SEA CHANGE

∎∎∎∎∎∎∎∎∎∎∎∎∎∎∎∎∎∎∎∎∎∎∎∎∎∎∎∎

Rumer Godden

William Morrow and Company, Inc.
New York

It is the policy of William Morrow and Company, Inc., and its imprints and affiliates, recognizing the importance of preserving what has been written, to print the books we publish on acid-free paper, and we exert our best efforts to that end.

Library of Congress Cataloging-in-Publication Data

Godden, Rumer, 1907–
    Coromandel sea change / by Rumer Godden.
        p.   cm.
    ISBN 0-688-10397-9
    I. Title.
    PR6013.O2C6   1991
    823'.912—dc 20   90-25847
                                                                    CIP

Printed in the United States of America

    2   3   4   5   6   7   8   9   10

BOOK DESIGN BY M & M DESIGNS

To Oscar—*Sir Owain Jenkins*—
my dear old "enemy," who has done
so much to help me

Acknowledgments

■ ■ ■ ■ ■ ■ ■ ■ ■ ■ ■ ■ ■ ■

My sincere thanks are due to Alan Maclean for his guidance over the book; my editor, Hazel Orme, for her constant care and patience; Tigger Stack for her expert help on Indian affairs and beliefs; Shahrakh Husain whose books and advice have been invaluable; Sir Owain Jenkins for his contribution of precious tidbits; and, as always, Ena Logan Brown and Sheila Anderson who typed and retyped without flagging.

R. G.

Contents

■ ■ ■ ■ ■ ■ ■ ■ ■ ■ ■ ■ ■ ■ ■

*"They come for the sea change," said
Auntie Sanni and she might have added . . .
"into something rich and strange."*

List of Characters

■ ■ ■ ■ ■ ■ ■ ■ ■ ■ ■ ■ ■ ■

Auntie Sanni	Miss Sanni to her servants, owner of Patna Hall
Colonel McIndoe	her husband

Staff at Patna Hall

Samuel	butler and majordomo
Hannah	his wife, housekeeper
Kuku	the young hotel manager
Thambi	lifeguard on the beach and general guard
Moses	lifeguards on the beach
Somu	
Ganga	the wine waiter
Mustafa	waiters
Abdul	
Ahmed	
Alfredo	the Goanese cook

houseboys, sweepers, a washerman, gardeners, etc.

For the election

Gopal Rau	candidate for the Patriotism Party
Mrs. Padmina Retty	candidate for the People's Shelter Party
Krishnan Bhanj	candidate for the Root and Flower Party
Dr. Hari Coomaraswamy	leader of the Root and Flower Party's campaign
Mr. Srinivasan	his aide
Sharma	their young district agent
Ravi	young party workers
Anil	
the disciples	other young men and women of the Root and Flower Party campaign

Guests at Patna Hall this week

Sir John and Lady (Alicia) Fisher	
Mrs. Olga Manning	
Professor Aaron	leader of the International Association of Art, Technology and Culture
Professor Ellen Webster	lecturer to the group
Mrs. van den Mar	leader of eighteen American lady archaeologists, professional and amateur
Mrs. Glover	archaeologists
Mrs. Schlumberger	
Julia Lovat	
Miss Pritt	
Mr. Menzies	
Blaise St. John Browne	on honeymoon
Mary Browne	

Others

Kanu	a small fisherboy

Shyama	Thambi's wife
Chief Inspector Anand	police officer
Krishna	god and goddesses
Radha	
Lakshmi	

Animals

Slippers	a donkey
Birdie	an elephant
Udata	a squirrel
Christabel	Auntie Sanni's mynah bird

Time

any time

Saturday

■ ■ ■ ■ ■ ■ ■ ■ ■ ■ ■ ■ ■ ■

Saturday was changeover day at Patna Hall.

"Two hundred sheets," shouted the *vanna*—the old washerman was close to weeping. "Two hundred pillowcases *and* the towels. That is too much."

"It is because of the election." Auntie Sanni was unmoved. "So many people coming and going besides our own guests."

Usually guests, as Auntie Sanni liked to call them, stayed at least a week or ten days, two weeks sometimes three, even three months like Mrs. Manning. Sheets were changed three times a week and always, of course, when a guest came or went, but now, "Too many," wailed the *vanna*.

"It is for the good of your country." Hannah, the Madrassi housekeeper, was always a reconciler; she also happened to be a strong partisan for the new and hopeful Root and Flower Party. "Don't you care for your country?"

"I care that I can't wash two hundred sheets."

"A contract is a contract." Auntie Sanni was unrelenting. "It does not say how many or how little. Take them and go."

"And none of your ironing without washing them first," sharp little Kuku put in.

"Wash them yourself," said the *vanna*, and left the bundles lying on the floor.

*   *   *

The three women in the linen room took no notice. They knew, as the *vanna* knew, that there were many *vannas* in Shantipur, even more in the port of Ghandara four kilometers away, all with swarming families, all poor; not one of them would let a contract with Patna Hall be taken from him. "He will soon be back," Hannah prophesied.

The linen room at Patna Hall was in a small cloistered courtyard built at the side of the main house for administrative offices and linen room, storerooms, a pantry or confectioner's room where Patna Hall's own specialist puddings and desserts were made with, nowadays, a refrigerating room. These were to be expected but Auntie Sanni's office was part business, part conservatory, part menagerie. The convolvulus blue of morning glory tumbled over the window, pots of canna lilies and hibiscus stood in corners; tame birds, cockatiels and mynahs, flew around the room. One mynah, Christabel, had learned to call Kuku so cleverly that Kuku never knew if it were Christabel or Auntie Sanni. There were doves; bright green parakeets flew in from the garden and mingled with them all—often they perched on Auntie Sanni's desk, watching her fearlessly, their scarlet-topped heads on one side. It was not only birds: two cats, tabbies, slept stretched on a mat in the sun; a brown-spotted goat was tethered outside while her kids wandered in and out, one white, one brown as if the colors had been divided. "But don't let the monkeys in," Hannah had warned Kuku, "they take too many things."

The monkeys were small, brown, and wild; their brown faces and bright eyes peered from the trees. They ran across the courtyard on all fours, their tails lifted, their small skinny hands quickly into anything—"and everything," said Hannah—and always, all through rooms and cloister, the soft Indian sea breeze blew bringing the sound of the waves crashing on the beach below.

*   *   *

Auntie Sanni—Miss Sanni to her staff and servants—was called Auntie because in Eurasian parlance that is the title given to any grown-up female whether she has nephews and nieces or not. Auntie Sanni had none by blood but, over the years, had acquired many—Auntie of the universe would have fitted her. She dominated the linen room as she dominated Patna Hall. "Why?" Kuku often wondered. To her Auntie Sanni was only an unattractive massive old woman, nobody knew how old. "No shape to her at all," said Kuku, looking at her in one of her usual cotton dresses like a tent reaching to her feet, its voluminous folds patterned with blue flowers; Auntie Sanni called them her "Mother Hubbards" from the garments missionaries used to hand out to the natives. On her feet were country-made sandals. Auntie Sanni's face looked young because of her head of short curls like a child's, their red still auburn. Her skin was true Eurasian, the pale yellow brown of old ivory against which her eyes looked curiously light, sea-color eyes, now green, now blue, set wide, again like a child's, but Hannah, even Kuku, could have told that Auntie Sanni was no child.

Hannah, almost her bondswoman, began piling the bundles tidily together, her silver bangles slipping up and down her arms. Hannah liked everything to be tidy, clean, exact, as did her husband, Samuel. They, for Auntie Sanni, were the twin pillars of Patna Hall.

Hannah was a big woman—though not beside Auntie Sanni. Kuku, when she was with them, looked wand slim, quick and brilliant as a kingfisher in her electric blue sari with its lurex border. Hannah had eyed that sari. "Muslin for morning is nice," she had said, "and practical."

"This, too, is practical," Kuku had retorted. "It is drip-dry."

Hannah herself wore a crisp white sari edged with red and an old-fashioned red bodice high in the neck, her scant gray hair pinned into a knob. In spite of this simplicity she was laden with silver jewelry: bangles; the lobes of her ears hung down with the weight of earrings; she had finger rings and toe rings on her gnarled bare feet; everyone knew where Hannah was by the sound of clinking. Kuku's *choli* stopped in a curve under breasts that were young and full, it left her midriff bare, supple, and brown; her hair which could have made the usual graceful coil was instead frizzed into a mane that reached her shoulders; she had a flower over her left ear. "Miss Sanni, why let her go about so?" Hannah often said to Auntie Sanni. "That hair! Those nails! And a sari should be muslin, silk, or gauze," and Auntie Sanni always answered, "I don't think Kuku has saris like that."

Kuku was an orphan, brought up in St. Perpetua's Home in Madras. "St. Perpetua's, very good," Hannah had always maintained. She and Samuel were English-speaking Thomist Christians. "St. Thomas, apostle, came to Madras and is buried there," they said. Kuku, though, was now proudly agnostic. No one knew what Auntie Sanni believed; perhaps all religions met in her as they met peaceably in Patna Hall; the gardeners were Brahmins, the sweeper women, Untouchables, the waiters, all Muslim while the head bearer, Colonel McIndoe's personal servant from Nepal, was a Buddhist. Nothing seemed to disturb any of them and, "Yes, St. Perpetua's is very good," Auntie Sanni endorsed Hannah. "It gives all its girls an excellent education and trains them for work but I don't think they get many saris."

Kuku had been trained in hotel management. "I didn't have to be trained," said Auntie Sanni. "I knew."

Auntie Sanni's grandfather had started the hotel in the eighteen nineties but the house was older than that, "Built by some nabob of the East India Company in the eighteenth century to catch the sea breezes," she had told Kuku.

"Could they have come so far without cars or the railway?"

"Far from Calcutta but there were plenty of East India Company men in Madras. They would have had horses and palanquins."

"What are palanquins?" asked Kuku.

"My grandfather made a fortune out of indigo in Bihar," Auntie Sanni would tell the guests. "That's why the hotel is called Patna Hall. Patna is the capital of Bihar." She herself had never seen the acres of the leafy flowering shrub that brought such riches as, processed—"My grandfather had his own factory"—the flowers turned from olive to orange and finally to the intense blue of indigo. "All sailors' livery used to be dyed with it, all blue cloth until chemical dyes became rife." "Rife" as Auntie Sanni said it was a dirty word. "My grandfather got out just in time. They were lovely colors, indigo, madder, sepia, those greens and turmeric yellows," she said softly. "It is seldom nowadays that you get colors like that."

Patna Hall was the only substantial house on that stretch of the Coromandel coast; its stucco, as befitted the property of an indigo planter, was painted blue, now faded to paleness; it rose three stories high to a parapeted roof. The porticoed entrance faced inward toward the village of Shantipur with its palms and *simile* trees, their cotton flowers scarlet; behind them low hills, where coffee grew, cut off the horizon. There were servants' quarters, the courtyard offices, a gatehouse, a large vegetable garden, a small farm and poultry yard, even a private cemetery.

On the other side of the house facing the sea, a garden of English and Indian flowers sloped to a private beach that had a bungalow annex. On every side dunes of fine white sand stretched away, planted with feathery casuarina trees; on the right the dunes led to a grove of mango and more *simile* trees; on the left they rose to a knoll that overlooked the demesne. On the foreshore of hard sand, the great rollers of the Coromandel Sea thundered down, giant waves that rose to eight, even ten feet, before they crashed sending a wash far up the sand. Farther out, by day, the sea was a deep sapphire blue.

The hotel beach was forbidden to fishermen or their boats; indeed, the sea there was netted to a distance of five hundred yards not only against fishermen but sharks; every night Thambi, the lifeguard, and his assistants, Moses and Somu, unfolded a high strong-meshed fence across the private beach padlocking it so that the beach was cut off from the sea. "Unless there is bathing by moonlight," said Thambi.

"Please," Auntie Sanni would say seriously to each guest, "please remember it is dangerous to go out alone to bathe. With the force and power of those waves, you must take a guard."

Women bathers usually had to have a man on each side to hold them and bring them up through the wave to ride gloriously back on its crest of surf. Thambi would let no one go into it without wearing one of the fishermen's pointed wicker helmets bound firmly under the chin; the helmet's peak would pierce the waves that otherwise might stun. "Ours is not a gentle sea," said Auntie Sanni, "and please," she said again to her guests, "no one must swim unless Thambi is on the beach."

Patna Hall looked tall from the beach, the blue of its stucco ornamented with decorations of scrolls and flowers like daisies, oddly inconsequential. The flat roof was bounded by its balustraded parapet, which had a wide ledge on which young adventurous guests liked to sit. At night the house lights shone far across the sea; a small glow came, too, from the gatehouse where Thambi and his wife, Shyama, lived. Thambi was another of Auntie Sanni's right hands, hotel guard as well as beach lifeguard; it was Shyama who was supposed to open and shut the gates but as they were always open she had nothing to do except to cook a little, dry chilies in the sun, and wash her hair. "Lazy little slut," said Kuku. "Thambi ought to beat her."

"I thought you were a feminist."

"I am but I don't like to see her."

"I do," said Auntie Sanni with a vision of the scarlet of the chilies and the blue-black hair.

Overlooking garden and sea, verandas ran the full length of the house above a basement of cellars and fuel stores that was half buried in sand. The lower veranda was the sitting place for the whole hotel, with cane chairs and tables, cane stools, and old-fashioned steamer chairs with extended boards on each side on which feet could comfortably be put up. There was a bar at one end; at the other, Auntie Sanni's swing couch had bright chintz covers and cushions; before lunch—which she called *tiffin*—and before dinner she liked to sit there and reign.

Inside, behind the veranda the rooms were high, floored with dark red stone which Samuel saw was polished; every morning a posse of village women came in to sit on the floor moving slowly forward on their bottoms as they pushed bottles, their ends wrapped in a waxed cloth, until the stone shone. The upper air was stirred by *punkahs*—electric flat-bladed fans; when the sea breeze was strong they stirred by themselves. If the wind was too high, sand blew in over the floors to Samuel's grief.

There was a billiard room; though few houseguests played billiards, gentlemen, chiefly Indian, came in from Ghandara to play and have drinks—there was a bar in the billiard room as well. The veranda was reserved for resident guests.

The drawing room, away from the sea, was immense, a double room; the stone floor here was green. It was so little used that the electric fans overhead creaked when they were switched on. "So much empty space," mourned Kuku.

"Which is always useful," said Auntie Sanni, "and

makes for peace and health, two things that are uncommon in this country which is why people come."

Hannah reigned over the bedrooms with, under her,
not women servants but men, bearers or houseboys in
brass-buttoned white tunics, white trousers, black caps,
while Samuel was king of the dining room behind the
veranda.

Samuel was regal, white-whiskered, white-bearded,
his clothes immaculately white and starched, his turban
huge with, around it, a red-and-gold band on which, in
brass, was Auntie Sanni's family crest—"My grandfather's
crest." The waiters wore modest imitations—woe betide
any of them who had a spot or smudge on their tunics or
trousers.

The food was delectable, the service unhurried; neither Auntie Sanni nor Samuel had heard of unions and,
though luncheon was served at one, dinner at eight, the
dining room kept no hours. The food was brought in from
the cookhouse outside; in the magical way of Indian servants it was kept hot by the old-fashioned use of packing
cases lined with zinc in which were gridded shelves with
a brazier burning red below.

From the first day she came there had been battles
between Kuku and Samuel. "Always objecting. Never do
as she is asked. Why not?" demanded Samuel.

"I suppose an orphan girl without money has to
fight," said Auntie Sanni. "Poor little Kuku. She hasn't
learned that the best way to fight is by not fighting. Also,
we are getting old, Samuel, perhaps we need fresh
blood"—and, seeing disbelief in his eyes—"but I think
Kuku will soon go on to something else, she won't be
satisfied here. Besides St. Perpetua's asked me to take her.
Kuku needs a chance."

"I think we are full up," said Auntie Sanni in her office
this Saturday morning.

"Full up! My God!" Kuku had brought the ledger from

the reception desk in the hall. "I don't know where to put them all."

"Let me see." Auntie Sanni opened the big register. There were, of course, permanencies, in chief, Colonel McIndoe, Auntie Sanni's husband, though no one called her Mrs. McIndoe. They had a suite on the first floor overlooking the sea. There was Kuku's small room on the floor above. "The first room I have ever had of my own," she had exclaimed in delight when she came. Samuel and Hannah had their own neat house, kept apart from the other servants' quarters by a hedge of poinsettias. "Let me see," said Auntie Sanni.

"Sir John and Lady Fisher?" Kuku peered over her shoulder.

"Number one," said Hannah immediately.

"They are our oldest, dearest guests." Auntie Sanni's voice dropped into a singsong which, like most Eurasians, she did not recognize as part Indian though it made Kuku wince—Kuku had tried to acquire an American accent. "Sir John says they can only stay a week this time. You will put flowers in their room and fruit and order a taxi to meet the connection from Delhi.

"Professor Aaron and his ladies . . ."

"Eighteen of them," added Hannah.

"One tourist professor, eighteen tourist ladies!" Kuku giggled but Hannah looked at her severely. "This is Patna Hall," said the look. "We don't take tourists."

Auntie Sanni explained, "It is a cultural group. The International Association of Art, Technology and Culture. Professor Aaron brings a group every year, sometimes for archaeology, sometimes it is botany. Sometimes there are men but all are highly qualified. Last year the group was French, this year they are American."

"Americans are the worst tourists," said Kuku.

"You say that because you have heard it." For once Auntie Sanni was wrathful. "What do you know about it? The British can be every bit as bad, also the Germans, and you will not call these ladies tourists, do you hear? Some of them themselves are professors."

"Old?" asked Kuku without interest.

"Usually middle-aged. Young people haven't the time or money—the tours are very expensive."

"They come from all over," said Hannah. "They will bring books, notebooks, maps, binoculars, magnifying glasses, cameras, what all."

"This time it is archaeology. They will visit the new diggings at Ghorāghat, also the cave paintings in our own hills but, especially, the great Dawn Temple at Ghorāghat, the temple of Usas, the Dawn Goddess." Auntie Sanni, who had never seen the Dawn Temple, still said it reverently, then, "A single for Professor Aaron," she said, returning to the ledger. "Nine doubles for the ladies, they will not mind sharing. They are usually not fussy," she told Kuku.

"Mr. R. Menzies," Kuku read out. "He does not say when he is arriving."

"Well, then, we cannot meet him. Give him a first-floor back, and later tonight, Dr. Coomaraswamy and Mr. Srinivasan will be here."

"What again?"

"Of course." Hannah at once grew heated. "Isn't Dr. Coomaraswamy the leader of our campaign? Isn't Mr. Srinivasan his aide? Isn't this the week of the election? The campaign starts tomorrow. Of course they are all coming back."

"Except Krishnan Bhanj, your candidate," said Kuku.

That slowed Hannah. "I do not know why," she said, "so often he has stayed here since he was a little boy, he and his parents, very good high-up people. He was here last month. Why not now?"

"No one knows but Krishnan," said Auntie Sanni, "and we can be sure he knows why."

"God almighty Krishnan!" mocked Kuku. "He's not

going to win you know. It said so on the radio. Padmina Retty has held the seat for so long. Mrs. Retty, Mother to the People of Konak."

"Much good has it done them." Hannah was fierce.

"Krishnan Bhanj is an upstart. They all say so."

"Hardly an upstart," said Auntie Sanni. "Krishnan has been in politics since the day he was born, but in any case, I could not have had Mrs. Retty here with Dr. Coomaraswamy. He booked first. Also, with him," Auntie Sanni told them, "will be at least ten, maybe twenty young electioneering assistants."

"My God!" but Auntie Sanni was unperturbed. "They will be out on the campaign all day and they can sleep in Paradise."

Paradise was a line of cell-like rooms on Patna Hall's roof. Once upon a time European or American chauffeurs were put there, now and again ladies' maids. "When we had people from the embassies," said Auntie Sanni, and, of the men, "They are young. They can sleep three or four to a room. Buy *charpoys*," she ordered Kuku.

"Mrs. Manning?" asked Kuku.

There was a pause, then, "She stays where she is," said Auntie Sanni.

"Taking up two rooms when we are so full and she hasn't paid for a month!"

"I think she cannot pay at present," said Auntie Sanni.

"Manning Memsahib is not like a memsahib," said Hannah. "She washes her own things in the bathroom to save the *vanna*'s bill."

That seemed sense to Kuku. "We were encouraged to do that at St. Perpetua's."

"You are you," Hannah's look said plainly.

"Mrs. Manning still orders whiskey, your whiskey . . ." Kuku came out against Mrs. Manning. "Olga," she mocked. "I thought only Russians were called Olga and showing off with the piano.'' If Kuku had admitted to what had hurt and rankled in her with Mrs. Manning it was that Olga Manning had called her ''housekeeper.''

''The housekeeper is Hannah. I am hotel manager.''

''Indeed!'' The hazel eyes had looked at her amused. ''How long have you been that?'' and, ''Six weeks,'' Kuku had had to say, and now, ''Where is Mr. Manning, I should like to know?'' she asked.

''Kuku, we do not pry into our guests' affairs.''

''Perhaps better if we did, and they are not guests, they are clients and supposed,'' Kuku said defiantly, ''supposed to pay.''

Auntie Sanni did not choose to answer that. Instead, ''Mr. and Mrs. Browne,'' she read out. ''They will not arrive until Sunday afternoon. Lady Malcolm recommended them. The girl is freshly out from England. They are, I believe, on honeymoon.''

''Aie!'' said Hannah. ''They should have had the bridal suite.''

''Dr. Coomaraswamy and Mr. Srinivasan have booked the bridal suite long ago for the whole of the campaign.''

''What a bridal pair!'' Kuku giggled again.

''Mr. and Mrs. Browne can have the second half of the bungalow,'' said Auntie Sanni. ''So close to the beach and away from other guests, they should be happy there.''

That made Kuku brood again over Mrs. Manning in the bungalow's other half, the half that had a sitting room.

''Miss Sanni,'' she said, ''you will never make a profit.''

''Profit?'' asked Auntie Sanni, as if to say what could she do with a profit. ''Patna Hall pays its way very nicely,'' her singsong went on. ''Colonel McIndoe and I, Samuel and Hannah and Thambi have all that we want.''

Kuku's exasperation broke. ''You should put up one of those hotel notices on your gates, 'Do Not Disturb.' ''

''That would be very nice,'' said Auntie Sanni.

* * *

Professor Aaron and the cultural ladies, as Hannah called them, were the first to arrive, in time for luncheon; eighteen ladies. "They can match with the young men in Paradise." Kuku giggled again.

The big red-bearded professor kissed Auntie Sanni, bowed to Hannah, and introduced the group, which was led by Mrs. van den Mar from Michigan—not with the waved blue-gray hair Kuku had automatically expected. Mrs. van den Mar wore hers in a plait around her head and, for all her elegance—"I think she is rich," whispered Kuku—was plump, comfortable, "and I think comforting," Auntie Sanni would have said. "A good leader." She introduced the most distinguished archaeologist of them all, Professor Ellen Webster, thin, earnest, brown hair cut in a fringe, spectacles. "She is a senior professor in the Department of Archaeology at Yale University. She will give us our lectures," said Professor Aaron. "And who," he asked, "is this charming young person?"

"Miss Kuku Vikram, who has come to help me," said Auntie Sanni.

"You don't need any help," the professor said gallantly.

As Hannah had predicted they had much paraphernalia: satchels, shoulder bags full of notebooks, shooting sticks, campstools, binoculars, cameras, dark glasses. To Kuku they seemed, too, all dressed alike; each carried a light raincoat; they wore cotton short-sleeved shirts, skirts, or trousers in neutral colors, one or two in blue denim; some had eyeshades, others cotton-brimmed hats, and all were eager, happy, intent. Impressed in spite of herself, Kuku murmured to Hannah, "They must be very cultured."

Mrs. van den Mar's first eager question to Auntie Sanni, though, was anything but cultural. "We're looking forward to your famous mulligatawny soup Professor

Aaron has told us so much about. We hope it will be for lunch."

"The soup of the day is vichyssoise," Kuku said with pride.

Their faces fell. "I can have vichyssoise in Michigan," said Mrs. van den Mar.

"I told you so," Samuel hissed at Kuku, his mustaches bristling with fury. "Do you think, after so many years butler at Patna Hall, I do not know what sahibs like to eat? You . . ." If Samuel had known the word "chit" he would have used it, all he could say was "upstart."

"We shall have mulligatawny tomorrow," and Auntie Sanni softened the blow further, "Today we have our equally famous prawn curry, prawns fresh from the sea. Now, may Miss Kuku and Hannah show you to your rooms?"

Half an hour later, the ladies gathered on the veranda where Kuku served at the bar. "Coffee, tea, and soft drinks only," Auntie Sanni had laid down. "Indian young ladies do not serve hard drinks or wine," but to Samuel's anger Kuku often transgressed, usurping what belonged to Ganga, the wine waiter. Now she served the cultural ladies with a favorite suggested by Professor Aaron, "Gin and ginger beer, taken long, with plenty of ice," but, "Do you know how to make mint julep?" one of them asked Kuku. "So refreshing!" Kuku, to her chagrin, had to ask Samuel. Some had iced tea. "That's a very beautiful sari," another said to Kuku, seduced by the color. Samuel sniffed.

"Well, have you settled in?" Professor Aaron went from one to another.

"Indeed," said a gentle Mrs. Glover. "We are charmed, Professor, truly charmed. We never expected anything like this."

"I certainly did *not* expect anything like this," an indignant voice came as a stout lady stumped on to the veranda. "Have you *seen* the bathrooms?"

"They are primitive," Mrs. Glover had to admit.

"Primitive! Never did I think that to take a bath I should have to sit on a stool and pour water over me with a *pitcher*." Mrs. Schlumberger was the group grumbler. Now she looked up sharply. Kuku had not been able to restrain a giggle.

"Isn't it good to do as the people here do?" pleaded Mrs. Glover.

"And it's far more hygienic than lying in a bath using the same water over and over again," that was Dr. Julia Lovat. "The Indians say that we Westerners with our baths are like buffalo wallowing in their own dirty water."

"Julia! How can you?"

"All the same, I shall miss my shower." Miss Pritt, the only unmarried one and handsome, tried to placate.

"We'll miss far more than that." Mrs. Schlumberger was not to be appeased. "That sweet little manager agrees with me. Says the lady refuses to modernize."

"Oh, come! There is air-conditioning . . ."

"No telephone in the rooms . . . no room service . . . I wouldn't have come if I had known."

"We can always arrange to send you back," Mrs. van den Mar said sweetly. "Ah, lunch! I expect you'll feel better after lunch."

Two large round tables had been set up for them in the dining room, Professor Aaron hosting one, Mrs. van den Mar the other. "For lectures they will use the drawing room," Auntie Sanni had said, "so open it properly," she told Kuku. "Put flowers."

When opened, the drawing room looked well with its Persian carpets—"Kerman," said Auntie Sanni—on the dark green floor. Potted palms stood in polished brass pots, also on the floor; chairs and sofas were covered in a sweet pea chintz. Around the fireplace, which had an enormous grate, a fire seat made a circle; the mantel above held Victorian china and over it was a painting, a portrait of Auntie Sanni as a child with the same short chestnut curls; other paintings of the indigo plantations hung on the walls. There was an upright piano with pleated silk above the keyboard and brass candlesticks; antique as it was, Mrs. Manning liked to play it in the evenings, even when the room was shrouded.

"Well, she can't do that while the conference is on," said Kuku with satisfaction. Then an idea struck her. "Couldn't she play something catchy for us during dinner? We could move the piano into the dining room. I will ask her."

"You will *not*." Auntie Sanni came down on Kuku like the juggernaut at the Dawn Temple which came out on festival days to carry the goddess and could crush mere humans under its wheels. "In our dining room people can still enjoy their food in *quiet*." All the same, Auntie Sanni was uneasy about Mrs. Manning's playing in the evenings. "It sounds so lonely," she had said more than once to Hannah.

"It is lonely," said Hannah.

"You have not change one i-o-ta." Auntie Sanni greeted Sir John and Lady Fisher.

"Nor you." Lady Fisher kissed Auntie Sanni. "You never change."

Sir John, on the verge of his sixties—"I retire next year"—was, in Auntie Sanni's canny diagnosis, all that was elegant and excellent: still slim, upright, his voice was quiet and firm; his sun-tanned skin, after years in the tropics, contrasted oddly with his silvered hair, while Lady Fisher had kept a complexion that looked as if it had never felt a rough wind. "I don't suppose it has," said Auntie Sanni.

In any case Lady Fisher preferred not to go on the beach or bathe or lie in the sun. "Then why does she come?" asked Kuku.

"To be with Sir John," with which Lady Fisher and Sir John would have completely agreed.

"Have you never heard," asked Auntie Sanni, "that men need rest? The more successful they are, the more in the public eye, the more they need it. There was never a more restful and calm person than Lady Fisher or one who listens more," but now, "I am sorry," she told the Fishers as she led them from the hall to the veranda, "sorry that the election should have come at this time. The house is so full, I am afraid you will have little peace."

"I don't think it will disturb us," said Sir John, while, "Dear Aunt Sanni," said Lady Fisher—she and Sir John gave her the dignity of "Aunt"—"with you there is always peace."

"They have been coming here for fifteen years," Auntie Sanni told Kuku. "I am proud to say they are our friends, Colonel McIndoe's and mine."

"A tin-pot little election, how could it disturb them?" Kuku asked on the veranda that evening and was overheard by Dr. Coomaraswamy.

"Tin-pot!" He was indignant. "An election that concerns at least a quarter of a million people?"

"Perhaps a million people," put in Mr. Srinivasan. "There are too many people."

Kuku seemed able to flirt even with the ends of her sari; Dr. Coomaraswamy's brown eyes, already so prominent that they looked like a fish's or seemed as a snail's to have come out on stalks following Kuku's every movement. "Yes, too many," Mr. Srinivasan was saying. "If we have a million, soon there will be two million. Not long and there will be four. For-tun-ate-ly one of the most important things in our Root and Flower Party's program is restriction, the making popular of the use of condoms—"

"Srinivasan! Not in front of Lady Fisher and Miss Kuku," cried Dr. Coomaraswamy.

"I think, dear Doctor, both Kuku and I have heard of birth control," said Lady Fisher.

Dr. Coomaraswamy knew that he was elderly, as his wife, Uma, was always telling him; elderly and unlovely, he thought. He was bald, overstout, obviously well-to-do, well-dressed—his suits were made for him in London. He flashed gold, gold-rimmed spectacles, gold pocket watch on a gold watch chain that stretched tightly across his stomach, the diamond in his little golden finger ring. By contrast, Mr. Srinivasan was a little man, thin and light as an insect, always anxious, dressed in an ill-fitting European suit and what seemed to be overlarge shoes, meticulously polished.

With them had come a cohort of young men. "No young women?" Auntie Sanni had asked in surprise.

"They are staying in Ghandara in our headquarters. Females," said Dr. Coomaraswamy, "do not mind discomfort so much—they are more dedicated, I think. Besides Krishnan has a special mission for them. At the moment he will not tell me what but they are to go among the women which is good—the women's vote is important to us."

"Of utmost importance," said Mr. Srinivasan.

The young men were in national dress, "For this week," said Dr. Coomaraswamy. "And for our young women, I myself have provided for them saris in green and white edged with yellow, our party colors. They are to go in sandals, marigolds in their hair. Padmina Retty's women go in trousers! We shall be traditional which, strangely, is nowadays more modern."

Charming as the young men were, they threatened to overrun Patna Hall until they found Paradise. "They will be out at Ghandara or in the country most of day," soothed Auntie Sanni. Besides providing *charpoys* and cotton quilts she had ordered braziers to be lit on the roof and she told Samuel, "Send two of the waiters, Mustafa and Ahmed, up with pots and pans so they can cook. Give them kabobs."

"Kabobs are not on the menu," Kuku objected.

"They are now," said Auntie Sanni.

Mr. Menzies came late that evening in a small red car, appearing out of the dark. "From where?" asked Kuku, trying to be friendly, at the reception desk. He did not answer.

It was the first time she had seen, in actual flesh, a gentleman wearing a hair ribbon, his hair tied back in a bow. Sometimes men wore them on television—"Oh, why, why, won't Auntie Sanni allow television?" had been Kuku's moan—but those men were young; if Mr. Menzies had known it, he was, for Kuku, too old to be of any interest. She did not either like his overpink complexion, yellow-pink, like the little crabs on the beach when they are cooked. Kuku could not suppress a giggle, though Auntie Sanni had impressed, "Best manners only while you are at reception." Still less did she like the way his eyes—again, as if from the beach, they reminded her of small gray pebbles—looked her over and at once dismissed her. She did not know that Mr. Menzies was not interested in girls unless they were in society which would have made them, for him, likely fodder.

He gave a London club as an address. "Savage Club?" Kuku could not believe it but, "He must be respectable to have a club," she said afterward to Auntie Sanni. "Club" to Kuku meant exclusiveness.

"For how long will you be staying?" she asked.

"I'll see. Don't bother to come up," he said. "The boy can show me. The 'boy,' one of the bearers, picked up his briefcase, typewriter, and suitcase.

"I'm afraid there is not a garage for your car."

"Doesn't matter. It's only hired."

"Most clients not coming by car," Kuku explained

At that he smiled. "Ah! But, then, I am not most clients."

Sunday

■ ■ ■ ■ ■ ■ ■ ■ ■ ■ ■ ■ ■ ■

Kuku was never to forget her first sight of the Brownes
or, rather, Mr. Browne: She hardly noticed the girl.

They arrived in the peace of Sunday's late afternoon
when everyone and everything seemed quiet before the stir
of dinner; it was as if the little dust of the new guests had
settled. "It always does at Patna Hall," said Auntie Sanni.

Dr. Coomaraswamy, Mr. Srinivasan, and the cohorts
had removed themselves to the party headquarters at
Ghandara—they had their own hired coach. Mr. Menzies
had followed them not long after. "He must be something
connected with politics," Kuku had guessed. The cultural
ladies and Professor Aaron had set aside Sunday for resting after their long journey and stayed in their rooms. Sir
John and Lady Fisher were on the veranda, she stitching,
he reading; they might never have been away. Mrs. Manning was walking along the beach. All was quiet when the
Shantipur taxi drew up.

"Browne with an *e*," the young man instructed as he
signed the register at the desk, but Kuku hardly heard:
She was gazing at his height, his fairness that was to her
dazzlingly fair.

The young wife seemed no match for her husband—
she was so slight, her overlarge spectacles making her
look like a schoolgirl—but she too was fair, gray-eyed with
mouse-pale brown hair that fell to her shoulders and hid
her face as it swung forward like a soft bell. Both, though,

had what Kuku called English complexions. "Apple blossom," murmured Kuku in despair.

Kuku was dark-skinned and had been schooled to think that, above all, fairness was desirable, all beauty had to be fair. The marriage advertisements in the newspapers showed that clearly: "Educated England, returned young barrister seeks fair girl." Sometimes it was the other way around: "Highly educated, executive-positioned, fair Brahmin young lady wishes to contact eligible young gentleman in similar employment," or more naïve and old-fashioned: "Wanted: young man, preferably in Government Service for fair good-looking girl. Knows music and knitting." There did not seem much hope for the Kukus of this world.

He signed the register "Blaise St. John Browne." "Blaise! What an uncommon name!" Kuku dared to say. He looked at her with such surprise that she saw she had transgressed, and flushed. The girl saw it too and stepped forward. "You don't have to sign," he told her. "You come under me."

Auntie Sanni, who had appeared in the doorway, caught the look she gave him, caught, too, a sight of a small firm chin when the hair swung back as she firmly signed her name, "Mary Browne."

There was more to it than that. "When my husband was born," the girl told Kuku, "his parents could not decide on a name uncommon enough for him, so they compromised with Blaise."

"Mary!" He had turned crimson. "For God's sake . . ."

But the clear voice went on. "When I was born the nurses asked my father what I should be called—it had to be the nurses, unfortunately my mother had died. He said the first name that came into his head, 'Mary.' You can't wonder"—the girl would not stop—"we were in Rome, you see, and Rome is full of Marys, though there they say 'Maria.'"

"Mary, Reception isn't even remotely interested—"

"Oh, but I am, I am," cried Kuku.

"All those churches: Santa Maria degli Angeli, Santa Maria dell' Assunta, Santa Maria Maggiore, Santa Maria Rotondo . . ."

Now what, wondered Auntie Sanni, could have provoked all that?

Mary could have told her: It was the journey from Madras. It had enchanted her, especially after three weeks spent in Ootacamund, "Which might have been England," she had said, disappointed. "It even has a vicar."

"My dear child, most Indian towns of any size have an Anglican vicar," Blaise had told her. "Why not?"

"I . . . just didn't expect it." Mary knew she sounded naïve.

From Madras the train had gone through forests where sun filtered between tall trees and creepers; villages, golden-thatched, the houses often on stilts, appeared and disappeared. Mary saw elephants, the first elephants she had seen working. "Bumble, look. Do look"—she had always heard Blaise called Bumble— "Look," but he was reading the *Madras Times.*

The elephants pulled logs; the small brown men around them gesticulated as they fastened chains or goaded the huge animals, swaying in their strength to strip trees with their trunks or push against them with their foreheads. In the groves she saw flowers growing along the tree branches in festoons. "Bumble, could those possibly be wild orchids? Come and look."

Indulgently he had come but carrying his paper. "I wouldn't know an orchid from a daisy."

"You must know."

"I know those big purple ornate things you buy in florists."

"These are wild," but he had gone back to his reading.

On ponds or village tanks, water lilies floated. Often monkeys, small and brown, swung away from the train among the trees. When the railway left the forests to run along the shore, nets seemingly as fine as gossamer were spread on the white sand and there were boats. Mary had sat entranced by the color and sun but she did not ask Blaise to look again.

Now, at Reception, Auntie Sanni thought it time to intervene and sailed into the hall. "Good evening. Welcome to . . ." but, "What's this?" Mr. Browne was saying to Kuku. "Share a bungalow? An out-bungalow? I booked for the main hotel."

In agitation Kuku began hastily to turn the pages as if she were looking for another room but Auntie Sanni went on as if Blaise Browne had not spoken. "Welcome to Patna Hall. I am Mrs. McIndoe, the proprietor. The main hotel is full, but quite apart from that, we always put our younger guests in the bungalow if we can." She made it sound like a favor. "They like to be on the beach and so do away with formalities."

"Yes, Blaise, it would be much nicer." The girl's tone was conciliating, almost coaxing; obviously she did not want a scene.

"I booked—"

"I am sure you will find the bungalow most suitable." Auntie Sanni put an end to the argument. "Miss Kuku will take you there."

"How handsome he is!" Kuku whispered to Auntie Sanni as the Brownes collected coats and hand luggage. Thambi picked up suitcases, tennis rackets, a big bag of golf clubs. "So big and blond, like a young god. Is it Apollo?"

"Apollo?" Auntie Sanni looked sharply at Kuku.

Kuku took them down a small path that wound through what seemed a large garden: a path of white sand that glimmered in India's sudden dusk and was edged with shells and lit by old-fashioned lampposts. The sound of the sea grew louder as they came nearer. The bungalow was almost on the beach, only separated by a narrow strip of garden from the foreshore; the roof was of palm thatch. The veranda rails shone white in the lamplight. Wicker chairs and a table stood on the floor of polished red stone. The bedroom had little but a wide bed. "An *almirah*," said Kuku, opening the cupboard door to show hanging space and shelves, a chest of drawers with a looking glass, and two chairs. *Durries* were on the floor.

To Mary it all gave a feeling of lightness and freedom but she could tell Blaise was not pleased, less pleased when he saw the bathroom, a dark little room, divided by a low kerb behind which was a single tap. "Only cold water," Kuku had to say in shame. Tall *gharras* were filled each morning from it, "So that the water stays cool," Auntie Sanni would have explained. Beside the *gharras* was a stool and an outsize zinc mug "For pouring water over yourself," but "An Indian bathroom!" Blaise was as dismayed as Mrs. Schlumberger.

"Our waterman will bring plenty of hot water," Kuku hurried to say, "if you telephone."

"At least we have a telephone," said Blaise.

"Only a line to the house, I'm afraid," Kuku apologized, but Mary could not think why they needed a telephone or hot water. "We can bathe in the sea."

"And there is a bar." Kuku could show that in its small refrigerated cupboard with pride. "You can help yourselves. There is ice but anything you want I shall bring."

Blaise, who had not really looked at Kuku, said, "*Atcha*" as when dismissing a servant. Kuku, hurt, flushed darker, gathered up her sari, and went. "She hasn't even given us a key."

"Why do we need a key?" asked Mary. "It's all wide open." Though the bungalow had heavy full-length wooden shutters to close against a storm, they were left folded back and the doorways had only half doors set midway; made of light wood and woven palm, they swung slightly in the breeze. Now Mary pushed through them on to the veranda and stood there looking.

From the moment they had driven up to Patna Hall she had known she loved it; it seemed to breathe a new air. In those three weeks at Ootacamund the time had dragged so they had seemed like three years. They had stayed at the club and only met the club people, retired English or else Westernized Indians; Blaise had played golf; Mary walked around with him. In the evening there was bridge; she had sat beside him until, desperate, she had wheedled, "For the last week of your leave couldn't we go somewhere Indian, in India?"

"Little silly. Ooty is in India."

"No, it's *not*," but she did not say it, only coaxed, "Lady Malcolm says there is a hotel farther north by the sea, 'India unchanged,' she says."

Blaise frowned. "Lady Malcolm is the only person I have not liked here in Ootacamund."

Mary had looked at him, startled. Lady Malcolm was the only person she had liked.

Now, out on the veranda, she felt the sea breeze which was strong but warm. In India, night falls quickly, and now, as the bungalow lights fell on the beach, she could only make out the pale crests of the rollers. Their noise surprised her; as they crashed on the sand the whole bungalow shook. Looking along the beach and the wet sand she could see small lights, lanterns or fires, under a darkness of trees. She lifted her face to look up at the stars, at one in particular which shone over the sea, Hesperus, Venus, the evening star. My star, thought Mary. Behind it was the shape of a growing moon. Suddenly, an immense happiness filled her. What does anything matter? thought Mary. I'm here.

"No hangers." Blaise was walking about, peering into the cupboard, opening drawers. "This really is a run-down place."

"It doesn't feel like that. I like it." Mary did not say "love." "Funny," she said, "I never heard you called Blaise until Bombay. I thought you were Bumble. We were Bumble and Merry."

"I have always been Blaise."

"Yes," and she said sadly, "I suppose we've gone public."

"I should hope so. You're my wife." Blaise came and gave her a swift hug but she sensed that he was stiff as he always was when he was embarrassed—Mary had already learned that. It seemed he did not want to remember a certain little hidden garden hut in Norway, a memory she had clung to all these days. "They're much nicer before you marry them." Who had said that? Lady Malcolm . . . But I wanted to marry, thought Mary.

The sadness was interrupted by a clip-clopping sound, like heavy horse hooves on a hard road, but, How can anything clip-clop on sand? thought Mary. Then she saw a small brown shape with a white nose: A donkey had come up on the veranda.

"Bumble, Bumble. There's a donkey on the veranda."

"A *donkey!* Get it out at once," but Mary had seen why it clopped: The donkey's hooves had never been trimmed or cut so that they turned up like Turkish slippers.

"Oh!" cried Mary. "Oh, poor thing. Bumble, come and look."

Long ago when in Rome, the small Mary had had an Italian nurse, Giovanna. Darling Giovanna, thought Mary as she remembered now how Giovanna had told her that because Jesus Christ sat on a donkey colt for his entrance into Jerusalem—it was somehow mixed, in Mary's otherwise pagan mind, with palms—'Ever since," Giovanna had said, "all donkeys bear stripes like a cross on their backs." Mary had not known if the story were true but she had always honored donkeys and here, on this one's back, was the striped cross, plain to see. "Bumble, look. Do come and look. Poor little thing."

A laugh came from behind a white painted wicker-work partition. "He isn't poor. He's a perfect little pest."

The laugh, the voice, were musical and deep for a woman but it was a woman who appeared on the garden path below the veranda. In the gathering dusk Mary could not see her plainly but had the impression of someone tall, thin as the wrapped skirt of her dress showed—an elegant dress—of dark hair pulled back into a coil at the nape of the neck. Mary could not see her face. "A pest?" she said. "He's sweet."

"He's not at all sweet. No one has ever been able to shoe him or even catch him. Yet he likes people. He's here all the time. He comes up the side steps."

"That he won't." Blaise appeared in the doorway but, "What's his name?" asked Mary.

"He hasn't a name. He's one of Auntie Sanni's pensioners."

"Auntie Sanni? Do you mean Mrs. McIndoe?"

"Auntie Sanni to us. You'll see." The woman—lady, Mary corrected herself—paused, looking at them, taking them in. "How do you do? I am Mrs. Manning, Olga Manning. I have a sitting room. Come around and have a drink and I'll tell you all about everything."

"Thank you," Blaise said quickly, "but we have to change for dinner or we'll be late. Come along, Mary." Mary gave a defiant little shrug, went down the steps, around the partition to Olga Manning's sitting room. The donkey clopped after her.

"Tonight is the inaugural meeting of our campaign." Dr. Coomaraswamy, Mr. Srinivasan behind him, had come out on the house veranda for a drink before the gong sounded for dinner and found Sir John and Lady Fisher already there.

"Our inaugural meeting," repeated Mr. Srinivasan. "Would you not come, Sir John, and give us your blessing?"

"My dear man"—Sir John laid his hand on the doctor's shoulder—"the last thing I feel like is a political meeting."

"That is a pity. I am to make my inaugural speech." Dr. Coomaraswamy smiled at the thought: He loved oratory. "I must make it exactly explicit. This is a rural district—"

"The people are extremely rural," put in Mr. Srinivasan.

"So that everything has to be explained, but everything, in Telegu as well as Tamil. Fortunately I, myself, am multilingual." Dr. Coomaraswamy visibly swelled. "In European languages as well . . . I shall begin . . ."

"Does Dr. Coomaraswamy have to make his inaugural speech twice?" Kuku asked audibly. Fortunately the doctor was called to the telephone.

"Constantly he is called to the telephone." Mr. Srinivasan scurried after him.

"Same dear old Coomaraswamy," said Sir John when they had gone. "But I should have been interested to hear young Krishnan."

"So would I," said Lady Fisher.

"Where is your candidate?" Sir John asked when Dr. Coomaraswamy and his echo came back. "Where is Krishnan?"

There was a pause. The doctor and Mr. Srinivasan looked at one another with a slight unease, then, "Krishnan Bhanj has chosen to remain at our headquarters in Ghandara."

"In Ghandara," confirmed Mr. Srinivasan, and Dr. Coomaraswamy gave a sigh, such a sigh that, clearly, it came from the depths of his being. "I confess to you, Sir John, I am profoundly disturbed. We do not understand at all what Krishnan is doing."

"Or not doing," Mr. Srinivasan said piteously.

"Yet I have to accede as if there were some mystery force. For instance, only last week I allowed him, from party funds, to spend ten thousand rupees on umbrellas."

"*Umbrellas?*"

"Precisely."

"To be distributed," explained Mr. Srinivasan.

"In Konak?" asked Sir John.

"No, not in Konak. That I could have understood but Krishnan ordered as far away as possible, actually in Bihar. It has something to do with the mission of our young women but now he asks a further twenty-five thousand rupees which he needs to carry this project out. It looks as if"—Dr. Coomaraswamy was still more glum—"I myself will have to supply that."

"But an umbrella," said Sir John, "is the symbol of Padmina Retty's People's Shelter Party."

"I have told Krishnan that. Besides, of course, he knows it perfectly well."

"Hmm," said Sir John.

The knoll to the left of Patna Hall was an unexpectedly high mound, topped by palm trees whose fronds rattled in the wind; a small path went up to where, under them, Auntie Sanni had put a seat. Every evening, when she had bathed and washed her hair, she would put on another clean, freshly ironed Mother Hubbard dress, also her pearl necklace, the pearls real and beautifully matched, take her palm leaf fan from Hannah, who had attended her, and then come out on the wide veranda where Colonel McIndoe, dressed too for dinner in linen trousers, a cummerbund, and jacket, waited for her. He would make an arm, she would put her hand in it and slowly, because of her weight, they would walk up to the knoll. "Walk! She lumbers," said Kuku.

From the knoll they could survey all that was Auntie Sanni's: the hotel, the demesne, and the beach—she had to acknowledge she could not own the sea.

On the other side of the hotel, in the grove, the trees were dark against the white sand. The fishermen had shrines under the casuarinas and sometimes lit *dipas* there. They made the pricks of light Mary had seen.

Below, Patna Hall itself was lit into brightness, its lights, like a necklace, going down to the shore. A red light shone from the roof so the cohorts could cook—Sir John had nicknamed them "the disciples." Auntie Sanni could see smoke going up, pale in the dimness of the young moon and a sudden flame where the braziers were fanned. An answering glow came from the gatehouse where Shyama was cooking, Thambi keeping watch, but tonight, there was another glow, red and living from the mango grove. "Someone has lit a fire there," said Auntie Sanni. She looked toward the village where a drum was being beaten. "Something is in the air," said Auntie Sanni.

It was always a proud moment for Samuel when he sounded the gong for dinner.

Though dinner might go on being served until ten or eleven, the gong for the residents was rung punctually at eight. "That is late for Americans," Kuku had pointed out. "In the Taj Hotel they begin serving dinner at half past six."

"If they come to Patna Hall," said Auntie Sanni, "they must do as we do."

At five to eight, Samuel turned on the dining room lights so that the starched white of the tablecloths was reflected in the polished dark red of the floor, which reflected, too, the white clothes of the waiters with their cummerbunds and turban bands of red and gold. The wine waiter, Ganga, an Ooriyah who served only wine and drinks, not food, was further distinguished by gold buttons and epaulets. "We have a wine waiter," Samuel had told Kuku. "He will fetch the drinks. There is no need for you to come from the bar." Kuku still came, the end of her evening sari flowing as she moved between the tables, outdoing Ganga. Like Samuel, this was the best time of the day for Kuku.

At eight, everything was ready, the waiters at their stations, every table set, napkins fluted in the glasses, silver glittering, fresh flowers on every table. Soup was waiting in the hot cases where the small braziers shone red; final touches were being given in the kitchens. A small army of dishwashers was ready to run with hot food between kitchen and pantry. Samuel made a quick round of dining room, pantry, kitchens, pantry, dining room; then he sounded the gong.

The tables began to fill; Dr. Coomaraswamy and Mr. Srinivasan had darted in as soon as the first gong beat sounded. After them Auntie Sanni and Colonel McIndoe led the way; their table was nearest the veranda, Sir John and Lady Fisher's opposite. Professor Aaron and his ladies took their already familiar places at the two round tables; smaller tables at the back were for Mr. Menzies, Mrs. Manning, and, a little secluded, a honeymoon table for the Brownes. Dr. Coomaraswamy's table was midway between the Fishers and Auntie Sanni. "Too close," she said to the colonel, "I don't like politics in my dining room. Those two hardly waited for the gong!" She frowned: They were not eating, they were gobbling.

"Yes. Yes. We are in a hurry," Dr. Coomaraswamy told Samuel. "We have to get to Ghandara. Tonight is our inaugural meeting."

He was excited, talking volubly but, "Eat. Eat," begged Mr. Srinivasan. Auntie Sanni turned her eyes away.

For the Brownes she had ordered a bottle of white

wine; Samuel had it ready in a silver bucket. The flowers on the table were like a bouquet; the head *mali* had sent an underling inland to gather orchids so that even Kuku was satisfied. "Though, of course, there isn't a florist even in Ghandara," she had complained. Samuel was eagerly hovering but Blaise Browne came into the dining room alone.

He did not notice the flowers, ignored the white wine, and nodded curtly to Samuel. The soup was brought and left to grow cold. It was not until ten minutes later that Auntie Sanni saw him stand up—"He has good manners," she said softly to Colonel McIndoe—as the young wife came in, following Mrs. Manning. "Oh, dear!" said Auntie Sanni.

The soft brown hair fell forward as the girl bent to look at and touch the flowers. Then she saw the wine. "Bumble! You ordered wine! How exciting and how sweet of you," the clear young voice sounded across the room.

"Nothing to do with me. Mary, sit down."

"Are you cross?" asked Mary.

"Of course I'm cross. Think what it looks like."

"Looks like?"

"Our first night here, a honeymoon couple, and I have to appear in the dining room alone."

"You should have come to Mrs. Manning." Mary refused to be upset.

"Sit *down*."

Lady Fisher looked across the room. "So that's Rory Scott's Mary."

"Didn't he call her Merry?" Sir John was looking too. "I thought she was still at school."

"Schools," corrected Lady Fisher. "I seem to remember there were several—Rory was always moving on so that Mary never settled. No wonder he had trouble. Well, a girl without a mother . . ."

"Yes." Sir John had seen the tilt of the head beside

Blaise, the turned shoulder. "I can guess she's a handful, a plain little piece."

"Not when she smiles." Mary had smiled across at Auntie Sanni. "Not with those eyes. She has her mother's eyes. Do you remember how Anne's bewitched Rory?"

But Sir John was frowning. "Surely she's young to be married?"

"She must be . . . let me see . . . eighteen."

"Still too young. He's old Archie Browne's son, you remember them in Istanbul?"

"Yes. The boy was born there. I remember the fuss. So this is the wonderful Blaise! What a nest of diplomats we are! But, John, you must admit he's very good-looking."

"So was his mother, in a florid way. Archie's a good chap, if humdrum," which for Lady Fisher confirmed again what she already knew, that Sir John did not care for Mrs. Browne but he was looking again across the room.

"It's what they call a good match," said Lady Fisher.

"Except that it isn't a match. I can guess that girl isn't ordinary, any more than her father," by which Lady Fisher knew that Sir John did care for Rory's Mary.

The cultural ladies were looking too. "Charming, quite charming, though not what you'd call a beauty," they murmured. "These English girls have *such* complexions."

"She looks quite dewy." Dr. Lovat sounded almost dreamy.

"Dewy?"

"As if the dew was still on her," explained Mrs. van den Mar.

"Can't we drink the wine?" Mary was saying, but Samuel had already taken matters in hand. A waiter had removed the cold soup, another slipped hot plates in front of each of them while Samuel proffered a dish from which rose a delectable smell, "*Koftas*, Sahib. Little fish balls of fresh crayfish. Very good. I think Sahib hungry," he said, deftly serving Blaise while Ganga filled the wineglasses; when he had opened the wine it had set off clapping from the other tables. "From Miss Sanni, best wishes," said Samuel.

"We should drink to her"—Mary raised her glass—"and to them all." Flushed, she stood up and drank to the dining room. Blaise had to follow. A pleased hum answered them. After the *koftas* came partridges, plump, each sitting on its square of toast, with a piquant bread sauce, gravy, fresh vegetables. Blaise began visibly to be appeased. The old butler is right, thought Mary, men are better when they have been fed.

Lady Fisher could have told her that.

At first Olga Manning had watched the Brownes' table with a hint of malicious amusement in her eyes, which changed to a curious sadness. When she had finished— she ate far too quickly and too little—she got up and went out; she went so fast the gauze of her sleeves brushed the backs of chairs and the potted palms. She stopped at the veranda bar, ordered a double whiskey, and avoiding any talk with Kuku, took it into the drawing room which was not being used that night as the cultural ladies were going out.

Every year at the outset of his tour, Professor Aaron's group was invited to a reception at the old palace of Konak. "Not that the Maharajah is there," Professor Aaron explained. He had stood up to brief the ladies while they still sat at dinner. "He lives in the South of France now. Here he has to be plain Mr. Konak but he keeps his titles abroad. It is his steward who will entertain us."

The palace, built on a steep slope of the Ghandari Hills, was falling into disrepair, "But you can still imagine its life." Professor Aaron tried to conjure it up: "Though there is a grand staircase, there are ramps between different levels so that the court ladies could be transported in miniature rickshaws. One or two rickshaws are still there. They are inlaid with mother-of-pearl."

"That sounds utterly romantic," cried Mrs. Glover.

"But we won't be transported in rickshaws." Mrs. Schlumberger was ready to object. "Does that mean we'll have to walk? I can't manage uphill."

"You can always spend a quiet evening here," Mrs. van den Mar stemmed the complaint.

"And there might well be elephants." Dr. Lovat was an experienced traveler.

"True, the gateways were built high to let elephants through," said Professor Aaron, "but I'm afraid there are no elephants now." If the ladies were disappointed they did not show it; they had not come to India to see elephants, but Mary, who had been listening, sighed.

"I expect the Raja's private court will be lit for you." The professor was still trying to beguile. "That's where the dancing girls danced for their lord alone." Mary seemed to hear the strange Indian music, the tinkling of anklet bells. "The courtyard is so high that at night it is said to be roofed with stars."

"Oh, I should like to go," said Mary but, "Has the palace any architectural interest?" asked Miss Pritt. "Should we bring our notebooks?"

"Perhaps I wouldn't like to go," said Mary.

In the big empty drawing room next door, Olga Manning began to play.

"Now what's happening?" asked Sir John.

A young man in flowing white had come hurriedly into the dining room.

"Who's he?" Lady Fisher wondered.

"A boy called Sharma. Coomaraswamy introduced him to me. The party's district agent."

"He doesn't look like a district agent," said Lady Fisher. "More like a dusky angel."

"A messenger from the gods," Sir John suggested. "But I think he has only come to tell them the party's coach is ready."

Dr. Coomaraswamy reluctantly put down his knife and fork. Mr. Srinivasan took a last mouthful; he was still chewing as he went after the doctor and Sharma.

In a moment or two, Mr. Menzies followed them. "He must be in politics," said Lady Fisher.

"Or journalism." Sir John did not seem quite at ease. "I can't imagine that a journalist of any prominence would find this campaign of importance. Yet I seem to have heard . . ."

"I don't like middle-aged men who try to look like girls." Lady Fisher had noted the hair ribbon.

She and Sir John were used to long-haired men. Their own son, Timothy, "Looks like one of the apostles," said Sir John.

"But he's young and the beard fits it." Lady Fisher smiled. "But this . . ."

"Not very attractive, certainly, and—bold," was the word that came to Sir John from the way Mr. Menzies had given orders to the waiters and spoke across the room to the cultural ladies. He was a short man, barely reaching to Sir John's shoulder yet, "I can guess he's potent." Sir John still felt an unease.

"They haven't waited for the trifle." Samuel was grieved for Dr. Coomaraswamy and Mr. Srinivasan.

"No, I don't like politics in my dining room," Auntie Sanni said. She did not like quarreling either.

Dinner at Patna Hall always ended with dessert, homemade sweets, crystallized fruit, fresh nuts, on especially fine porcelain plates, each with a finger bowl filled with warm water and floating flower petals. "No one has finger bowls nowadays," Kuku had said, "and these are silver. They have to be *cleaned*."

"Kashmiri silver," said Samuel. "Old Master Sahib brought them from Srinagar." The silver was chased with a design of chenar leaves and iris, lined on the inner side with gilt.

"Of course they must be cleaned and polished," said Samuel. Generations of polishing had worn them thin but, "No one in my dining room," said Samuel, "has a dessert plate without a finger bowl."

He placed them himself in front of Blaise and Mary. "How pretty," said Mary of the finger bowls, and Samuel smiled.

"Samuel likes that girl," Auntie Sanni said to Colonel McIndoe as Mary looked up at the old butler.

"Do you think I could have a few carrots and sugar lumps for my donkey?"

"Of course, Miss Baba."

Miss Baba had slipped out and Blaise's displeasure was back. He said to Mary, "Miss Baba! You're not a child. It's not your donkey and you're not going to adopt it," and to Samuel, "*Memsahib* doesn't want any carrots," and then, "Talking of which, I would rather you wouldn't be so friendly with this Mrs. Manning."

"Why not?"

"There's something about her, Mary. I'm a good judge of character," said Blaise with satisfaction. "You must let me know best."

"Even when I don't think you do?"

"They don't look very happy over there." Lady Fisher had been watching. "Rory's an old friend, John, and we knew Archie Browne."

"Slightly."

"Slightly or not, go and ask those young people to have coffee with us on the veranda."

*   *   *

Mary had not wanted to have coffee on the veranda; she wanted to be out in the night but Blaise was flattered at being asked by Sir John Fisher. "He's really my chief—by remote control," he had whispered to Mary. Blaise had completely recovered himself and now, as he stood talking, the lights showed off his fair hair. Kuku, her vivid sari showing off the brown plumpness below the tight gold of her bodice, brought his coffee, fluttering her eyelashes as she served him; he took the cup without noticing her and went on talking to Sir John. Blaise was palpably enjoying talking to Sir John—Because he is Sir John, thought Mary, which was captious but she knew it was true. Well, why not? she told herself and, It's you who are cross now. We're both tired. Yet she did not feel tired, it was only . . . I didn't want to spend my first real Indian night in chit-chat.

She was sitting on a low stool beside Lady Fisher, who, in courtesy, was asking her about her father—"It's a long time since we saw Rory"—about England and the wedding in Bombay . . . Just what I don't want to talk about.

If only I could get up and walk away, thought Mary, be back on that other veranda where I can watch those waves coming in roller after roller, sending their wash far up the sand. If I could look over them and see how the sky comes down over the sea to meet the horizon, a great bowl of stars. If I held up my hand against it, all around my fingers would be nothing but air, emptiness. I don't want to say Rory is well—as far as I know; that Bumble and I were married in Bombay's cathedral. I don't want to say I like India. *Like!* When I'm . . . what *is* the right word? Yes, enthralled. Then she looked at Lady Fisher, who had discreetly returned to her embroidery and was listening to her husband and Blaise—or thinking her own thoughts? And what must she be thinking of me? thought Mary uncomfortably. Why, tonight, am I not able . . . ? Oh, I wish something would happen, or somebody come to rescue me.

A sudden hubbub filled the veranda. Dr. Coomaraswamy had come back surrounded by some of the young men but, "Go. Go," he cried to them. "Go now. I must think," and mopping his bald head he came along the veranda giving small moans.

"My dear fellow!" Sir John helped him to a chair. "Let me get you a drink. Brandy?"

"Iced water. Please. Please."

"And for me," Mr. Srinivasan was even more disheveled and distressed, "if you would be so kind. Water."

"I'll get it," said Blaise, but Kuku had already gone. "What has happened?"

"*Catastrophe!*" Dr. Coomaraswamy sank into the wicker chair, his head in his hands, while Mr. Srinivasan beat his together. "Catastrophe? Utter catastrophe."

"What kind of catastrophe?"

"Krishnan . . . Krishnan Bhanj . . ." Dr. Coomaraswamy could hardly speak. "Candidate in the state of Konak for the Root and Flower Party, our party, our candidate—"

"Was our candidate," moaned Mr. Srinivasan.

"Was?" Sir John was startled. "Is he dead?"

"No. No."

"He has withdrawn?"

"No. Oh, no! No. No!"

"Better if he had," wailed Mr. Srinivasan.

"Then?"

"Worse than that," and Dr. Coomaraswamy said in a voice hoarse with shock, "*Krishnan Bhanj has taken a vow of silence.*"

Silence. How lovely, thought Mary as a torrent of talk broke out above her. Auntie Sanni and Colonel McIndoe had joined the group; Kuku came with tumblers of iced water as Dr. Coomaraswamy began to tell the tale.

"We were all on the platform. Every influential person. All such important people. I, the chairman of the Root and Flower Party—"

"And Krishnan?" asked Lady Fisher.

"Nat-u-ral-ly. Krishnan—on the platform. I myself was speaking, only to introduce him, you understand—I myself—"

"For long?" asked Lady Fisher.

"Oh no, not at all. Perhaps ten minutes."

"Ten minutes *is* long for an introduction," said Sir John.

"It was the inaugural speech." For a moment Dr. Coomaraswamy had dignity, then the injury welled up. "Speaking—on the platform when Krishnan got up and—and—"

"And?"

"He walked out."

"Well, Indian politicians often do walk out," said Lady Fisher.

"Yes, Lady Sahib, but he left a note."

"It was I who picked it up," Mr. Srinivasan moaned again.

"What did it say?"

"It said," came the unfailing voice of Mr. Srinivasan, " 'This is enough. I am not speaking tonight. I am not speaking throughout the campaign. I have taken a vow of silence.' "

A sound, quickly smothered, came from Sir John, a sound that made Dr. Coomaraswamy look at him sharply.

"This Krishnan Bhanj," Mary, in a low voice, asked Lady Fisher, "what is he like?"

"Blue-black," said Kuku derisively.

"Kuku! I know he's dark—" Lady Fisher protested.

"Blue-black," Kuku insisted. "Which doesn't suit his name."

" 'Krishnan' comes from the Hindu god Krishna," Lady Fisher explained, "one of the avatars or manifestations of Vishnu, second god of the Hindu Trinity—Brahma the Creator, Vishnu the Preserver, and Shiva, Death, who is also Resurrection. Whenever there is trouble on earth Vishnu comes down, at first he was a fish, then an animal, later as a man or god like Krishna, who is usually shown with a blue skin."

"Blue? A *blue* skin?" asked Mary.

"Pale blue," said Lady Fisher. "Krishnan is dark but he is a man and he can't help his color. After all, he isn't Krishna. The god is blue because he drank poison in the milk of his wet nurse. She was a demon in disguise but the milk did not harm him, only her. He sucked so fiercely that he emptied her body of all energy and she fell dead. That's what they say. Old folk tales," said Kuku in contempt.

"They're not exactly folk tales," and Lady Fisher smiled. "When Krishna came down on earth, he was, of course, a baby. He had to be abandoned by his royal parents but was found by a cowherd who brought him up, like Perdita in *The Winter's Tale*."

"William Shakespeare," said Kuku, proud to know.

"Yes." Lady Fisher's needle went in and out with a gentle plucking sound that made this, to Mary, fantastic conversation of gods and demons mixed up with cowherds and poison, everyday.

She looked up at Auntie Sanni who had come to sit with them, towering among them; Mary was reminded of a mountain with small towns, villages, and farms and their innumerable occupations and preoccupations held safely in its folds. Auntie Sanni obviously loved to hear Lady Fisher talk, and Mary guessed that Auntie Sanni would be indulgent to any belief—as long as it is belief, thought Mary. And why am I so interested? she wondered. Usually I hate being told things, but now she wanted to know more about these strange immortal beings and, "Go on, please," she said to Lady Fisher.

"As Krishna grew older he sported," Lady Fisher chose the word carefully, "with his foster father's *gopis.*"

"*Gopis?*"

"Milkmaids."

"Sported!" Kuku was indignant. "Imagine, Mrs. Browne, the *gopis* were so much in love with him they longed to be his flute so that his lips would perpetually caress them. Silly girls! Like all men, he was heartless."

"All men?" Lady Fisher laughed. "Certainly not all men. Take Krishnan Bhanj."

"Like all men." Of course! As Lady Fisher said, this Krishnan Bhanj is a man. That thought gave Mary a slight shock, and looking at Kuku, she wondered if perhaps he had "sported," that exact word, with her. "You know Mr. Bhanj?"

"He was staying here when I first came." Kuku gave a still indignant little snort. "He called me Didi—sister. I am not his sister."

"I'm sure he said that as he would have said Bhai—to a young man." Lady Fisher defended him. "Bhai means brother," she told Mary.

"Exactly," said Kuku with venom, and I can guess it was you who tried to sport with Krishnan, thought Mary with a sudden astuteness, which was confirmed when Kuku said, "Krishnan. Krishna. What is the difference? All Krishna did was to play tricks on poor girls."

"Not always," said Lady Fisher. "Remember, there was Radha."

"Radha?" asked Mary.

"Krishna met his match with Radha in more ways than one. She seemed to be a *gopi* but Radha was a god as well."

"Goddess. She shone among the *gopis.*" Though she was contemptuous, Kuku had seen pictures from the

Hindu scriptures. "Anyway, Krishnan Bhanj may think he is a god but he's not Krishna."

"That's not what the villagers think." Mr. Menzies had come up the veranda and was standing beside them.

"Krishnan Bhanj was so good, so excellent," Mr. Srinivasan lamented. "A barrister, he is particularly versed in law, England returned." Mr. Srinivasan's English belonged to the thirties and forties. They talk differently, thought Mary. They don't take shortcuts—"is not" instead of "isn't"; "will not" instead of "won't"; they break up syllables . . . "Par-tic-u-lar-ly." "Krishnan also speaks English per-fect-ly," Mr. Srinivasan was going on. "Also his great advantage to us is that he speaks Tamil as well as Telegu."

"What advantage is that if he will not speak at all?" Dr. Coomaraswamy was in despair.

"Where is Krishnan now?" asked Sir John.

"We do not know. We do not know *anything*." Once more Mr. Srinivasan beat his hands together.

"I, myself," said Dr. Coomaraswamy, "am going now to look for him. He was at Ghandara, where, for the election, as I have told you, he preferred to stay."

"One little room," Mr. Srinivasan went on, "a *charpoy*, table, and chair, not even a fan when he might have stayed here. He cannot be in his right mind. To go off and leave us in this fixation."

"We went straight to headquarters. He was not there," explained Dr. Coomaraswamy. "He left his clothes, his suit, shirt, tie—"

"Even his shoes, his socks!"

"So what is he wearing?"

"I suppose national dress. Maybe only a *lunghi*. It would not be past him, our candidate!" Dr. Coomaraswamy cried bitterly. "What has come over him? Where is he?"

"Have you asked in the village?"

"Nat-u-rally. They are a wall."

"You mean, they stonewalled?"

"Yes, walls of stone!"

"They knew in the village before you knew." It was the first time Auntie Sanni had spoken.

"But why should he have come here, except to Patna Hall? What is there for him here in Shantipur?"

With quiet footsteps, the young Sharma came along the veranda, made a graceful *namaskar* to the company, and handed the doctor a note.

"I ab-so-lute-ly do not understand," Dr. Coomaraswamy cried when he had read it. "Why? What use?" and he read it aloud. " 'Tomorrow, by first dawn, you will get a lorry and in it set up a small *pandal* . . .' "

"What is a *pandal*?" Mary whispered to Lady Fisher.

"A sort of tabernacle. The people make them on festival days for an image of one of the gods. They are usually bamboo, decorated with banana tree stems and garlands of lucky mango leaves and marigolds."

" 'A *pandal*,' " read Dr. Coomaraswamy, " 'as for a god. I will sit in it. The people will see me.' But this is idiotic!" he cried. "This is i-di-o-tic."

"It is brilliant," said Mr. Menzies.

"Surely," Blaise said to Sir John when the Indians had gone, "it can't be serious. This Krishnan must be some sort of jumped-up play actor who has taken them all in?"

"On the contrary, Krishnan Bhanj has not only been canvasing for weeks throughout Konak, for the past five years, he has been steadily and culminatively working toward this election in his own way here in Konak and doing untold good, how good we shall not know for perhaps decades. Besides, his father is perhaps the most respected politician in all India, of absolute integrity," said Sir John. "I know of no one who would not trust him."

"And extraordinarily good-looking, with a great presence," came from Lady Fisher. "Krishnan is very much his son."

"Vijay Bhanj has been ambassador in Washington and has represented India in conferences everywhere from Sri Lanka to Moscow. No young man could have a better background."

"Partly because," said Lady Fisher, "his mother, Leila, is a deeply spiritual woman, some of which, I think, is in Krishnan too. She comes from near here, from South India which perhaps has the deepest roots. I love Leila," and Lady Fisher told Mary, "When I came out to Delhi, as a new bride, she would not let me be the usual English wife, blind to the country. She taught me Hindi and about Hinduism for which I shall be eternally grateful. I hope, Mary, someone will do the same for you."

"Sir John laughed. He laughed. I am sure of it." Dr. Coomaraswamy was standing by the window of the first-floor room in the party's headquarters at Ghandara. The room, usually used as his office and usually buzzing with activity, was silent; the whole of the two-story stucco-faced house, important in this town of bazaar shanties, corrugated iron, cheap concrete blocks, was empty. Every helper had been sent far and wide, some to look for Krishnan, some in search of the required lorry.

On the outside, the house veranda and balconies were swathed with muslin draperies in the Root and Flower Party's colors, green, saffron yellow, and white: "Green for hope, saffron for holiness, white for pure intention," Dr. Coomaraswamy liked to explain. Over them hung the party's posters; for weeks the disciples had been putting them up all over the state—it was a point of honor between all parties not to tear down each other's posters. They were pictures with a symbol. "You must remember most of our people cannot read, so the party symbol is of

utmost importance." Dr. Coomaraswamy always empha-
sized, "And it must be recognizable instantly." Krishnan's
symbol was of three wise-looking cows lying among flowers; they would be on the voting papers too and instantly
identifiable with Krishnan. "There is," Dr. Coomaraswamy said in satisfaction, "not one man, woman, or child
who does not know the Krishna story." At headquarters
every poster was garlanded with fresh lucky mango
leaves; their very freshness seemed a mockery to Dr.
Coomaraswamy.

He was not even sure now about his inaugural
speech. He heard Sir John's voice, "Ten minutes is long
for an introduction." "But I like to speak," said Dr.
Coomaraswamy piteously to the empty room. "Also, what
I had to say, was it not important?"

"Yes, but it still depends on the way you say it,"
Krishnan had cautioned and, "He knows me," Dr.
Coomaraswamy had to admit. Krishnan had also forbid-
den any expletives: "No foul words or abuse."

"But Gopal Rau has denounced you as 'cheat,' 'liar,'
'hypocrite'; Mrs. Retty as 'dirty humbug,' 'ignorant
swine'—"

"And in return you will call them 'gentleman,' 'lady,'
'benefactor,' 'mother,' even 'prince.' "

"But those are kindly."

"It depends on how you say them." Krishnan had
smiled.

"Yes, but"—Dr. Coomaraswamy had been sad—"my
words were so beautifully foul!"

He had opened his speech with what he thought was
simple directness—and in the current fashion: "Friends,"
and then went on, as Mr. Srinivasan told him afterward,
to spoil it by "people of Konak, men, women, and our
beloved children: Accustomed as I am to public speaking,
tonight when I come to open this, the final week, of our
Root and Flower Party's campaign for which we owe so

much to so many of you, my heart is so full that I can hardly speak . . ."

"Speak. Speak," hissed Mr. Srinivasan who, as always, had been close beside him.

"The few words I have to say to you tonight are of such import, such freshness, newness of approach that they awe me and make my very lips to tremble . . ."

"Don't tremble. Go *on!*" mouthed Mr. Srinivasan.

"We shall begin with the root. The root goes on to flower, the flower will bring you fruit, much fruit. For you, for all Konak, perhaps for millions, our new manifesto offers this hope. Men and women, for you, at this very moment, hope is hovering with bright wings . . ."

Dr. Coomaraswamy had particularly liked "bright wings" but Mr. Srinivasan was making frantic accelerating gestures and Dr. Coomaraswamy had gathered momentum—too much momentum. "You must think before you speak," Uma, his wife, had always urged but at speed, "Friends," he had cried, "you are aware that for decades, if not generations, our beloved country, through the corruption, avarice, greed, exploitation of the few in power, has been standing on the edge of the precipice of utter disaster. Let us"—and here he had raised his fist in exaltation as his voice rang out—"let us take the first step forward."

Too late he saw Mr. Srinivasan collapse; too late knew what he had said but the most bitter mortification of all had been that no one had noticed. They had not been listening, Dr. Coomaraswamy thought now in anguish. My words might have been hot air. Perhaps they were hot air but he had not lacked courage; he had continued but then Krishnan had walked out.

Yes, he has made me a laughingstock, Dr. Coomaraswamy thought bitterly now of Krishnan: umbrellas, a lorry, a *pandal* as for a god. "I will sit in it," Krishnan had said. "You will not," Dr. Coomaraswamy had vowed, but then Sir John had laughed—he, Dr. Coomaraswamy, was certain it had been a laugh. Not only that, there were other cryptic things that had been said. "What did they *mean?*" asked the doctor.

"Krishnan is bats. Bats," Mr. Srinivasan had been moaning.

"Bats hang upside down, which seems topsy-turvy to us but it's their way." Sir John had been perfectly grave.

"So he should have been." Dr. Coomaraswamy was momentarily incensed. "It is no laughing matter. I, myself, have invested two *crores* at least in this cam-paign . . ."—"And did I not tell you not to?" Uma had said, over and over again, thought Dr. Coomaraswamy wearily.

"And why care so much about Sir John?" Uma had said that too, also over and over again. "You are a Doctor of Medicine, MA, MRCS, Edinburgh," she said this continually. "Also, I do not care, at all, for Lady Fisher."

"You mean she does not care for you." Dr. Coomaraswamy had not said that; Uma was formidable, bigger than he. "Lady Fisher is an inveterate snob," said Uma, but, I believed Sir John and I were friends, Dr. Coomaraswamy thought now. He calls me Coomaraswamy, I say, Sir John . . . He winced, remembering the terrible time when he had said, "Sir Fisher." "Solecism! Solecism!" he could have cried aloud to the unresponsive walls of headquarters.

He had taken off his jacket to ease the tiredness of his shoulders, had let his braces hang down. My God, my belly! thought Dr. Coomaraswamy—he could not see his feet and could feel the rolls of fat around his neck and face; to add to his misery he knew sweat was glistening on the baldness of his scalp. I am thoroughly unlovely, no girl would look at me, thought Dr. Coomaraswamy.

"Girl? What girl?" Uma seemed to pounce even on his thoughts. "What is this I hear about a girl?"

"My angel, you know there is no one else but you,"

and at once, as if in reality he had said it, there came into Dr. Coomaraswamy's mind a vision of Kuku as she had been this night: the sweet scent of her hair, the enticing girl flesh between *choli* and sari—he could have put his hands around her waist—the shadow of the long eyelashes on her cheeks. "Those eyelashes did not flutter for you," he told himself cruelly. "They were for that young Blaise Browne, you old fool." Still he found he was listening for the soft swish of a sari—Uma wore hers kilted up to show thick ankles and sensible nurse's white canvas shoes, which made her feet look larger than ever, whereas Dr. Coomaraswamy could not help having, in his eye, the sight of little feet with slender bones, the nails painted red, delicate sandals held by a thong between the toes. Each time he saw them a quiver of delight had run through Dr. Coomaraswamy. No one has ever written a poem to toes, he thought. He had a mind to try, but again, "Old fool, keep to what is your business," he told himself, and his thoughts returned to the deserted party, the lost *crores* of rupees—worst, the loss of face. He could have wailed aloud, "What to do now? What, in heaven or earth, to do?"

It was late, almost on midnight, when Dr. Coomaraswamy came back to Patna Hall. The breeze was soft, benign, as he left his taxi and crossed the courtyard. The house slept; the moon had gone. Then, as he came out on the veranda, he saw a figure sitting quietly in a chair.

"At last," said Sir John.

"You . . . you have been waiting for me?"

"I was getting worried. You look all in. You need a stiff drink."

"Whiskey peg, Srinivasan still calls it," Dr. Coomaraswamy tried to joke.

When they had their glasses, "Well, have you found him?" asked Sir John.

"Nowhere. Not anywhere."

"Hari, what are you going to do?"

"I don't know. I *do not* know. John"—Sir John had said Hari—"John, you tell me."

"There's only one thing you can do. You haven't time to get another candidate. In any case, Krishnan Bhanj has not withdrawn, so—" Sir John interrupted himself, "Are you sure it's not nerves? Young candidates often have a case of nerves."

"Krishnan has no nerves. I wish he had, it might make him more amenable. Nervous? On the contrary . . ."

"Then," said Sir John, "you can only do as he says."

"This antic? You mean the lorry, the *pandal* and all? This nonsense?"

"I mean the lorry, the *pandal*, this nonsense—to the letter—and now, Hari, my friend, go to bed and try and get some sleep."

"Hari. My friend." It was as if all the sore places had miraculously healed. Tears came into Dr. Coomaraswamy's eyes. "John—" he began.

"Hallo," said Sir John, "who's that?"

He had gone to the veranda rail. Dr. Coomaraswamy joined him. Someone was running along the beach, a slim someone in a pale blue dress, hair flying. "That is Mr. Browne's young wife," said Dr. Coomaraswamy, "and alone."

"Alone?" Sir John scanned the beach. "So it seems."

"She should not be out alone this time of night."

"She should not," said Sir John, "but she is."

Sunday — Monday:
Midnight Hour

■ ■ ■ ■ ■ ■ ■ ■ ■ ■ ■ ■ ■

"I should have said no in Bombay."

Sunday's evening had grown better as it went on; Blaise, unusual for him, had joined the women: Auntie Sanni, Lady Fisher— and me, thought Mary. Kuku had gone to bed. Sir John was talking to Professor Aaron who, having brought his ladies safely home from the palace, had come onto the veranda to say goodnight. "Professor Webster and I have our lectures ready." He stretched and yawned. "Tomorrow we go to see the cave paintings in the hills."

Mr. Menzies had disappeared to do some telephoning. "Always he is telephoning," Kuku had said as she watched him go.

Sitting in a chair by Auntie Sanni, Blaise had drawn Mary, on her stool, to lean against his knee. He was listening, not talking, and every now and again he ran his fingers through her hair—he might have been Bumble again. Auntie Sanni's voice was soothing too in its quiet singsong; she was telling Blaise the history of Patna Hall and of her grandfather's estate in Bihar, his factory, and indigo fields. Indigo. Indigo: Mary seemed to see acres of a strange plant brilliantly blue—but it's Krishna who is blue, or is it Vishnu? Vishna? Krishu? The names began to merge into a maze. "Mary, you're half asleep," said Blaise. "Come, I'll take you to bed."

"It's very late, almost midnight." Lady Fisher folded

her embroidery. As Blaise pulled Mary to her feet and steadied her, she bent and kissed Lady Fisher and Auntie Sanni.

Outside in the garden it was magical, the air balmy, the sky a dome of stars. The long flower beds were spangled with fireflies. Fireflies and stars, which are which? wondered sleepy Mary, while there was a scent of such sweetness that it made her more sleepy still. Then, at the foot of the steps, they heard the piano. "She's still playing," said Mary. It made her uneasy and as she listened, "Chopin," she whispered. The nocturne ended; Olga Manning began the little A major prelude with its pleading and, "I should go and say goodnight to her." Mary moved toward the steps.

"You should not," said Blaise, and caught her back. "Don't you see, she's desperate for friendship."

The music seemed an echo of that; it made Mary say, "Haven't you ever felt desperate?" but Blaise was in a peaceful mood. "I'm desperate to go to bed."

A waiter on late duty came down the steps. "Memsahib," he called, and handed Mary a basket of carrots and sugar lumps. "Samuel say for donkey."

"Throw them away," said Blaise, but forgetting Mrs. Manning and the playing, Mary had run down the bungalow path. "How do you call a donkey if you don't know its name?" She tried a whistle. There was an answering whicker and when Blaise caught up with her most of the carrots and sugar were gone. "I don't believe anyone has been kind to him before," she told Blaise. "I'm going to call him Slippers."

"Call him Gum Boots, if you like," Blaise said, yawning, "as long as he stays in the garden and doesn't come on the veranda."

While Blaise undressed in the bathroom, Mary went out to look at the sea. The thundering of the waves seemed to have a lulling sound now; the breeze, gentle tonight, blew through the room. "That's why," Auntie Sanni had told Blaise when, among other things, he had asked for a mosquito net, "at Patna Hall we do not need them. We do not have mosquitoes, which is a boon." The big double bed, without a net, had its sheet and light quilt turned back—Patna Hall had thin Indian cotton quilts, "Not proper blankets or eiderdowns," Kuku had lamented. Mary's short nightdress had been laid out; she looked at it and felt a sudden distaste.

"Where did you meet that outrageously handsome husband of yours?" Mrs. Manning—Olga—had asked.

"In Norway. Rory, my father, has a lodge there, like a chalet above one of the fjords. He likes fishing, when he can."

"Your father's a diplomat?"

"Yes. Bumble—Blaise was his second secretary in Kuala Lumpur. When they came on leave, Rory asked Blaise to Norway to fish. I joined them. I had just left school, my last, thank God."

"So . . . Blaise is in the service too?"

"Yes," and now, It has not really dawned on me, thought Mary looking at the nightdress, how important to Blaise his work is, yet he jeopardized it, or thought he did, for me. Well, he had been out of England for a year, perhaps he was starved. She knew now that, when in any foreign posting, Blaise would never have considered any of the native girls. And I? thought Mary. I had not been really close to a young man before—she could see that schoolgirl Mary—and I suppose I was feeling emancipated, grown-up . . .

There was a little hut where we put overflow guests . . . she had not, of course, told Olga Manning this—never, never anybody, thought Mary. Blaise and I used to go there, mostly at night. Nobody knew. It was fun, thought Mary, with longing. We made love—and it was love. There was only a single bed; once Bumble fell on the floor. He just laughed. It was good. It never seemed wrong, but . . . Mary's nails dug into the flesh of her palms. In these double beds, I can't.

"Merry, are you coming?"

"Don't call me Merry."

"Does it matter what I call you?" Blaise had come amiably out of the bedroom; he was wearing only a *lunghi*—many young Western men new to India had taken to sleeping in them—it wrapped his loins and stalwart legs. His torso still shone from the ladling of water from the mug; as he bent his knees to look in the looking glass, his hair glistened too. He was young, fresh, powerful, but Mary asked, "Blaise, in Norway, what made you tell Rory about us and the hut?"

"It was the only honorable thing to do."

"Wouldn't it have been more honorable to ask me first?"

He ignored that and went on, "Besides I had to, you weren't like other girls."

"I was exactly like other girls."

"Not for me." For a moment, Mary thought it was Bumble speaking, her Bumble, but then, "Rory was my chief," Blaise explained. "In my very first posting which was vital. If I hadn't told him and he had found out, he might have wrecked my career before it really started."

"I see." Mary said it slowly trying to keep down her dismay. Then she blazed, "Rory wouldn't have done that. Even if he had minded—and I think he did mind—he would never have done that. He's not that sort of man. Don't you know *anything* about people?" and Save me, save me, beat in her every nerve.

An answer came, a clip-clopping, and Slippers appeared on the veranda. He gave a whicker when he saw Mary, came confidently through the doorway and began nosing around the chest of drawers, clopped to the bed, nuzzling the pillows. "He's looking for more carrots and sugar!" Mary's laugh was cut short.

"Get out! Out, you little beast," yelled the already angry Blaise. "In our *bedroom!*" and, as the little donkey looked at him in surprise, a shoe came hurtling across the room. Slippers shied in fright, slipping, and slithering on the stone floor; hampered by his hooves, he could not get his balance and half fell across the bed. Blaise took up the other shoe.

"Blaise, don't! Don't!"

"I'm only trying to get him out."

"You needn't *hurt* him," but, "Get off the bed," Blaise shouted at the donkey. "Get *off!*"

Slippers righted himself and stood trembling. "Don't. *Don't!*" wailed Mary again but, holding the shoe by the toe, Blaise advanced on Slippers and beat him with the heel on his rump and sides. Blaise had not meant it but the shoe flew out of his hand and caught the soft nose. "He's bleeding!" screamed Mary.

Blood had begun to ooze from one nostril; the ears went back as with terrified brays, stumbling over his distorted hooves, Slippers fled to the veranda. Slipping and sliding again, they heard him crash down the steps. "He may have broken his legs!" and Mary shouted at Blaise, "I'll never like you again! Never!" as she ran down the steps. "I'm going," she shouted, "and I'm not coming back!"

Slippers had not broken his legs. He was stumbling along the beach. She ran after him.

"Mary, don't be silly. Come back. Come back at once." Blaise's words floated back to him on the breeze.

Mary ran along the beach past fishing boats drawn up, nets stretched to dry, until she caught up with Slippers. For a while he would not come to her but at last the bruised and bloodied nose touched her hand. Taking off her shoes, holding him by the rope around his neck, she led him into the sea, hoping the water would ease his legs—they must be bruised. With her free hand, she patted him, talking to him; the trembling eased to a quivering. Then she led him back to dry land.

There, her arms around his neck, Mary began to cry, cry as she had never done before. I should have said no in Bombay, gone with Rory to Peru . . . Peru, London, the North Pole, anywhere. She sobbed against Slippers's rough neck as the donkey stood quietly, holding her weight. I should have been warned, thought Mary. Hadn't Blaise said that very first time when he got up from the ridiculous bed, "I shall never forgive myself, never. I must see your father at once." She had only pulled him down, "Don't you dare," and kissed him. And there was magic, she insisted now, a sort of magic, in the long Norwegian summer days, hardly any night. Then how had it come to this? She did not know. I suppose in Ootacamund I kept my eyes shut tight. Now they were painfully open and, "Oh, Rory, Rory, I wish you were here."

Far out to sea there was a steamer, its lights making a chain of pinprick reflections across the water; the steamer looked as small and lonely in that vastness as Mary felt. She turned to go back but behind the beach was a line of what seemed to be small trees, soft and feathery with, behind them again, taller trees; though Mary did not know it, this was the casuarina and mango grove. As she looked, she saw a glow that flickered. A fire, thought Mary.

Her shoes in her hand, her bare feet making no noise on the sand, she walked up slowly through the fuzzy trees, their feathery branches brushing her face. Vaguely she could see, among them, bushes of what seemed to be scarlet flowers, hibiscus; holding the bell of one of them, she stood at the edge of a clearing among the taller trees.

There was a roof of palm matting stretched between two slender trunks of trees; below it, animal skins, deer and goat, lay on the sand before a seat or a couch—or was it a throne? To the side was a big earthenware pitcher for water, a brass *lota*, a few brass platters and long-handled spoons—Mary had come out without her spectacles yet every detail seemed printed on her eyes. A washing line was stretched, too, between two trees—a line hung with loincloths and, incongruously, a sweater. Behind the washing was a pile of brushwood and green-brown stems—could they be sugarcane? wondered Mary.

The fire was in front, a fire of wood; tending it was a young man, blue-black—Mary felt as if she recognized him. He was wearing a loincloth with another cloth across his shoulders. His hair looked oddly white; then, as the fire flared up, Mary saw his hair was full of ashes. On his face, two arched eyebrows were drawn in white with, between them, a white U shape that Lady Fisher had said was the sign of the god Vishnu; the lips were scarlet.

He stood up. At that moment, Slippers, who had followed Mary, gave her such a sudden shove with his nose that she dropped her shoes.

At the sound, quick as a cat, the young man had leapt to the couch and was sitting in the lotus position—legs crossed, each foot up to rest on the opposite knee, looking exactly, thought Mary, like one of the gods in the pictures she had seen in the bazaar.

"Come," a voice called, a mellifluous voice that had an echo of a flute. "Come."

Her arm around the donkey's neck, Mary came. "Oh, it's you," the young man said, and got off the throne.

Mary had stepped into the circle of light; there was a small lantern set on the sand. He picked it up, holding it to see her. Mary knew her face was tear-stained, her eyes red from crying, her hair in tangles, her skirt soaked with salt water from washing Slippers and that she smelled of donkey. "Never mind. Please sit down," he said, as if he had read her thoughts, and then, not a question but a statement, "You are from Auntie Sanni's."

"Yes."

"Mrs. Blaise Browne."

"Yes." Mary was reluctant to say it.

"On honeymoon."

"Yes."

"Not much honey, I think." He was holding the lantern closer. "Too much moon."

"Yes." That was like a sob.

"Moons wane," he said, "not like ours tonight which will grow bigger. That is propitious. If you start anything new always do it on a waxing moon. Perhaps your husband would say that is superstitious?"

"Yes."

"It is not superstitious to take notice of seasons, tides, sun, and moon. So, you ran away to be with the donkey instead?"

"Yes."

"If you can only say one word"—he laughed—"undoubtedly yes is better than no."

Was he mocking her? No. His voice was tender—and, You could trust him to be tender, she thought, instinctively. She was beginning to unwind from the hard little ball she had made of herself. There was something about the gaiety that was irresistible; she found she was responding. "They are looking everywhere for you," she told him.

He laughed. "Looking far and wide. They will not think of looking close."

"But why are you talking to me?" she said. "I thought you had taken a vow of silence."

"A public vow. This is private. The makeup is public too; underneath it, I assure you, I am a most presentable person."

More than that, Mary could have said. There was something magnificent about him—a curious word to use for a young man. She found she was looking at him with an again curious minuteness; he was not tall but was so slim he looked taller. She could see, in the firelight, how the muscles moved with rippling ease, almost like a great cat's, under the dark skin—Yes, blue-black, thought Mary. The shoulders were broad, the head well set, his face fine-boned, a straight nose with sensitive nostrils; his eyes were brown not black as with many Indians—they looked light in the darkness of his skin.

"You ask me why—the vow, I mean." He bent down and scooped a little of the sand and let it trickle through his fingers. "I think you know," he said, "what it is to be out of love?"

"Yes." That was so fervent that they both laughed, happy, easy laughter.

He threw more wood on the fire which leapt up, sending sparks high in the air. Sparks, fireflies, stars. Mary felt dizzy; the sand though, warm and dry, was firm under her as she sat, her wet skirt spread around her; he was opposite, sitting Indian fashion on his heels.

"Your name is Krishnan from Krishna?"

"That is so."

"Do you play the flute?"

"No, only the fool." He laughed, then conceded, "Well, I play a little but not as well as Krishna, who could? And your name is?"

"Mary."

"Mary Browne." He tried it over.

"Browne with an *e*," Mary mocked, which she knew was disloyal.

"Then, Mary Browne, how did you come here?"

"Blaise, my husband, was posted to India. I followed him."

"He wasn't your husband then?"

"No, not until Bombay."

Blaise had insisted, "It must be properly arranged."

"Properly?" She had laughed but to her surprise, Rory, who had always allowed her to do as she wanted—almost, she had to admit, there had been those schools—

and who did not care a fig what his world thought about him, took the same view but, "I . . . I'm not ready to be married yet," Mary, even in her ardency, had said.

"Exactly what I think," and Rory had urged, "Merry, come with me to Peru." Rory, too, had a new and even more senior posting. "Then if in two or three years' time you still . . ."

"Two or three years!" the young Mary had cried in anguish, at eighteen that seemed aeons, and, "So I came," she said now to Krishnan.

"*Atcha!*" He accepted that with the ambiguous Hindustani word.

There was a sound of crashing: Something heavy was coming through the trees. Slippers, who—contributing to the peacefulness—was lying near on the sand, his legs bent under him, his ears still, pricked them and gave a whicker as, behind the shanty shelter, a big hulk appeared. "An elephant!" cried Mary.

"My elephant," said Krishnan. "At least she belongs to the Maharajah but as he is absent she has been lent to me for the campaign."

"I didn't know there was a maharajah."

"His Highness Tirupatha Deva Raja of Konak. He has other titles but not as lovely for instance as, best of all, the Seem of Swat. The Maharajah used to own the state. He had palaces, three forts, an army, foot and horse."

"And elephants?"

"Yes, especially one elephant, very fierce, the Maharajah kept for trampling people. In those days that was the usual punishment and every now and then the fierce elephant was sent into towns and villages to trample a few peasants and officials to remind them the Maharajah was the Maharajah."

"That can't be true."

"I do not always speak the truth," said Krishnan. "Who does? But this is true. Now the current Maharajah is plain Mr. Konak, the treasury is forfeit, most of the palaces are colleges or hospitals, the forts and armies gone. He has only this one small elephant—she is small because her mother discarded her. She has become a pet."

"Where is her—is it a *mahout?*—the man who drives her?"

"Drunk, I expect," said Krishnan. "She wanders at night."

"But is that safe?"

"She wouldn't trample a chicken, she's far too wise. The villagers give her sweets."

"Will she come if you call?"

"If I have sugarcane. Fortunately I have," and in his fluting voice he called, "Come, come, Birdie."

"*Birdie?* That's not a name for an elephant."

"It is in remembrance," said Krishnan. "When I was a little boy I had an English governess, Miss Birdwood. We called her Birdie. She, too, was an orphan."

"Is that why you speak English so well?"

"Well, I was at school in England, then went to Oxford."

He let these small details about himself fall into the conversation. Is he showing off? thought Mary. Yes, he is, to me. It made her feel pleasingly important. She tried to see the small dark boy he must have been with the governess, Birdie; he would have had the same brown eyes, probably mischievous, the haughty face. Miss Birdie could not have had an easy time except that, Mary was sure, he was affectionate. At Oxford he must have worn a suit, at least a jersey and trousers, which seemed incredible, and at once, as if she had spoken aloud, Krishnan said, "I assure you, I was perfectly proper."

Mary blushed but the elephant had come, standing, swaying on the other side of the fire from the donkey who stayed in quiet comradeship.

Krishnan had said Birdie was small but to Mary she loomed large. She looked at the width of her back with its gray, wrinkled skin, the ridiculously small tail, the outsized toenails on the big feet, half buried in the sand, and lifted her eyes to the head with its curious dome—again, she was looking in detail. The ears were not as big as the elephants she had seen in Africa. "Indian elephants are more elegant," said Krishnan. "Perhaps because they are used for state occasions and for walking in processions." Birdie's ears were shapely, mottled pink and brown on the underside. The eyes looked—tiny, Mary thought in surprise, yet elephants' eyes are supposed to have a hundred facets. More surprising were the eyelashes—"I never knew elephants had eye-lashes!"

"Like a film star's," said Krishnan. The trunk was reaching toward him, its tip lifted to show small pink divisions. A stem of sugarcane came, was accepted whole with leaves; the trunk stuffed it into the mouth with its absurd underlip, came back again while Krishnan crooned words in Telegu. How gentle he is, thought Mary.

"You give her some," said Krishnan.

"Would she take it from me? Would she?"

"Don't be so doubting, try."

The trunk came toward Mary, accepted, then suddenly slapped the ground, sending a shower of sand over her. "*Ayyo!*" cried Krishnan. "That's enough. That was play," he explained. "She's the only elephant I know who amuses herself. The palace uses her to fetch marketing and firewood. For that she has to go inland, across a river, wide and shallow. To while away the time, she puts her trunk just under the water and blows bubbles but she would much rather walk in processions—they hire her out for weddings," and he sang:

> *With rings on her fingers*
> [*though they would have to be earrings*]
> *And bells on her toes,*
> *She shall have music*
> *Wherever she goes.*

His voice was full and sweet; it filled Mary with a happiness as light as the bubbles Birdie blew. What did it matter if they broke and disappeared? "It seems so strange," she said. "Nursery rhymes and bubbles. To be at Oxford you have to be clever."

"Naturally. I got a first."

"Then politics—and you know about elephants?"

"At the moment I know everything," said Krishnan. "My father says when I am older I shall know that I don't know anything but I haven't reached as far as that yet."

"My father says," Mary was not to be outdone, "that you should always pretend to know less than you do about things. With me, that isn't difficult. I don't know anything. One of my headmistresses wrote in my report, 'Mary has a marvelous capacity for sitting in a class and absorbing absolutely nothing.' But I can speak French and Italian—servants' French and Italian."

"You talk to the servants, you won't talk to our friends," Rory used to reproach her.

"*Your* friends," even as a child, Mary had retorted that. "We move about so much, I don't have time to make any."

"I don't think," she told Krishnan now, "I ever had a friend but the servants stayed with us. They took me to market. Markets are much more interesting than drawing rooms. I suppose there have to be drawing rooms."

"For you, yes," said Krishnan. "You see, I know your father's name: Roderick Frobisher Sinclair Scott."

"That's not half as grand as it sounds. It's only because in Scotland, if you inherit land, for instance from your mother or grandmother—"

"On the maternal side?"

"Yes, you add her surname to your own. You could end with four but Rory's only a younger son."

"They are proud old names, yet you would rather be Mary Browne?"

"That's what I thought," and Mary quickly turned the talk away from herself. "Sing something again," she said, "something Indian."

He sang in Tamil first, then in English:

A cradle of chaudan
A cord of silk.
Come, little moonbird
I'll rock the cradle,
Rock you to sleep
Sleep.

"That," said Krishnan, "is one of the lullabies *ayahs* sing to children when they are in bed." He stood up. "Now, before you go to sleep, moonbird, or they send out a search party and raise a sensation, I must take you back."

"I'll leave you here," he said when they came near the bungalow. "I don't want to be shot."

Mary watched him go. Suddenly he began to dance in and out of the waves, taking long leaps over the stretched-out nets and the prows of boats. Slippers and Birdie had come out of the grove to watch, standing one behind the other at the foot of the dunes; as he turned to join them, he looked along the beach and raised his hand.

Mary raised hers in return.

Monday

■ ■ ■ ■ ■ ■ ■ ■ ■ ■ ■ ■ ■

"Rory's family couldn't be bettered," Lady Fisher said in satisfaction. Sir John had told her about seeing Mary on the beach late last night. "Her mother was a Foljambe, a Devon Foljambe. That ought to be all right."

"Alicia, you are a constant joy to me." Sir John in his dressing gown was standing at the window. "You never change."

"I see no reason to change." Lady Fisher was as placid as ever. "I believe in good breeding—at any level—and it's a comfort to know people's backgrounds . . . it helps one to understand why they behave as they do."

It was a perfect morning. Early mornings in India are not like mornings anywhere else; they have a purity, "Perhaps," Sir John often said, "because they begin with ritual washings and prayer." In every town and village the people were making their morning ablutions, going down into the rivers or village tanks or pools, standing waist high in the water, pouring it over themselves, lifting their hands in prayer. In Shantipur the villagers did not go into the sea like the fishermen—the waves were too strong—but all were at prayer, purifying themselves.

There were smells: of dew on leaves and grass, of smoke from small fires of dung, of cooking in mustard oil; sudden whiffs of sweetness came from flowers opening in the first sun and, oddly mingling, European smells of toast for the early morning teas being made in the pantry at Patna Hall.

The wind was only a breeze. Along the beach, the waves were almost gentle; black dots of fishing boats were out on a calm sea. "They must have gone out early," said Sir John.

Auntie Sanni's doves were calling from the dovecote in the courtyard while parakeets swung and chattered in the jacaranda and acacia trees; monkeys were industriously searching one another for fleas. There was a tumble of bougainvillea and of morning glory along the walls, their convolvulus-shaped flowers brilliantly blue. As Sir John looked, Hannah came down the upstairs veranda, bringing their morning tea with toast and plantains, small bananas, extra sweet. "Who could want breakfast after this?" asked Lady Fisher.

"I do," said Sir John, "at Patna Hall."

Hannah, in a clean white sari, her bracelets clinking, put down the tray and made *namaskar*. Lesser guests had their trays brought by the houseboys.

"Thank you, Hannah." As Lady Fisher poured, she began again where she had left off. "Anne, Mary's mother, Anne Foljambe, remember, would never have countenanced this marriage. Mary should have stayed at that excellent convent in Brussels. She had seemed settled. Do you remember we took her out while we were there?"

"Rory always let her do what she liked."

"Yes, but to marry so young."

"Probably couldn't stop her," said Sir John. "Pity the young man's not up to her."

"Most people would say the other way around. He's an only son, there's plenty of money but . . . How does he stand with you, John?"

"Steady, therefore dependable. Completely honest, of course. Excellently briefed—up to a point—but I detect"—Sir John winced—"a certain arrogance, or is it pretentiousness?"

"That's from Mother," Lady Fisher said at once.

"Yes. Archie Browne's a good chap, as I said, invaluable in secondary places where, I can guess, Master Blaise will follow him."

"Poor Mrs. Browne."

"But, Alicia, that girl! She's quicksilver. I was watching her last night when you were telling the Krishna story, response in every line."

"Probably too much response." Lady Fisher sighed. "Well, she married him, she'll have to conform, though it seems a pity to clip her wings."

"I don't think she'll let them be clipped," said Sir John.

Dr. Coomaraswamy, in his shirt sleeves, without a tie, his fringe of hair ruffled, was on the telephone. "Since six A.M. have I been on the telephone," he told Samuel, who was supervising the tables for breakfast, while Mr. Srinivasan frantically looked up numbers. "Hallo. Hallo." Another stream of Telegu, then the doctor hung up. "No contractor has a lorry free. Not one."

"And what, anyway, are we doing with a lorry?" Mr. Srinivasan seemed to beseech heaven.

"Only what we have to do," said Dr. Coomaraswamy—"Gloomaraswamy," as Krishnan often called him.

"What we have to do? And what will that be?"

Gloomaraswamy lost his temper. "I only know if this fool antic has to be done at all, it must be done properly."

"Pandal, garlands and all?"

"Pandal, garlands, posters, loudspeakers, bloody well all."

"We cannot do it without a lorry," said Mr. Srinivasan in despair.

"I have a lorry." Fresh as the morning, his white clothes immaculate, his ringleted hair oiled, came Sharma, once more a messenger for good. "A beautiful lorry."

"Who got it?"

"I," said Sharma. "Am I not District Agent?"

"Whose is it?"

"Surijlal Chand's."

"Surijlal's? But he's opposition."

"No longer," said Sharma with his angelic smile. "No longer."

"But . . . how?"

"I took him to see Krishnan. Surijlal is a highly religious man. He was up at dawn saying his prayers. Do you know where he is now?"

"How could I know?" said Dr. Coomaraswamy crossly. "I am not Surijlal's keeper."

"He is taking *darshan*," said Sharma. *"Darshan* of Krishnan . . . sitting, not saying a word, filled with joy and we have his lorry."

"But . . . what is it costing?"

"Nothing. He has given it."

"Surijlal has *given* it? And he a *bania*. I do not believe . . ."

"There it is," said Sharma, leading them through the hall, and there, by the portico, stood a full-size lorry, almost new and already decorated with tassels, beads, and paper flowers.

"But this is excellent." Mr. Srinivasan was hopping up and down in excitement.

"Call everyone!" a recovered Dr. Coomaraswamy shouted. "Srinivasan, go up to Paradise and gather everybody at once. Tell them to hurry."

Auntie Sanni heard the lorry drive up, then, later, Coomaraswamy's voice shrilly exhorting as the young men came hurrying down the outside staircase with a hubbub of excited voices as orders were shouted from under the portico. The other side of the house was in peace, and as Auntie Sanni on her swing couch was sipping her tea, Hannah, in full clinking, massaged her legs.

"Kuku not up yet?" asked Auntie Sanni. "She should be."

"Let her sleep," said Hannah, "for all the good she is."

Mary wanted to sleep too but, "Wake up," came Blaise's voice. "Tea. We're going to have a swim before breakfast."

Their tray had been set down on the veranda table; rolling over, Mary could see the teapot in its cozy, the pile of toast, bananas, and thought of her electric Teasmaid of the hotel in Ootacamund and smiled. She was too lazy to get up and lay blinking in the light—Blaise had opened the half doors, sunshine lay on the stone floors, and Blaise, holding his cup of tea, was in his bathing shorts. "Come and swim." Generously he made no allusion to the night before. "Come on."

"No, thank you," said Mary. She was lying on the far side of the bed, the farthest she had been able to get from him, but by his friendliness, he seemed to have forgotten everything or decided to put it out of his mind—he had been asleep when she came in.

Now, as she lay, she was still filled with the happiness and ease of the grove and, "Krishnan, Krishnan," she whispered into the pillow.

"Mary, a good swim . . ."

"No, I don't want to have this buffeted out of me," but she could not tell that to Blaise and, "You go," she said, trying to sound half asleep.

"Right, I will."

Beyond the partition, Olga Manning had been listening to the news. She clicked the transistor off and, standing in the doorway, looked at the waves. She could not see them though; her eyes were blind with tears. As if she had to prevent them spilling down her cheeks, she clenched her hands hard.

A furious altercation broke out on the beach.

"Sahib wish to swim?" Thambi had come up to Blaise. "I call Somu."

"Somu?"

"Lifeguard. Very good young man. He swim with you."

"For what?"

"At Patna Hall," said Thambi, "no guest swim in our sea alone and must wear helmet, Sahib." He showed the pointed, strong wickerwork cap. "For break wave force. Necessary, Sahib."

"Absolute bull! Don't be silly, man. The sea's perfectly calm."

"Look calm," said Thambi, "but deep, has currents, waves in one minute get too strong. Sahib, please to wait while Somu come."

"Why should I wait? I swim when and how I want."

"No, Sahib." Thambi stood firm. "It is rule. No guest swim alone. I call Somu."

"Damned impudent cheek!"

Blaise was back in the bedroom putting on his toweling bathrobe.

"Where are you going?"

"To have this out with Mrs. McIndoe."

"Auntie Sanni?" Mary had been listening, willy-nilly: Blaise had been shouting. "Blaise," she tried, "why not just do as they say? Wouldn't it be more simple? When they see what a strong swimmer you are, of course they'll let you be alone."

"I won't take this from anyone," declared Blaise.

Mary had to sympathize. His swimming was the thing of which Blaise was most proud and with reason; she remembered him in Norway and how impressed she and Rory had been. "Blaise," she began again, but was not surprised to find that he had gone.

"Mr. Browne, my grandfather kept the rule and so do I," said Auntie Sanni. "Each bather takes a man, sometimes two, and wears the helmet. It is wise."

"Quite, for most people. I don't want to boast, Mrs.

McIndoe," said Blaise, "but I was chosen for training to swim the English Channel."

"The English Channel is not the Coromandel coast, Mr. Browne." Auntie Sanni was unimpressed. "I am sorry to disappoint you but no visitor swims alone from our beach."

"Then I'll go farther up the beach."

"If you like." Auntie Sanni's singsong was calm. "Patna Hall beach is netted and enclosed far out to sea. Elsewhere there are sharks. That is why the fishermen go out four at a time," and seeing Blaise look like a small boy balked, echoing Mary, she coaxed, "Mr. Browne, why not, this first time at any rate, go in with Somu? I expect you swim like a man but he swims like a fish, in-stinc-tive-ly. Try him this morning, Mr. Browne, then if he and Thambi think—"

"How kind!" said Blaise, which irony was lost on Auntie Sanni. "I prefer not to swim at all."

The lorry could not have been better: Like all Surijlal Chand's possessions it was flashy, painted bright yellow, "For-tun-ate-ly one of our party's colors," crooned Mr. Srinivasan. Green was provided by mango leaf garlands, the white by the background of the posters, of Krishnan's symbolic three cows among stylized flowers.

"It could not be more eye-catching," Dr. Coomaraswamy had to admit both of the lorry and symbol. Two loudspeakers were connected to a battery; in case it failed, there was a megaphone. Dr. Coomaraswamy was to stand on the tail of the lorry. "Yes, I myself must speak all day, since Krishnan . . ."

The *pandal*'s throne seat was raised, "So everyone can see him," said Sharma, and was handsomely set off by whole banana trees, their wide long leaves fresh, their stems swathed in yellow and green. When Krishnan took his seat, naked except for a small loincloth, his skin shining blue-black—Sharma had used plenty of oil—his face painted, the U mark of Vishnu on his forehead, the garlands around his neck—white mogra flowers that had a heady jasmine scent—he looked a veritable god.

He sat in the lotus position. "You will get cramp," Mr. Srinivasan predicted.

"I never get cramp," wrote Krishnan. He had a pad and ball pen beside him on which he put down his orders.

Everyone was ready. "But will the people take it?" the doctor worried—"buts" were flying about like vicious small brickbats.

"Surijlal took it," said Sharma.

With a sense of occasion he had found a conch; as the lorry swept out on the sandy road outside the grove, followed by a small fleet of Jeeps, motorbikes, and ambassador cars filled and spilling over with the disciples. "Ulla ulla, ullulah." The conch sounded its holiness as the cortege drove past Patna Hall, then slowly through the village. "Through all villages we must be slow, then away to Ghandara, slow through the bazaar, then other villages, other towns," cried Sharma. "Ulla, ulla, ullulah. Ulla."

"What shall we do?" asked Blaise after breakfast.

"It was a glorious breakfast," said Mary. She had eaten papaya, a luscious fruit, large as a melon but golden-fleshed, black-seeded, then kedgeree, and, at Samuel's insistence, bacon, sausages—"At Patna Hall we make our own"—with scrambled eggs, which Auntie Sanni called "rumble-tumble." Finally, toast and marmalade, all with large cups of coffee.

"I've never seen you eat like this," said Blaise.

"I've never eaten like this."

"Are you sure you've had enough?" he teased as she laid down her napkin. "Well, what can we do today?"

"I'm too full to do anything," and not only with breakfast she could have said. "I'm going to lie on the beach in the sun like a lizard." These dear little Indian lizards, thought Mary . . . There was one now, climbing up the dining room wall—she had heard that if anyone touched their tails, the tails would fall off . . . I don't want anyone to touch me, thought Mary.

Back at the bungalow, she took a towel, spread it on the beach, and lay facedown, basking.

"I think I'll play golf." Blaise's bag of clubs was bigger than Mary. "The brochure says there is a golf course."

He was soon back, disgruntled. "Call that a golf course. Absolute con! All on sand! Not even nine holes."

"Better than nothing." Mary was half asleep.

"Anyhow I can't play alone." Blaise sounded lost. "Sir John won't come out. I tried Menzies but he's at his bloody typewriter. Mary, I'll give you a lesson."

"No."

"Merry . . ."

"I can't." Mary shut her eyes and her ears. "I can't."

Blaise was reduced to putting on the flattest sand-green he could find.

Mary lay idly watching the small crabs that scuttled down the beach to meet the highest ripple of each wave; each crab threw up a minute flurry of sand. Crabs, lizards, the elephant Birdie, the sea, and the sky seemed to merge and come into one, be "cosmic," thought Mary. That was a big claim yet true. I am cosmic, she thought, so is a crab or a lizard. If she shut her eyes she seemed to see circles of light that moved, changed, and fused. Cosmos, thought Mary, or is the plural "'cosmic"? But "cosmos" can't have a plural, you silly. She went back to being a lizard and was soon asleep.

Mary was woken by Hannah's planting a beach umbrella beside her in the sand. "Not good, *baba*, to lie in sun too long. You have sunstroke, brain fever. Too hot." She opened the umbrella. It was true, Mary was too hot and was grateful for the shade. "And you drink," commanded Hannah. Besides the umbrella, she had brought a jug of still lemon. "We make our own lemonade . . . drink, *baba*."

It was plain that Hannah, Samuel, and now Thambi, who had come up too and was smiling down at her, had a conspiracy to look after her but *"baba,"* thought Mary sitting up, her arms around her bare knees. *Baba,* child. Yes, I am behaving like a child. She put a lock of hair behind her ear; her hair felt soft, like a child's but, "You must try to be older," she told herself sternly. "You're a married woman. Be generous." That was a word she had not used before and as Thambi asked, "Missy swim?" she said, "I must go and tell my Sahib," got up, and went to look for Blaise.

They swam. "Sahib strong swimmer," Thambi said in admiration, but Mary noticed the young Somu swimming beside Blaise.

Moses and another fisherman held Mary, diving with her under a towering wave. For a moment she felt her feet standing on a floor of sand—the sea floor?—then they swept her up through the wave; it fell like a weight of thunder on her head but the point of the wicker helmet pierced it and she was up; deftly they turned her, their brown hands strong and quick, then, with them, she was riding in on the crest. On the shore they let her go, gasping, laughing in exhilaration, as the wave trundled her up the beach. "I've never felt anything like this," she called to Blaise.

"I must say the bathing *is* marvelous," he shouted back above the noise of the surf. For the first time at Patna Hall he looked happy . . . as a sandboy, thought Mary—he was covered in sand. "Let's go in again."

"Yes," called Mary. He dived back into a wave, followed at once by Somu while Mary held out her hands to Moses and the fisherman.

Towels around their necks, she and Blaise walked back to the bungalow, then up to the house for lunch in friendliness.

They played tennis all afternoon.

"Isn't there something very dear about this place?" Mrs. Glover asked the other ladies, stretching her feet luxuriously as she sat in the comfortable veranda chair. "Unlike the other hotels we've stayed at, coming back here in the evening is like coming home."

The group had spent the day driving out into the hills to see the newly discovered cave paintings; now they were resting on the veranda and, "Yes," said Mrs. van den Mar in content, "it is like coming home! Such a welcome."

"That nice Hannah made me sit down, took off my shoes, and massaged my feet," said Mrs. Glover, "pressing them, pulling out the toes. Exquisite."

Mrs. Schlumberger shuddered. "I can't stand her bangles, rattle, clink, chink. Anyway, she never came near *me*."

"I'm not surprised," but Mrs. van den Mar refrained from saying it.

"And my feet are more swollen than Mrs. Glover's. There was far, far too much walking." Mrs. Schlumberger glared at Professor Webster.

"But those cave paintings, those colors still there after all these centuries." Miss Pritt was rapt. "The old true colors, crimson and brown madder and turmeric, indigo— those violets and greens."

"They looked very dirty to me." Mrs. Schlumberger was still cross. "Shabby and old."

"Old! I should say! Two thousand seven hundred years!" Dr. Lovat had been as moved as Miss Pritt.

"Maybe later, second century B.C.," Professor Webster had to caution.

"Before Christ! Think of it! And as your eyes get accustomed, the faces seem to speak to you, so expressive, witty, and eloquent. Those *apsaras!* The heavenly dancing girls, the verses in their honor scratched on the walls." Professor Webster had translated them and Dr. Lovat quoted: "The lily-colored ones. The doe-eyed beauties . . . Mystical!"

"Mystical! Utterly disgusting. Obscene! That multiple sexual intercourse!" Mrs. Schlumberger said in outrage. "How dare Professor Aaron expose us to such things?"

"Multiple intercourse was supposed to be the paradigm of ultimate bliss." Dr. Lovat was deliberately taunting Mrs. Schlumberger. "It's an allegory for the way sex is revered in Indian culture. That's why the girls are enchanting," and she quoted, "If the senses are not captivated the lure will not work."

"Lure! I'm surprised at you, Julia."

"But did you see those student workers?" Mrs. van den Mar skillfully changed the conversation. "Students cleaning those wonderful murals with acetone. *By order!*"

"Yes"—Professor Webster was wrathful—"the colors will be ruined. I shall write to the department of archaeology."

But Miss Pritt was not concerned with departments. "Those paintings seemed to distill all these centuries of art as if they had been five minutes."

"Centuries in which, by comparison, we have gained nothing, nothing," said Mrs. Glover.

"Something happened to painting," said Dr. Lovat, "when it came off the walls. With murals and frescoes it was pure."

"You mean, as soon as it turned into pictures, buying and selling came in and something went out," said Ellen Webster.

"Joy and, yes, awe, you're right," said Dr. Lovat.

"Just as something happened to men's minds when they built office blocks higher than a spire . . ."

Kuku gave an enormous yawn.

It was toward dusk when Mary and Blaise were leaving the tennis court that they heard the soft beating of drums and with them a chanting; looking up, Mary saw lights moving, people carrying lit torches. A procession was coming down the hill beyond the village. She could make out men in white—they carried the flares—and, less distinct because of their colored clothes, women who seemed to be carrying round baskets on their heads heaped, she saw when the torchlight fell on them, with fruit and flowers. The light fell, too, on chests carried on poles laid on each side of them and painted scarlet. "Marriage chests," said Olga Manning.

She had come out in the late afternoon to watch them play. "Uninvited," Blaise had muttered. As soon as they came off the court she had come up to them, whereupon he had picked up the rackets and presses and left.

Olga had taken no notice. "It's for a wedding," she explained to Mary. "There must be one near, in some village. This is the bride's dowry being brought down to the bridegroom's house. She must be a hill girl. Poor little thing, probably married to a man she doesn't know," and Mary, startled, thought, I'm married to a man I don't know. Almost she said it aloud, but as if she had, Olga said with curious passion, "None of us should marry, unless we love a man so much we would go through hell for him, which we shall probably have to do."

"Well, Hari, how did it go?" Sir John asked on the veranda that evening.

"It did not go. Not at all. Not at all." Dr. Coomaraswamy again was in despair. "Everywhere we went Padmina Retty was before us, so skillfully she had arranged it. She is eloquent, so eloquent." Dr. Coomaraswamy had tears in his eyes. "They tell me one speech lasted over an hour, while Krishnan—"

"A contrast indeed!"

"Everyone was so much astonished," came Mr. Srinivasan's moan.

"Good," said Sir John, "good."

"What good?" Dr. Coomaraswamy had become angry. "What if they are astonished into inertia? Inertia! I myself spoke and spoke but I am no match for Padmina. They did not listen, only looked."

"Isn't that what they were supposed to do?" asked Sir John.

Lady Fisher, changed for dinner, came out, and sat by Sir John. She was smiling. "Kuku," she told him quietly, "asked me if there were really a man's club in London called the Savage."

"How did she come to hear of it?"

"Apparently Mr. Menzies gave it as his London address. I think she had a vision of men in skins, tearing meat with their hands and teeth."

As if she had fathomed Kuku's dearest longings, Lady Fisher had given her, to Hannah's intense disapproval, a pure silk sari. "Even sent to Ghandara for it. Sharma bought it," Hannah told Samuel.

"That was dear of you, Alicia," Auntie Sanni had said. "I am most glad." In consequence Lady Fisher now was Kuku's confidante.

"The Savage Club is real enough." Sir John was thoughtful. "I'm not as sure about Menzies."

"Mr. Menzies has been at least half an hour on the telephone," an indignant Kuku told Auntie Sanni. One of Patna Hall's two telephones was in a kiosk that stood in the hall; the other in Auntie Sanni's office was available only to her and Colonel McIndoe. "I needed urgently to order a few stores. Twice I came back. He was still there. When I stood to show I was waiting, he shut the door."

"I expect he had some business to do." Auntie Sanni was not disturbed.

The International Association of Art, Technology and Culture was having a lecture that night given by Professor Webster. "And they have been out in the hills since eight this morning. Where do they get the appetite?" Auntie Sanni marveled as she marveled each year. "Kuku, you must warn Mrs. Manning—I'm afraid she can't have the drawing room tonight but tell her that, though the lecture is for the group, anyone who cares to is welcome to come."

"No, thank you," was Olga's answer, "and, Kuku, will you tell Auntie Sanni I have to go to Calcutta in the morning and, please, order a taxi for the station."

"Another of those mysterious trips," Kuku told Mary, who had come with Blaise to wait for dinner.

"Why mysterious?"

"She keeps on going, coming back. Why so often? She tells no one."

"Why should she?"

That to Mary was one of the best things at Patna Hall. Except for Kuku, no one asked that perpetual why? why? why? No one asked you why you wanted to lie alone in the sun, only brought you a beach umbrella and a drink of lemon but Kuku's eyes were bright as a little snake's. "She travels second-class," said Kuku.

Kuku's spite was partly born of a sense of hopelessness; Blaise was wearing white linen trousers, a primrose-colored silk shirt, a deeper yellow-and-gray striped tie. They set off his hair, his fresh tanned skin, and his height. "Not Apollo, Adonis," murmured Kuku. She could have scratched Mary's eyes out, especially when, as if purposely, Mary stopped at Mrs. Manning's table in the dining room and asked her to have coffee with them after dinner.

"Mary, you've forgotten," came the inevitable from Blaise. "The Fishers have already asked us. I'm sorry, Mrs. Manning," and after he had steered Mary away, "I told you to stay clear of her. She's a leech."

On any other night, when after dinner they came back to the veranda, Mary would have gone defiantly and sat down by Olga but, I must keep Blaise in a good mood tonight, she thought. Then he'll sleep—she had not known she could be so guileful. He must sleep because I'm going to see Krishnan.

Krishnan. Krishnan. All day the thought of him had

come back to her, Krishnan—happiness. There was a poem she had learned at one of those schools, a poem she loved:

My heart is like a singing bird
whose nest is in a watered shoot . . .

It had sung in her mind all day. Am I in love? wondered Mary. No, I've been in love. I don't want that again, thank you. This is different, unimaginable, like the waves here that are quite different from anywhere else on earth. Outwardly, on Patna Hall's veranda, the young wife of this eminently suitable young man appeared to be listening to the talk that was going on around her while all the time she only heard "*My heart is like a singing bird . . .*" and, "Soon it will be time," she told herself. "Soon."

It was Sir John who broke up the talk early. Mary had already seen him go quietly down the veranda to Olga Manning—to ask her to join us. Mary was grateful but Olga, though she smiled, shook her head. Soon after she had left and now, "I must drop in on this lecture," said Sir John.

"The culture lecture?" Blaise was surprised. "I thought the group . . ."

"Were a bit comical?" asked Sir John. "What those who knew no better used to call culture vultures?" Blaise blushed. "In actuality, they are giving India the compliment of trying to understand her art and civilization." Oh, I like Sir John, I like him, thought Mary. "I think we should honor that and I suggest, Coomaraswamy, you come with me and," said Sir John, "you might invite Professor Aaron's ladies to come to one of your rallies and see how you run your election. Take them around with you."

"With things as they are?" cried Dr. Coomaraswamy in acute pain. "Also you have forgotten, Sir John, tonight Padmina Retty's inaugural rally is going on with great display. *She* knows how it should be done. I should have been there already to watch, God help me. So—no lecture for me."

As he and Mr. Srinivasan went, Lady Fisher left her embroidery. "I'll come, John," but, "Miss Sanni, Colonel Sahib, Lady Sahib," Samuel burst out of the dining room in excitement. "It is the radio. I have been listening to the radio. Come. Come quickly. They say Padmina Retty's rally in utter discredit."

The voice was going on. "Poor Mrs. Retty. A huge audience was sitting, many on the grass—the rally is being held in Ghandara's botanical park. Bands had been playing as the decorated platform was filled with dignitaries while over it was suspended Padmina Retty's symbol, a giant open umbrella which slowly turned showing the party's name, the People's Shelter Party, and the slogan promise: 'I will shelter you.' Mrs. Retty, a commanding figure in a billowing blue-and-silver sari—blue for promise—standing at the microphone was in full eloquence. Certainly she can hold her audience. 'I, Padmina Retty . . .' when suddenly, among the audience one figure after the other stood up, men, women, many women, and, yes, children, each holding an umbrella which they opened and held up, ancient umbrellas, stained, tattered, torn, some showing only ribs, some with ribs broken, all palpably useless. As their bearers stood steadily it was more eloquent than words!

"Mrs. Retty's own words faltered, in any case they would not have been heard because a ripple of laughter began which spread to a gale, the whole audience laughing in complete glee . . . but under the glee old resentments flared. There were catcalls, shouts—something Mrs. Retty had not encountered before. I must add that, prominent among the umbrella holders were young women dressed in green, yellow, and white, colors, as we know, of another party. It was fortunate that they were protected by their fellow males because, as could have been predicted, fighting broke out. It could have become a riot but the police were prepared and quelled it swiftly . . .

"Mrs. Retty had left the platform. There was, of course, no sign of Krishnan Bhanj."

Samuel so far forgot himself that he clapped, Hannah clapped too, Lady Fisher clapped with her as did Mary, and even Colonel McIndoe. Mary was laughing with delight until Blaise spoke. "Wasn't that rather an antic in a serious election?" asked Blaise.

"Yes, you see, our young women had been all over," Dr. Coomaraswamy told later when he and his supporters came back. He was still shaking with laughter. His young men, some of them with black eyes, bruises, and cuts, were being tended in Paradise by Mr. Srinivasan, Samuel, and Hannah. "Krishnan planned it so well," the doctor went on. "A month ago to Bihar he had sent them. By Jeep, car, motorcycle, bullock cart they had traveled among the villages to carry out this trading, new umbrellas for old—what you used to call, I think, in England gamps. It took time to persuade the people—they could not believe a new umbrella for old. It also took time to persuade our Konak people tonight. Did I not tell you, just to stand up and open their old umbrellas, five rupees for each we had to give," but Dr. Coomaraswamy said it happily. "Once they understood, how they enjoyed! Our young men and women started the laughter but almost immediately everyone was laughing of themselves." Dr. Coomaraswamy laughed too.

"Just because I hit the donkey."

"It's nothing to do with the donkey."

The sound of the hard young voices came through the partition to Olga Manning.

"You might at least try." That was Blaise. Then Mary, "It's no use if you have to try." The voices rose as, "No!"

shrieked Mary. "No!" and, "God," shouted Blaise, "any-one would think I was trying to *rape* you. You are my *wife*."

"Do you think you could desist," Olga Manning's voice came from her side of the bungalow, "and let me get some sleep?"

A guilty silence. Then, "I apologize," called Blaise, "for my wife."

"Apologize for yourself!" shouted Mary.

"Very well. Goodnight." Blaise flung himself on the bed. Then, seeing Mary dressing, "Where are you going?"

"Out, if you don't mind."

"Go where you like. I don't care a damn," said Blaise.

Auntie Sanni, as if her thumbs had pricked her, had come out on the top veranda, looked down across the garden to the beach, and seen Mary fling out of the bungalow and down the steps to the shore.

"*Ayyo!*" said Auntie Sanni.

"Well, Doctor. What will you do tomorrow?" Sir John, Dr. Coomaraswamy with Professor Aaron were having a nightcap on the deserted veranda.

"You should not say, 'What will you do?' What can I do? God knows! God knows. Tomorrow Padmina Retty is holding a second rally. There will be thousands—"

"This Krishnan Bhanj," Professor Aaron ventured to say. "Have you, forgive me, but have you, shall we say, been mistaken, taken in by his charm—I hear he is charming—and perhaps his position? Vijay Bhanj's son?" and the doctor seemed to hear Uma's voice, "You see, Hari"—Uma was emancipated enough to call her husband firmly by his given name—"you see how you have been carried away by this Krishnan. It is always the same: If they are beautiful, sweet-mannered, you are over the moon. Isn't it the old call of the flesh?" Uma had said "flesh" with distaste.

"Krishnan Bhanj is a most gifted politician," Dr. Coomaraswamy said aloud, adding silently to Uma, "Flesh has nothing to do with it," and at once had a vision of Kuku. "Please, please," he cried silently, "please, Kuku, get out of my mind."

She had glided between the tables at dinner, bending to set glasses down on his.

"We have a wine waiter," Samuel had growled.

"The doctor asked me to bring."

That was true. "What is that perfume you put on your hair?" It had almost touched him.

"Jasmine."

"I will send you a bottle."

"Do. It will be costly." Was there a touch of malice in that?

He had watched her as she went back to the bar, his fork halfway to his lips. "A great booby you must have looked," Uma would have told him, but the walk was so smooth, sinuous, the hips undulating. "Is it my fault our candidate has good looks?" he cried now to invisible Uma, yet he could not rebut Professor Aaron and said bitterly to Sir John, "The campaign is dead loss. Dead loss."

A car drew up. Then Mr. Menzies came along the veranda.

"Where have you sprung from?"

"Madras."

"That's a long drive."

"Yes." He looked tired but his eyes were alert. "You've had a bad day," he said to the doctor as he poured himself a whiskey.

"Desperate. Dead loss!" moaned Dr. Coomaraswamy.

"I should cheer up, if I were you," said Mr. Menzies.

Mary had to wait on the beach to let her anger die down—instinctively, I can't bring anger into the grove, she thought—waited, too, in case Blaise had, after all, followed her. There was a sound but it was only Slippers. After his tidbit, he had waited hopefully outside the bungalow; now he had plodded after her until he came close enough for her to pat him and pull his ears.

Suddenly he lifted his nose and brayed. At the same time, Mary heard an excited chattering and laughing. A group of boys was standing around one boy who was holding something; their dark skins, black heads, tattered clothes, told Mary they were fisherboys. More excited laughter broke out; above it she heard a piercing shriek, then another, a small animal's shriek, and she started to run, Slippers lumbering after her. "What have you got there? What are you doing?" She cried it in English, scattering the boys, "Devils! *Shaitan!*" she screamed, because the boy in the middle held a small gray squirrel, one of the squirrels that abound in India.

They had tied a rag over its head to prevent it biting; it cried and squirmed as they poked it with slivers of pointed bamboo, fine and sharp as skewers. Blood was over the boy's hands. "Give it to me," stormed Mary. She snatched the squirrel, rag and all, as, with the flat of her other hand, she hit the boy hard across the face, then slapped the other boys, *"Jao!* Go! *Chelo—"* the first words she had learned of Hindustani. *"Chelo . . . Hut jao! Shaitan!"*

But these were fisherboys, not town boys easily quelled. She was one among seven or eight of them, not little boys but ten and eleven year olds. Caught by surprise, at first they had stood dumb; the slaps roused them. With an outbreak of furious voices they closed in around her. Holding the squirrel close, Mary stood as hands and fists came out to hit, scratch, pinch, claw. Then Krishnan was beside her. He did not speak but took the squirrel from her. The frantic squirming stopped instantly and it was still as he raised his hand over the boys, only raised it; as one, they bent, scooped up sand, and poured it over his feet, touching them with their heads. "Kanu," he said to the ringleader boy. "Lady," and unwillingly Kanu did the same to Mary, who, as he lifted his head, gently laid her hand on it. He shook it off at once and with the others ran away through the trees.

"Is it badly hurt?"

"We'll see."

He led the way to the fire. Mary's knees seemed to give way and she sank down on the sand. "How could they? How could anyone be so cruel?" She hid her face so long that Slippers poked her with his nose.

"Look," said Krishnan. He was sitting cross-legged on his goatskin throne and on one folded knee was the squirrel, sitting upright. Its wounds showed red in the firelight but it was nibbling a nut held in its small claws, its head cocked on one side, its black eyes brilliant. "We call squirrels *udata* in Telegu," he said. "She has had some milk. Now this little *udata* will get well, thanks to you."

"Not me. Thanks to you. They would have taken her back. Oh, why must people be so cruel? Even children!"

"Particularly children." He spoke gently. "They don't know any better," and now Mary did not see the evil, pointed sticks but the small heads bent to touch Krishnan's feet.

Her angry trembling ceased. "What are those marks on her back?" she asked.

"Long long ago," said Krishnan, "the young god, Prince Rama—another incarnation of Vishnu—had a beautiful wife, Sita. Indian girls, when they are married, are told to be a 'little Sita,' she was so perfect. But Sita was stolen by a powerful demon—he had ten heads—who carried her off in his terrible claws to Sri Lanka.

"Rama was in despair as to how he could get her back. How could he take his army across that wide sea? But Hanuman, who is the Monkey God, called all the monkeys of India to build Rama a bridge. Thousands of great powerful apes and strong quick monkeys carried stones, rocks, boulders from the mountains to the shore. Quarries were dug, mighty rocks brought down to the sea, great boulders hewn into blocks. It was such a gigantic task that the very gods of heaven marveled while Rama himself watched amazed.

"As he watched he saw a great monkey almost trip over a squirrel who was on the beach too. From his height, the monkey looked down a long, long way at the tiny squirrel and saw she had a pebble in her mouth.

" 'What are you doing?'

"The little squirrel looked up. 'I am helping to build the bridge to Lanka so that Rama may bring back his beloved wife, Sita.'

" 'Helping to build a bridge!' The monkey burst into a roar of laughter and called all the other monkeys. 'Did you hear that? The squirrel says she is helping to build our bridge. Did you ever hear anything so funny in your life?' The others laughed too, then all of them said, 'Shoo. We've no time for play and the likes of you.'

"But the squirrel would not shoo. Again and again the monkeys picked her up and put her out of the way; she always came back with the pebbles until one of the monkeys grew angry and not only picked her up but flung her hard across the beach. She fell into Rama's hands where he stood.

"Rama held the squirrel close—just as you did—and said to the monkeys, 'How dare you despise her? This little squirrel with her pebbles has love in her heart that would move heaven and earth with its power.' And, lo!" said Krishnan dramatically, "Rama was transformed back into his origin, the great god Vishnu, the Preserver. Vishnu stroked the squirrel's back and as he put her down the monkeys saw, on her gray fur, these white lines that were the marks of the great god's fingers. Since when, Udata, you have those marks on your back, haven't you?"

Mary put out a hand and touched the stripes; the squirrel allowed her. "It's the same as Christ riding on the donkey," she said. "All donkeys have the mark of the cross, even Slippers far away in India. It's the same."

"All the same."

"Will she come to me?"

"I'll ask her."

He talks to her as if he were a squirrel, thought Mary.

"How do you know I wasn't?" Krishnan said with his strange power of following her thoughts. "I could have been a squirrel, couldn't I?" he asked the squirrel. "But," he said to Slippers, "I do not seriously think I could have been a donkey."

"You're conceited," said Mary.

"If I am, why not? A peacock struts and spreads his tail because he is a peacock. That would have suited me. Peacocks are sacred in India and I am about to become sacred. I could have been a peacock. That is what we Hindus believe," and he mocked, "Don't tread on that cockroach, it might have been your grandfather. Don't tread on a cockroach but let children starve because you have put chalk in flour, given short weight, foreclosed on a peasant's one little field before he has time to pay off the debt." His eyes blazed with indignation.

"Is that what your party is about?"

"Of course. Why do you think I'm doing this?"

"I don't know. I only know I like what you are doing."

"Not always. You couldn't. Remember all is fair in love and war. Politics now are a war, a bitter, greedy war and I have to fight Padmina Retty in every way I can. You don't know, Mary, thank God you have had no need to know, but Indian politics are corrupt, venal as never before. If Padmina Retty's manifesto had been truthful, it would have said: (a) the People's Shelter Party totally believes that, in the state of Konak, one family, the Rettys, should have total rule and that in perpetuity; (b) every member of the People's Shelter Party will give full material and emotional help to its leader in misappropriating funds; (c) the People's Shelter Party will support only those people who believe in hooliganism and slander."

"That's terribly damning."

"Not damning enough. The same goes for Gopal Rau, though he has not a chance. I tell you," said Krishnan, "no one from a family of integrity would dream of going into politics except a mopus like me. Even a mope, though, knows that no one can get into Parliament without so much wheeling and dealing that it disgusts. Not to mention spending money, floods of money, which is where our Dr. Coomaraswamy comes in."

"That funny old fat man?"

"That funny old fat man is a visionary. No one but a visionary would back me. I do not think," said Krishnan, "poor Coomaraswamy will get his money back. A candidate can only be elected for five years, but he or she can retrieve his money, even make a fortune, by way of taking bribes, cheating, pulling strings, dispensing patronage, which must be paid for. The people know very well, if a village helps to get a candidate elected, it will be the first to get electricity or a well. If it resists, no electricity, no well. Patronage! I couldn't patronize a bee, yet the dear doctor has worked with me and my ideas for years."

"Years?"

"Yes, you don't think I came to this in five minutes? And all the time he has had to put up with a barrage from his terrible wife." Krishnan mocked again, " 'So easilee you are bamboozled, Hari'—Hari is Dr. Coomaraswamy's name." Krishnan, whose English was smoother, more rounded than most Englishmen's caught the wife's accent to perfection. " 'And you are like a child with sweets so easily parted from your mon-ee.' But Uma is right," said Krishnan. "I am using Coomaraswamy but that is a good man, Mary. How he has helped us." Krishnan brooded again. "The fisherpeople should be all right, but they are, in fact, the very poorest, virtually bonded in debt to the middlemen and victims of the powerful fish market Mafia. Mary," he asked, "what do you think the village people most need?"

"Water," Mary said at once.

"Indeed, yes, and the wells will come faster if they work with us. I will not promise what I cannot do. What else?"

"Trees. Seed."

"Yes, but not first." His eyes darkened. "Outside people coming in, would-do-goods, could plant a million trees—a million million—and change nothing because it would all begin again, but someone who plants ideas, knowledge, respect for our earth"—Krishnan was deeply in earnest—*"might* just succeed." Now his eyes seemed alight.

"Mary, I have been trying to do that for the last five years and I know it works, otherwise I would never have presumed—yes, *presumed*—to be a people's candidate. Let me tell you: I got one villager to let us use his piece of land that was bare—he would have said, of no use. He and his wife and children built mud walls and channels so that we could irrigate from quite far away. Then we came with saplings and seedlings. Now on his scruffy land he has an orchard, with pineapples and tea growing under the trees and enough grass to feed his cow and buffalo.

"If," said Krishnan, himself visionary, "if we can teach one or two villages to feed themselves and their animals, that may spread and save the whole continent. If not"—the light went out of his eyes and he shrugged—"at least a few less villages have less hungry children."

"Lady Fisher told me," said Mary, "that when there is great trouble in the world, Vishnu comes down in one form or another. I wish he would come now."

"It is a belief," said Krishnan. "Some people would call it a delusion but I believe it is a good belief."

"Love and war," said Mary. "Can politics be love?"

"They can, thank God."

Mary watched his hand stroking the contented squirrel.

"I think you love everyone, everything," she said.

He laughed. "That wouldn't be possible." Then he was serious again. "It is that I am everyone, everything, just as everything, everyone is me."

"Even the hateful ones?"

"Particularly the hateful ones because I am very hateful, very often."

"But I . . . I like people and things—or dislike them—violently."

"That is because you are thinking of yourself, not them," which was true. "See, now," he said, "here is a creature"—he says creatures, created things, not animals, thought Mary—"a creature who does like you. Birdie has brought you a bouquet."

The little elephant—how can an elephant be little? thought Mary again, but Birdie is—held in her trunk a whole stem of plantains, at least thirty small bananas on a stem. "I think you have stolen that," Krishnan told her. "Bad girl!" but he patted her trunk. He broke off the plantains, gave two to Mary, took three for himself, bit off a small end for the squirrel, gave ten to Slippers, the rest back to Birdie. The stem he threw on the fire so that the flames leapt up. They munched in companionship. Mary liked the way Birdie ate, picking up a plantain in her trunk and delicately putting it in her mouth; Udata nibbled; Slippers's bananas went around and around in his mouth—he would keep his the longest.

"This is the last time I can speak with you," Krishnan said. "Tomorrow the vow must be absolute. I shall not know who might be listening."

He sighed. *"Ayyo!* How my legs ache with all that sitting."

"I ache too, inside me," but Mary did not say it. She must not think back over the day, "But the sea was wonderful," she said. "Those waves!"

"The sea. Yes. Let's go and get clean." He jumped up and held out his hand to Mary.

On the beach he unwound his loin and shoulder cloths, leaving him with only a cloth. Mary pulled her dress off over her head.

A pile of fishermen's helmets had been left by a boat. "Put this on." He put on his own. "Don't be afraid," he said. "Thambi and I have been swimming here since we were five years old." He took Mary straight through the waves, far out where he let her go. On the shore, Slippers, Birdie, and a dot that was Udata had come out to watch. Mary could hear the thunder of waves on the beach, here it was still; the water, warm and balmy, was dark blue. They swam, floated.

When Mary was tired, Krishnan came behind her, took her shoulders, and let her rest. "Let's stay here forever," she said.

"If only we could."

Back on the beach, dressed, he and the animals walked her back, but before they reached the bungalow, Mary stopped. "Don't come any nearer," she said, "it might be broken."

Krishnan did not ask her what "it" was.

Tuesday

■ ■ ■ ■ ■ ■ ■ ■ ■ ■ ■ ■ ■

"Would anyone object," Mr. Menzies asked the whole dining room at breakfast, "if, because of the election, we put on the morning news?" Without waiting for an answer he switched on the big veranda radio.

"This is the English Programme of All India Radio. Here is the news."

The news was always read in Tamil, Telegu, and English.

Now the voice, speaking in English, was reading the headlines: "The drought is beginning to be felt in the Gamjam district. In Sri Kakylam there have been riots . . ." The breakfasters listened with half an ear if they listened at all. "The bodies of two children, both boys, have been found in a field near the village of Palangaon. The trial, under Mr. Justice Rajan, of the Englishman, Colin Armstrong, charged with fraud, embezzlement, and trafficking in drugs, is drawing to a close . . . and now, the election in Konak."

"Aie!" cried Dr. Coomaraswamy and silence fell as everybody listened.

"The debacle that befell Mrs. Padmina Retty's People's Shelter Party last night could not help but leave traces this morning. For one thing, the symbol of the umbrella has disappeared. All posters have been hastily torn down and there has been some hand fighting in the square where these two rival parties' headquarters face one another. Mrs. Retty, as befits a professional and long-accustomed campaigner, is cool and unperturbed. Her headquarters is buzzing with activity while the opposite building is strangely quiet and, except for two secretaries, empty. Again, there is no sign of Krishnan Bhanj.

" 'I am not surprised,' says Mrs. Retty. 'After that antic last night' "—she used the same word as Blaise, who smiled in self-congratulation. " 'After that antic, Krishnan dare not face me . . .'

"But," asked the voice on the radio, "could he outface her? Mrs. Retty, it seems, has not heard of a lorry that, since dawn, has been driving through the countryside."

"I, myself, sent him out," Dr. Coomaraswamy interrupted; he had a ray of hope. "But"—once again "buts" were flying like brickbats—"but was I wise?" He sighed.

"You couldn't have stopped him," said Sir John.

"Have you seen the morning papers?" asked Mr. Menzies.

Patna Hall's Goanese cook, Alfredo, collected them when he went to do the marketing at Ghandara, as he did every morning. In time-honored fashion, the papers were ironed and then Kuku laid them out on the veranda tables for the guests; Colonel McIndoe's were taken by his bearer to his study. "Ah! The *Madras Times*. The *Nilgiri Herald*. *All India Universal*." Sir John picked up the *Madras Times*. "It's the leading article."

"Read it. Read it," begged Dr. Coomaraswamy.

Sir John read: " 'Is it disrespectful to ask if Krishnan Bhanj, candidate for the new Root and Flower Party, has taken his startling vow of silence in response to a direct commandment from the gods—in which case who dare say him "nay"?' That's a tongue-in-cheek remark if ever I heard one," said Sir John. " 'Or is this rising young politician playing a wily game of cards? If so, he is playing it well. Mrs. Retty was routed last night and without violence, simply by a superior display of that insidious and most deadly of weapons, ridicule, making a story that will be told as long as politics exist. Already a ripple is spreading through Konak, a ripple from town to town, village to village. It may be only curiosity, maybe it is reverence, but one can forecast that soon, Mrs. Padmina Retty's audience will have gone elsewhere, waiting for a garlanded lorry that has on it a *pandal* and, in the *pandal*, a young god silently blessing.' That," said Sir John, "was written, I'm sure, by Ajax."

"Ah!" Dr. Coomaraswamy gave a very different sigh.

"Who is Ajax?" asked Mr. Srinivasan.

"Probably the best political correspondent in India and the Far East. If he is covering this election, you are in luck but he is best known for his gossip columns which spread on occasions to London and Europe. He is adept at dirt."

"*Ayy!*" Dr. Coomaraswamy was well pleased.

"Looking to see if anything has been cut?"

Coming out from breakfast, Sir John had found Mr. Menzies at one of the veranda tables, studying the article in the *Statesman* and, as he looked up startled, "You are, of course, Ajax," said Sir John.

"I am." There was something more than self-satisfaction, insolence, in the way Mr. Menzies said that. "And I don't let them cut my stuff. Clever of you to guess," he told Sir John.

"Not at all. It was quite transparent," and with a nod Sir John went on down the veranda leaving Mr. Menzies slightly taken aback.

It is going to be a lovely empty day, thought Mary. They are all going away.

"I am taking Mrs. Manning to the train," Kuku told Mary. Her eyes were bright with the same brightness, Mary could not help thinking, that had been in the boys' eyes when they were tormenting the squirrel. "I think she will be meeting someone."

You want me to ask, "What sort of someone?" thought Mary. Well, I won't.

Kuku's look said, "Prig."

Professor Aaron was taking his group to see the famous Dawn Temple at Gorāghat, fifty miles along the coast.

Sir John, Lady Fisher, and Blaise were going too.

"I'd much rather be swimming or playing tennis," Blaise grumbled as he picked up his packed lunch, binoculars, and hat.

"Then why don't you?" asked Mary.

"If Sir John goes, I must."

"Why?"

"You're always asking why," Blaise was irritable. "He's a big noise, that's why."

"I think he'll know if you're pretending."

"Pretend what? The Dawn Temple is very fine, even from the point of view of history. It's marvelous how they carried those enormous blocks of stone to build it. It's one of those things one should see."

"Even if you don't want to? And it isn't only history, it's beauty," said Mary, "old, old beauty. Lady Fisher says it faces east and just at dawn, as the sun rises, the whole temple turns gold and rose-colored."

"If it makes you so lyrical, why don't you come?" But Mary shook her head. "I'd like to go there early, early in the morning before dawn, all by myself, not in a coach full of people with cameras and binoculars and notebooks."

Mary's day turned out not to be empty, not at all: It was filled with Patna Hall. "Samuel is taking me to the bazaar," she had told Blaise.

"You mean you would rather go with a servant to see an ordinary squalid bazaar than on a splendid excursion like this, with Sir John, Professor Aaron, his group—and me?"

"Much rather," said Mary.

"I find you utterly incomprehensible."

"I know you do," said Mary sadly. "And I you," but she did not add that.

Blaise hated all bazaars. "All those rows of shanty huts and booths, corrugated iron, stucco houses blotched with damp! Even the temples are tawdry. Their silver roofs are made of beaten-out kerosene tins."

"I think that's clever if you can't afford silver," said Mary.

"And the *smells!* Cess in the gutters . . . men squatting down to relieve themselves even while you pass. Rancid *ghee* from the cookshops and that horrible mustard oil they cook in. Rotting fruit and meat hung too long and flies, flies, flies. If you walk on the pavements—if they can be called pavements—you tread on phlegm and red betel where people have spat. Ugh! And all those beggars and children with swollen stomachs and sore eyes. Once, perhaps, one could find good things in the bazaar, muslins, pottery, but now it's all machine-made, plastic, ugly. Mary, I hate you to go there. I know there are wonderful things to see in India but there are some things it's better for you not to see."

"I want to see it whole."

But Blaise had made up his mind. "You're not to go," he said as authoritatively as Rory. "You're not to go."

"I'm going," said Mary.

Auntie Sanni had overhead. "You're not very kind to that husband of yours," she said.

"He shouldn't order me about. I'm not his child."

"Come. Come. He only wants to protect you," said Auntie Sanni. "If your husband is a real man, that is innate."

"I don't want to be protected. Don't you see?" Mary was hot-cheeked. "I've never been anywhere, seen anything . . ."

"Except, as I understand, Italy, Paris, Norway, Brussels . . ."

"I meant India. Besides in those countries Rory always sent me to *school*." Mary said it as if it were the ultimate betrayal. "You don't know, Auntie Sanni, what girls' boarding schools are like, so—so little. I was—choked." Mary could not find the right word. "There was one," she had to admit, "a convent in Brussels which was part of something bigger. The nuns had something else to concern themselves with apart from girls." She said that word in scorn. "Even at home, Rory never let me be really free to do things—or thought he didn't. Now Blaise thinks he won't allow me either. Well, he has another think coming."

"It's early days yet," said Auntie Sanni.

"I knew you'd say that."

"I do say it," Auntie Sanni spoke sternly. "Mary, child, be careful. You may cause more damage than you mean."

"I'd like to go to the bazaar every day and do my own shopping." Mary was to tell Blaise. It was an every day she had not glimpsed before yet perhaps had sensed. Everything Blaise had said of the bazaar was true: the stench, the shanty huts and booths, the flies . . . but the first shop she and Samuel came to was the shop where kites were made and sold costing a few *annas*, kites of thinnest paper, in colors of pink, green, white, red, with a wicker spool to fly them from, wound with a pound of thread. The thread had been run through ground glass so that the boys— Samuel told Mary that kite fliers were always boys—could challenge other kites, cross strings with them, cut them adrift, and proudly tie another bob of paper on their own kite's tail.

The front of the money changer and jeweler's shop was barred; he sat behind the bars on a red cushion, quilted with black and white flowers. Though this was South India he was a Marwari from Marwar in Rajasthan, known for businessmen and financiers. He had a small black cap on his head, steel spectacles, and many ledgers. There was nothing in his shop but a safe, a pair of scales, and a table a few inches high. In India jewelry is sold by weight, jewelry made of silver threads woven into patterns and flowers. Mary, watching fascinated, saw a man buying a ring—which the Marwari took out of his safe—and paying for it. The moneylender took the money and reckoned it by weighing.

"Miss Baba like something—a nice brooch, nice ring?" asked Samuel, but Mary did not want to buy, only watch.

A little black goat came by with twin kids; they butted their mother in vain because her udders were covered by a neat white bag.

"Goat milk very precious," said Samuel.

There was a bangle shop with most of the bangles made of glass in clear goblin fruit colors of green, blue, amber, and red. "Miss Baba not buy," Samuel cautioned. "They break and cut very bad."

The sari shop had the shimmering colors of heavy silk. "They expensive," said Samuel with feeling, remembering Lady Fisher's gift to Kuku: Cotton saris like Hannah's had plain borders. Children's dresses with low waists, cut square and flat, like paper doll dresses, hung outside in the street. The grain shops had grain set out in different colors in black wicker baskets and with them were sold great purple roots and knots of ginger, chilies, and spice. There was a stall devoted to selling only drinking coconuts which could be split there and then if the customer wanted. "Coconut milk very fresh," said Samuel.

"I'd like to taste them," said Mary.

"Not in the bazaar," said Samuel.

A tassel shop had silk tassels in vivid colors of scarlet, brilliant pink or blue, orange, violent yellow, and "What are those for?" Mary saw small velvet and gold thread balls.

"For missies to tie on end of pigtail, very pretty."

To Mary the temple was interesting and, Yes, clever, thought Mary, its outside walls and floors tessellated with broken pieces of china, countless pieces. The temple's gods were two big Western jointed dolls with eyes that opened and shut. They were dressed in gaudy muslin and tinsel and wreathed with paper flowers. "Priest puts them to bed every night, morning gets them up. Hindu worship," said Samuel with contempt, but Mary saw that in front of them was a low table with offerings of sweets and flowers. A woman came to pray; on the brass tray she put a little powdered sugar and with her thumb she made on it the pattern of the sun for luck.

She looked up at Mary and smiled.

A sound like a murmur began to run through the bazaar: It grew louder and, with it, music and the ululation of a conch blown in jubilation. A lorry was coming down the road, heralded by motorcyclists, carrying between each pair of them long scarves of green, yellow, and white. One held aloft on a pole a poster like a banner—the poster of "The Three Wise Cows," as Mary had began to call them.

She had seen them last night in the grove when Krishnan had shown a copy to her, three stylized cows, bells hung around their necks—clearly they were cherished—lying at peace among equally stylized flowers and looking out at the people with wise kind eyes. "Is the script Telegu?" Mary had asked.

"Yes. Telegu script is decorative for posters. It goes oodle, oodle, oodle." It certainly looked it.

"You speak Telegu?"

"I speak everything," Krishnan had said. "As required—Tamil, Telegu, Hindi, English, French, even a little Russian."

"Don't boast," Mary had said in pretended severity. Then, "Why did you choose cows?"

"Because they symbolize me," and as she had looked puzzled, he had said like Dr. Coomaraswamy, "Symbols are crucially important in an Indian election. Every party has one. You must remember that most of the men and women in Konak cannot read so that written names and slogans mean nothing to them and, when they come to vote, how can they tell which is the candidate they want? Only if the symbol is at once identifiable. You have heard Padmina Retty had an umbrella signifying 'shelter.' Well, we put an end to that. Now she has a star, which is not very wise for voters. Our third candidate, Gopal Rau, has a flower . . . so . . . 'The star,' they'll say, 'might be Padmina . . .' yet equally the flower might be Padmina but cows . . . There is no one," said Krishnan, "in towns or villages, near or far, who does not know the story of Krishna, the cowherds who adopted him, the *gopis,* so as soon as they see my cows, three for prosperity, 'Ah!' they will say, 'That's Krishnan,' and, notice, under the cows there is a flute."

Now, in the bazaar, Mary heard it.

All the people began to look, pressing nearer. Shopkeepers stood up on their stalls; small boys wriggled through the crowd to the front; other urchins ran to meet the sound. The murmuring was loud now and grew to a shout as the lorry came close and paused. On a throne Krishnan was sitting—How his legs will ache tonight, thought Mary. The blue-black of his skin shone—with sweat? she wondered. Or oil?—against the *pandal's* bright green leaves that fluttered as the lorry drove. It was the first time Mary had seen Krishnan in daylight and, with a shock, saw, even with the makeup, the Vishnu horseshoe shape in white on his forehead, eyes outlined in black, reddened lips, how beautiful he was. Not handsome or good-looking, beautiful, thought Mary.

Dr. Coomaraswamy, sweating and stout, stood on the tailboard of the lorry bellowing through a microphone; when he paused, out of breath, Indian music invisibly played while behind the lorry followed Jeeps and cars, one

behind the other, overflowing with young men and
women who immediately jumped down and came
through the crowd to give out small pictures of the god
Krishna. Sharma, in his flowing white, stood on the roof
of the lorry's cab. A man beside Mary gave a shout,
"Ayyo." The crowd took it up. *"Ayyo, ayyo-yo. Jai,* Krishna.
Jai, Krishna."

Krishnan's eyes looked. Has he seen me? wondered
Mary. She hoped he had.

Everyone was shouting now. Dr. Coomaraswamy put
down his microphone, he could not be heard, but Sharma's conch sounded over the noise. Still Krishnan did not
move except to raise his hand, palm toward the people,
fingers pointing upward in benediction, blessing them
while he smiled his extraordinary sweet smile.

The lorry passed on, Dr. Coomaraswamy talking again
through his microphone in a strident torrent of words.
The Jeeps crowded after and after them, bicycles, bullock
carts, the bullocks being urged on, the drivers whacking
them and twisting their tails so that Mary hid her
eyes. "Miss Baba, better you come home," Samuel said in
her ear.

All that morning, "It is too early to say," Dr. Coomaraswamy had told himself, "always you are too optimis-
tic," as Uma had said over and over again. "Always you
are carried away, either despair or huzzahs," but the doctor could not help seeing how, as the lorry approached,
people stopped at once on the road; men shut their umbrellas in respect—it could be reverence; one or two pros-
trated themselves in the dust; women bent low as they
peeped behind their saris.

"I am not huzzahing." In his mind, Dr. Coomaraswamy was telling Uma that. "But, my darling, I begin
to think . . ."

As Mary came up on the bungalow veranda on her way to
wash and change for lunch, she saw Kuku coming out of

Olga Manning's rooms. "Just checking to see everything is clean," Kuku explained, but there was an elation about her that made Mary pause. As if that showed she was curious, Kuku came closer. "I was right," Kuku whispered, "she has a lover."

"She's too old," was Mary's instant young reaction, then remembered what Blaise had said of Olga's desperation and, "How do you know?" she felt compelled to ask.

"Looking in her drawers, I found gentlemen's handkerchiefs," said Kuku with relish. "Not only that, gold cuff links, a gentleman's gold watch."

"She is keeping them for someone." The whole of Mary was drawn together in repellence. "Why were you looking in someone else's drawers? I have a good mind to tell Auntie Sanni," she said.

At lunchtime Mary found it strange to be in an almost empty dining room. Only she, Colonel McIndoe, and Auntie Sanni were there. "Come over and join us," called Auntie Sanni.

Mary enjoyed being with them; little was said except of quiet domestic things, which brought a feeling of well-being, of goodwill—toward everyone, thought Mary. It seemed, as with Krishnan, that if Auntie Sanni disliked anyone—Mary had fathomed she had a reserve toward Blaise—she managed to see beyond the dislike. I wish I could, thought Mary, but I can't.

"The stores have come from Spencer's," Auntie Sanni was telling the colonel. "Once a month," she explained to Mary, "stores of things one cannot get locally"—Mary was charmed by the way she said "lo-cal-ly" with a lilt up and down—"not in the village or Ghandara, come from a big shop in Madras. Samuel has unpacked them. Now Kuku and I must check them, make a list, and put them away. Would you like to come and help?"

Mary loved it; the stores seemed to bring an intimacy with Patna Hall that gave her an odd satisfaction. Why should it make her happy to call out to Auntie Sanni, "Twelve dozen tins of butter"? and "I never knew butter could be tinned."

"Here we can only get *ghee*," said Kuku in contempt. "Butter made with buffalo milk and clarified so it is oily." She shuddered. "Horrid!" Twelve dozen tins, that is a gross, thought Mary. The quantities were immense: "Two hundredweight of brown sugar, white sugar, caster sugar, icing sugar." Kuku's voice became singsong too as she enumerated: "Tea, coffee, chocolate. Tinned apricots, prunes."

Strawberries came from Ootacamund, as did cheeses, there were few imported wines, but there was Golconda wine from Hyderabad, liqueurs from Sikkim.

Auntie Sanni checked. Mustafa, the headwaiter, Abdul, the next, put sacks, bottles, tins away in cupboards and on shelves. "Goodness," said Mary, "I never dreamed what it takes to run a hotel. Kuku, I would like your job."

"Like my job?" Kuku was amazed. That anyone should want to work when obviously they did not have to was beyond her. She was particularly out of love with her work at the moment because she knew when the last tin or bottle had been checked and the storeroom securely locked, the keys would be given to Samuel. "I ought to have them," she said each time; each time Auntie Sanni seemed not to hear.

When at last Mary went down to the bungalow she found that Blaise had come back from the Dawn Temple, plainly anything but exalted. He was asleep on the bed; camera and binoculars had been flung down, he had not taken off his shoes, and, even in his sleep, his face was cross, over-pink with sunburn. Mary quietly changed into her swimming things, tiptoed out, and was soon laughing and playing in the exhilaration of the waves, Moses and Somu each side of her. When they had finished, Mary beaten by the rollers—"all over" she would have said—her hair dripping, Somu shyly produced a bracelet of shells threaded on a silk string. Each shell was different: brown-speckled ones, pink fingernail-sized ones, almost transparent, brown ones curled into a minuscule horn and fragments of coral, apricot red. She tied the bracelet on while Moses and Thambi applauded. "I shall keep this forever," said Mary, and Somu, when Thambi translated, blushed dark brown with pleasure.

She looked up and saw Blaise, awake now, watching them from the veranda. She waved, showing her arm with the bracelet. "Look," she called, "a present from the sea," but Blaise had gone into the bedroom.

"You don't want to get familiar with those chaps," he told Mary when she followed him. "They might misunderstand."

"Misunderstand what?"

"I believe that part of the tourist attractions in foreign countries are the, shall we call them, 'attentions of the locals'?"

"You mean fucking?"

"That's not a word I would use—and I wish you wouldn't—but yes, it's supposed to be part of the adventure, even for the elderly, or especially the elderly, women."

"In a group like Professor Aaron's?" Mary did not believe it for a moment. "Mrs. van den Mar. Professor Webster. Dear Mrs. Glover. Dr. Lovat." Mary laughed. "I can't believe it."

"It wouldn't surprise me," said Blaise. "That Miss—is it Pritt?"

"Miss Pritt is in love with India, not Indians." You spoil things, she wanted to say, then saw that, fortunately now, for her Blaise could not spoil anything. You don't disturb me one iota, thought Mary. These are my friends.

*   *   *

". . . This is the news." It was the middle of dinner and Auntie Sanni looked up and frowned but the voice went on. "The government has taken measures to bring relief to the effects of the Gamjam drought . . . Tons of grain, rice, fodder, and medical supplies are being flown in . . . Troops have been sent in to reinforce police in quelling the outbreak of riots and violence in Sri Kakylam. The two boys found dead in the village of Palangaon have been identified as Pradeep and Bimal, twin sons of Birendranath Hazarika, a local landowner. Police are treating it as a case of murder.

"In the trial of the Englishman, Colin Armstrong, charged with fraud, embezzlement, and trafficking in drugs, Mr. Justice Rajan has today begun his summing up and hopes to finish it tomorrow.

"In Konak, the candidate of the fancifully named Root and Flower Party, Mr. Krishnan Bhanj, has been touring the state today. It is said that his strange vow of silence is arousing great interest in towns and villages; his symbol of the three wise cows is everywhere, while the people flock to see him.

" 'I am not afraid,' his chief opponent, Mrs. Padmina Retty says. She has a new symbol—the defeated umbrella has disappeared—it is now a star. 'My star is rising, not setting.' She laughed. 'The people of Konak are my people. They look to me. They will not let me lose. I shall win.' "

"And she well may." Dr. Coomaraswamy was Gloomaraswamy again. "She is the mother figure, so potent in India."

"Mother is very dangerous." Mr. Srinivasan, too, was in gloom. "We must talk very ser-i-ous-ly to Krishnan."

Professor Webster's lecture was to begin at nine o'clock.

"Dear, are you coming to join us?" kind Mrs. Glover asked Mary.

"I'm afraid I can't. Auntie Sanni is going to introduce me to the cook."

"The *cook?*" Mrs. Glover's expression plainly said, "A cook, when you could listen to Professor Webster!" while Miss Pritt said gravely, "My dear, Professor Webster is world famous as a lecturer. It's a privilege to hear her."

"I—I promised," Mary stammered, and escaped. She had noticed that Auntie Sanni did not come on the veranda after dinner for coffee. "No, it's my time then to see Alfredo, our cook. We plan the menus and orders for the next day."

"I thought Kuku . . ."

"Kuku is not capable," Auntie Sanni said shortly. "She thinks she knows better." It was the nearest thing to condemnation Mary had heard her say. Then she asked, "But would you like to come sometime and listen?" Now Mary caught her just as she was going, like a ship in full sail, into her office.

Every evening when he had finished cooking, Alfredo from Goa left the kitchen to his underlings; he would come back later to see that it was spotless. He bathed, changed into a clean white tunic and trousers, a black waistcoat with red spots, a silver watch chain and a silver turnip watch far bigger than Dr. Coomaraswamy's. In the cookhouse it was kept on a shelf in its case with a steady ticking; in all Alfredo's now ten years at Patna Hall it had never lost time. With his lists he presented himself to Auntie Sanni.

They discussed food as two connoisseurs. For luncheon Alfredo suggested fish kabobs.

"*Fish* kabobs?" Mary was surprised.

"Yes, any kind of firm fish, made into cubes, marinated with ground onion, yogurt, and spices, then threaded on skewers and grilled. Very good," said Auntie Sanni.

"Then, as some sahibs liking English food," said Alfredo, "young roast lamb, new potatoes, and *brinjals.*"

Auntie Sanni rejected the *brinjals*. Peas would be better.

"What are *brinjals?*" asked Mary, as she continuously asked "What are. . . ?"

"Missy taste tomorrow." Alfredo smiled. Missy, Miss Baba, not even Miss Sahib, none of them calls me Memsahib, thought Mary, a little startled.

Dinner was to be carrot and orange soup—again, something of which she had not heard. "It is delicious," and Auntie Sanni laughed seeing her doubtful face. "Refreshing and light, which it needs to be because we are having tandoori chicken."

"Tandoori?"

"*Tandoor* means an oven, a large long earthenware pot which is buried in clay and earth—fortunately we have one. We put charcoal inside and when it is red-hot the coals are raked out; the chicken, spiced and ready, is put inside and sealed and it cooks with an un-im-ag-in-able taste." Auntie Sanni sounded almost rhapsodical. "People try and cook it as a barbecue or on a spit. Of course, it is *not* the same! And we shall finish," she told Alfredo, "with lemon curd tart . . . as an alternative, peppermint ice cream."

"I'm going to have both," said Mary.

When the menus were settled, to Mary's surprise, Auntie Sanni opened the bag she always carried and counted out notes, notes for a hundred rupees, not the usual twenties, tens, fives, and ones. "Do you give Alfredo money every night?"

"Every night," said Auntie Sanni. "He has to shop in the bazaar, here and in Ghandara, and must pay cash. In the morning he will give me his account. Then there will be a great argument, eh, Alfredo?" Alfredo smiled and nodded. "He himself will have bargained and so he has to have his 'tea money'—the little extra on everything where he has cheated me, but not too much," said Auntie Sanni in pretended severity. "He understands and I understand."

"How nice!" said Mary.

"Would you like to see the baskets of what he will bring?"

"Oh, I would."

"You will have to get up early."

"I will"—again there was that happiness. Is it, Mary asked herself as she went back to the veranda, because all this is something I haven't known anything about, making other people happy and comfortable? Then that was lost as, Soon, somehow, I will see Krishnan again, thought Mary. We might—we might swim, but she could not go until Blaise was asleep and Blaise was playing bridge with the Fishers and Colonel McIndoe, their four heads bent over the green baize of the table Kuku had set up. The cards gleamed in the electric light.

"Two hearts."

"Three no trumps."

"Four clubs . . ."

Bridge! thought Mary, while outside the night waited, the waves sounding on the beach, the moon, bigger now, shedding light on sea, sand, and on the trees in the grove. Is Krishnan waiting there? wondered Mary.

She knew, of course, he was not waiting for her—no one could be more self-contained—but, "Krishnan, Krishnan," all of Mary sent that call out silently over the veranda rails, to the sea, the sky, and the grove until, "What are you looking at?" Blaise asked from the table.

"I was wondering where Slippers was."

"Mary's like Titania," said Sir John.

"Titania?" asked Blaise, momentarily puzzled.

"Methinks I am enamored of an ass!"

"Don't be silly, John." Lady Fisher spoke with unwonted asperity. "She's simply sorry for that poor donkey. I do not understand how Auntie Sanni let him get like that."

"He belonged to the washerman." Mary had learned that from Hannah. "He has never been broken. When they tried to make him carry the washing, he kicked and bolted so the washerman let him go wild. By the time Auntie Sanni knew, his hoofs were like that because no one could get near enough to cut them. I shall have them cut one day," said Mary with certainty.

Lady Fisher looked at her over the cards.

The lecture was over. Professor Aaron and the ladies came out on the veranda—"For the cool air," called Mrs. Glover—but, seeing the bridge players, they hushed their voices as they collected around the bar for a goodnight drink and soft discussion. Professor Webster came to Auntie Sanni.

"We have finished."

"And I'm sure successfully."

"Yes, I'm glad to say." Professor Webster's cheeks were flushed from her efforts; her eyes shone.

"And what was your subject?"

"After today, at Goràghat and the Temple, it was about Usas, Goddess of the Dawn, one of the Shining Ones, the old nature gods." Mary was listening: It's these old gods, true gods, I believe in, she thought. "Usas is the daughter of the sky," Professor Webster went on, "sister of night and married to Surya, the sun god. She travels in a chariot drawn by seven cows; its huge wheels are carved in stone, the cows are there too. The temple faces the east so that when the sun rises its first rays touch the cows and they turn rose red. I have slides to show this and there is a path of gold to the sea."

"Oh!" breathed Mary. "Oh!"

But Lady Fisher broke the enchantment. "Dear," she called to Mary, "I feel a little chilly. Would you run upstairs and fetch me my wrap? It's on a chair, just a light shawl. Thank you, dear child."

As, noiselessly, Mary came up the stairs, she saw a small black figure sidling along the corridor toward one of the rooms. It was the boy on the beach, the squirrel boy. What is he doing here? wondered Mary. Next moment the same question came ringing down the corridor. "Kanu! Why you here?" and a stream of scolding Telegu. It was Hannah, come from turning down the guests' beds for the night. She strode down the corridor, her jewelry clinking, one hand uplifted ready to slap but the boy ducked and escaped down the stairs.

"That boy very bad, little devil. Evil!" and, "How dared he?" cried Hannah, her nostrils snorting. "Dare come into Patna Hall at all, then come upstairs. *Upstairs!*"

It was past midnight when Mary got to the grove.

"God, I'm tired," Blaise had said in the bungalow bedroom.

"I'm not," said Mary, "but then I didn't go all that way to the temple. I think, for a little while, I'll go along the beach." Perhaps she had sounded breathless because Blaise was suddenly alert. "Out? At this time?"

"Just to stretch my legs."

He accepted that, perhaps too tired to bother. "Don't be long," was all he said.

Slippers came as he always came but as Mary turned from the beach toward the grove, where the fire should have been leaping, there was only a dull red glow.

She stepped nearer. The grove was as she had always seen it: the fire, the roof of matting between the trees, the seat with its goatskins, the brass *lota* and pans shining as if someone had cleaned them, the pitcher of water, the line of white washing, the cut sugarcane, all there the same but the grove was empty.

She stood, sick with disappointment, balked. Then there was a sound, light as the wind, and a young man appeared . . . The same young man who came with a message into the dining room our first night, thought Mary. Swiftly he began to mend the fire, kicking the wood together with his bare feet until the branches flamed. He jumped when Mary came into the firelight, then stood holding a branch as if he were brandishing it.

"I think you are. . . ?"

"Sharma," he said, still on guard.

"I am Mary Browne, staying at Patna Hall. Do you speak English?"

"A little."

"Where is . . . Mr. Krishnan?"

"Krishnan Bhanj is holding *darshan* at Ghandara."

"*Darshan?*"

"Many peoples coming to see him. He will be there all night."

"All night?"

"Yes. I must hurry," said Sharma. "We get ready for tomorrow." He paused. "I think I see you in the bazaar?"

"Yes," said Mary. "Yes."

He was gone. Mary waited but it did not seem as if even Birdie would come; there was no sign of Udata. Perhaps Krishnan had taken the squirrel to Ghandara and Mary had turned to go when she heard voices, light young voices. Another fire was burning beyond the trees, the voices were singing in a gentle contented chant. Followed by Slippers, Mary went to see.

It was the boys, the same boys who had tormented Udata but now were squatting on their heels in a circle, faces illumined by the firelight, black polls bent, their hands busy making garlands, and, at once, Of course, thought Mary, garlands for the lorry. They are helping Krishnan. As she stepped nearer they looked up but without animosity; their eyes, bright in their dark faces, were merry, their hands did not stop and, "Show me," said Mary. As if they understood, the smallest handed up a garland. It was made of mango leaves, fresh, pungent, and surprisingly heavy.

"*Shabash!*" said Mary, another word she had learned.

"I'll help you," and she knelt to sit down as they made room for her. She looked around the circle. "Where's the big boy? Where's *Shaitan*, Kanu?"

"Kanu?" For a moment they stared at her, then they collapsed into laughter as if she had made a good joke. "Kanu!" The name went from lip to lip. "Kanu! Kanu!" they cried. "Kanu! *Ayyo! Ayyo! Ayyo-yo.*"

Mystified, Mary picked up a garland to see how it was knotted.

"Mary," came a voice. "Mary."

Quickly, still holding the garland, Mary stood up, like a nymph surprised.

"What the hell are you doing?" asked Blaise.

"Why did you come after me?" In the bungalow bedroom Mary turned on Blaise.

"Isn't it reasonable," asked Blaise, who was being extraordinarily patient, "reasonable for a husband, if his wife goes wandering night after night—"

"Only two nights," Mary interrupted.

"Three," said Blaise. "Tonight's the third."

"Why? Can't I do what I like?"

"Making garlands with fisherboys as if you were one of them seems a strange thing to like."

"I happen to be interested in the Root and Flower Party."

"How can you be?" Blaise asked. "You haven't been here long enough. Nor do you know anything about India."

"I knew more about India in five minutes than you would if you stayed five years," Mary wanted to fling at him. Yet, of course, what he said was true and, What do I know? she thought hopelessly.

"Anyway, I don't want you to be involved with any of this damned masquerade."

"If it's a masquerade I'm sure it's for a good cause."

"I doubt it and I don't want you to be involved."

"I would give anything to be involved," she told him flatly, but had to add, "I don't see how I can be." Had Krishnan not said, "This is the last time I can speak with you."

In Ghandara after the *darshan,* "We must find ourselves a mother figure," Dr. Coomaraswamy told Krishnan.

"Copycat," wrote Krishnan on his pad. For a moment he sat, wrapped in thought, then wrote, "Not a mother. Allure."

"*Allure?*"

"Yes. Goddesses. Two goddesses, Lakshmi for good fortune, Radha for love; both young, beautiful."

"Who?"

"Kuku," wrote Krishnan. "Kuku in the most brilliant most vulgar of her saris so that she looks like the *bania's* glossy catalogue pictures of Lakshmi. Lots of jewelry, you'll have to hire. Auntie Sanni will give her leave, I'm sure. Yes, Kuku for Lakshmi."

"And Radha?"

Krishnan smiled. "Little Radha?" and he wrote, "Mrs. Blaise Browne."

"But she is English! It would not be popular at all if Radha was a Western goddess."

"Dress her up," wrote Krishnan.

"We could, and hide her hair. She is sunburned." Mr. Srinivasan liked the idea. "She could pass for fair wheaten complexion which a goddess should have."

"But it's impossible," Dr. Coomaraswamy almost spluttered. "Can't you imagine? Sir John and Lady Fisher, they would never approve. Sir Professor Aaron, the ladies, Hannah, Samuel, and that young man, Mr. Blaise!" Dr. Coomaraswamy did not like Blaise. "He's her *husband.* He would never consent."

But Krishnan wrote, "Don't ask him. Ask her."

Wednesday

■ ■ ■ ■ ■ ■ ■ ■ ■ ■ ■ ■ ■ ■

"Dr. Coomaraswamy Sahib coming," said Thambi.

Thambi, who was alert to everything that happened in Konak to its very borders, was Krishnan's loyal supporter and knew exactly why Dr. Coomaraswamy was coming. Blaise and Mary had come out early for a morning swim; Blaise had already gone in, Moses after him. "Can't I once, even once, swim without these water rats?" Blaise had exploded.

"Sea can change any minute," Thambi had answered as always, "Moses knows this sea," and, "Wait, Miss Baba," he said as Dr. Coomaraswamy came puffing down the sandy path—Even walking downhill, he gets out of breath, thought Mary. It was not that; Dr. Coomaraswamy was agitated.

"Mrs. Browne, forgive me for intruding at this early hour. I hope I have not disturbed you."

"Of course not. I was just going to swim."

"No. No. Not now. Please not now, Mrs. Browne. I have an ex-tra-or-din-ary favor to ask you. Please do not take offense."

He mopped his forehead. Does he always have to mop? thought Mary as, "What favor?" she asked.

"One that I myself would never have asked, but Krishnan—"

"Krishnan?" Now Mary was surprised.

"As, at present, Krishnan Bhanj himself will not go

into society, you do not know him . . ." Mary did not
contradict the doctor, "but in India's mysterious way he
knows of you . . ."

"The ways of India are even more mysterious than
you think," Mary would have told him, but again did not
say it. Instead, "What does Mr. Bhanj want?"

Dr. Coomaraswamy cleared his throat—if Mary had
not been there he would have spat the phlegm out on the
sand. "It has happened that Mrs. Padmina Retty, candidate for the People's Shelter Party, Krishnan's opponent,
has come out as the Mother Figure for the state, that is the
Mother Goddess. Padmina is a very clever woman, Mrs.
Browne. Also, in all religions, the 'mother' is, I think,
potent but in India you do not know how potent."

"You mean, like the Virgin Mary?"

"Indian goddesses are not virgin, Mrs. Browne, not
at all and, so, more potent. We shall have to combat.
We, the Root and Flower Party, need for Krishnan a fem-
inine counterpart. Not a mother, that would be copycat."
Dr. Coomaraswamy quoted Krishnan with as much
satisfaction as if he had thought of this himself. "We
must be different, also challenging. So we shall import
goddesses. Mrs. Browne, will you come with us on our
lorry to be the goddess Radha? *Please.* We so need this
allure."

"I'm not alluring."

"Indeed you are, but it is the female element that is
more important, gentle, supportive, as are the Hindu goddesses."

"I thought they were fierce."

"Some, not others. Supportive, also beautiful."

"I am not beautiful, Dr. Coomaraswamy."

He did not think so either but, "As Radha you will be.
We shall dress you. All the clothes I have ready."

"What would I have to do?"

"Nothing but sit and smile most graciously. Hold your
hand so, Krishnan will show you. You will have a small

throne on the lorry. With bamboo and leaves we shall shade you. Please."

Mary did not waver anymore. Go with Krishnan, she thought. Be near him all day. See the villages and little towns and, "What can I say but yes." She smiled happily on Dr. Coomaraswamy. "Goddesses don't wear spectacles though. Give me a minute to put in my contact lenses and I'll come."

When she came back Blaise was far out to sea and, "Tell Sahib I have gone out for the day. I'll see him this evening," Mary told Thambi.

"Not for all the tea in China," said Kuku.

"I am not talking about tea, I am talking about cash."

"How much?" asked Kuku.

"She'll not consent," Dr. Coomaraswamy had told Krishnan.

"She will if you offer enough. Try three hundred rupees."

"*Three hundred?*"

"Kukus are expensive and we don't want to fail."

"We shall give you a hundred rupees. *One hundred,*" the doctor told her now.

Kuku gave a snort. "How much do Krishnan's girls at Ghandara get?"

"Our young women do it for love."

"I'm sure they do. Krishnan's *gopis!*"

"Miss Kuku, you may not sneer at our candidate. Three hundred."

Kuku settled for five—And I, myself, shall extort every *anna* of that, Dr. Coomaraswamy had peculiar pleasure in promising himself this. Yet, "If you had known," he told Kuku silently, "I would have given you a thousand rupees, two thousand. For you, I am weakness itself." Instead, he was able to say, "You will stand throughout."

"I shall faint."

"That will be ten rupees off. You will wear green with

yellow and white or yellow with green and white—party colors.''

"I will wear yellow and green, India's colors."

"You will wear what I say," said Dr. Coomaraswamy, "and you will not ogle Krishnan Bhanj."

"Ogle? What is ogle?"

"You know very well," and Kuku laughed.

She did not laugh when the lorry came and she saw Radha.

"Who is that?"

"Don't you know?" Dr. Coomaraswamy was delighted but Kuku had seen the gray eyes.

"Mrs. *Browne!*" she cried.

"Kindly, Mrs. Browne has consented to be the Radha goddess, your companion," said Dr. Coomaraswamy.

"For kindness, not for cash," Mr. Srinivasan put in.

Kuku said at once, "She is far better dressed than I am." It was Shyama who had dressed Mary in the gatehouse. The sari was green gauze patterned with gold-thread stars, the *choli* gold tissue—Mary was titillated to feel her midriff bare; fortunately, from wearing her bikini, it was tanned too. Her hair was hidden by a black slick cap gathered at the back into flowers, a plait hanging ended by one of the little velvet and gold thread balls she had seen in the bazaar. Below the cap her forehead had been painted white which made her skin look darker, the white edged with red dots; her arms were painted with patterns too, the soles of her feet and the palms of her hands red. There were strings of white flowers, a gold necklace, and bangles. Shyama had outlined Mary's eyes with kohl, painted the lids blue, and reddened her lips vividly red. "She says you must take this makeup with you, to freshen in the heat," Dr. Coomaraswamy had said, and, "She says to tell you now you are most beautiful."

Then, by the lorry, "Far better-dressed than I am. I'm not coming," cried Kuku.

Sharma picked her up and put her in the lorry. "You have come," he said.

"Thambi, that was a bad thing to do." Auntie Sanni had sent for Thambi immediately when, as was inevitable, she heard about the dressing up in the gatehouse. She spoke in English to be more severe. "Very bad."

"Bad?" Thambi was astonished. "It was for the party."

"I suppose that was what Krishnan felt," Auntie Sanni said when she told the Fishers. "Better you hear this from me than from Samuel or Hannah."

"All the same, I am surprised at Krishnan," said Sir John.

"I think Krishnan," said Lady Fisher, "is not averse to a little play. Think how mischievous the god Krishna was."

"But Mary must have known this was *not* right," Sir John was fulminating. "All those years with Rory . . ."

"She did not know," said Auntie Sanni, "because she did not give herself time to think. Nor would I—or you—have done at eighteen."

The decorated lorry made its way from small town to small town, village to village, a slow way because it was stopped again and again by the crowds. Soon each stop seemed joined to the other by the people along the roads as Sharma blew his conch, drums beat from the Jeeps and cars behind with the shrill whine of Indian music and Dr. Coomaraswamy bellowing from the microphone. Every time they stopped, a throng pressed forward.

"Where do they all come from?" asked Dr. Coomaraswamy.

"I think from everywhere." Mr. Srinivasan was almost cheerful.

It was a reverent crowd. Again men shut the umbrellas that had shielded them from the sun and made *namaskar;* women usually shy, hiding themselves behind their sari ends, now threw flowers, garlands, jostled forward to touch. "You *must not shrink*," Dr. Coomaraswamy said angrily to Kuku. "Stand up or else . . ."

He glanced at Mary who sat so still he thought she was asleep—but no, she bent a little to the crowd, let the women touch her, received the homage, dutifully kept the other hand in blessing. He saw her, now and again, look at Krishnan and Krishnan looked back with that irradiating smile but once Dr. Coomaraswamy saw what he could hardly believe: Krishnan gave young Mrs. Browne a . . . wink? wondered Dr. Coomaraswamy. Could it have been a wink? There was no time to think further. He had to go back to his microphone. "People of the State of Konak, men and women, friends . . ."

"Jai—Krishnan. Jai—Krishnan," and as the crowd swelled the cry grew into a roar.

"Stand up," he commanded Kuku.

"I want to blow my nose."

"That will be five rupees off."

"Out for the day!" On the beach Blaise had been incredulous.

"She say"—Thambi could not help enjoying this, he had heard "water rats"—"she say she see you this evening," and he volunteered, "She quite safe, Sahib."

"But where has she gone?"

And Thambi had pleasure in saying, "On Krishnan Bhanj's lorry."

"That young Blaise!" Sir John had said in wrath. "Not a word or, I can guess, a thought as to what is going on between him and Mary, only what people might think."

Blaise had come up to breakfast but had contained himself until the Fishers had finished. He followed them on to the veranda. "Gone on this fool lorry. Not a word to me only a message from that far too cocky fellow Thambi," and, "Suppose it gets into the papers?" Blaise said in agony.

"Well, it's bound to be on the news. They seem to be following this election step-by-step. The papers will, of course, copy."

"I meant the British papers."

"My dear boy, to the average Britisher, if they know where it is at all, Konak is a little patch, perhaps the size of a postage stamp on the map of India and about as interesting."

"Not if there's something unusual. This chap Ajax seems to be able to make anything unusual."

"It is unusual, one can't gainsay that. She is dressed up. They may not know it is Mary."

"In this blasted country everyone knows everything. No." Blaise set his teeth. "This time Mary has gone over the edge."

"Many people are bewitched on their first encounter with India." Lady Fisher tried to be soothing. "Bewitched or repelled."

"I'd far rather she was repelled."

"Still, if you're wise you'll take no notice."

"Notice!" Blaise had exploded again. "She's my *wife.*"

"Blaise have you thought," said Lady Fisher, "that the effect of this could be the reverse of scandal? If Krishnan Bhanj wins—"

"He can't win, surely?"

"Suppose he does, wouldn't it be a commendation—what Dr. Coomaraswamy would call a feather—for a rising young diplomat to have a wife with such understanding of Indian affairs, so percipient that she personally backed this election and went campaigning?"

Blaise looked at her dumbfounded, shook his head, bewildered, and left.

* * *

Mr. Menzies was again going through the newspapers and Sir John deliberately voiced what he had said to Lady Fisher. "I'm surprised that a journalist of your reputation should take such an interest in what, after all, is not a big or important election."

Mr. Menzies looked up. "To me all elections are important." There was a distinct swagger. "Not because of the politics. They're not really my game."

"Game?" asked Sir John. "In India they are vitally serious."

"Exactly. That is why, in my case, it's not the politics, it's the politicians at election times. They are so beautifully vulnerable." Mr. Menzies chortled.

"For your filthy column?" Sir John managed to keep his voice pleasant.

"Exactly," Mr. Menzies said with delight.

"So? I don't think you'll find much in the way of titillation in Padmina Retty, or poor old Gopal Rau—or Krishnan Bhanj."

Sir John added Krishnan deliberately and kept his voice mild.

"We'll see," said Mr. Menzies, highly pleased. "We'll see."

"John," Auntie Sanni called from her swing couch where she had come to sit quietly before going on with the day's round—"I like to take this time to consider my guests," she had told Mary, "and their needs." This morning the needs were troubling her and, "John, have you time to come and talk a little?"

"All the time in the world."

"For the first week in years," said Auntie Sanni, "I'm troubled, very troubled, about my guests—some of them."

"Such as?"

"Obviously, Olga Manning."

"With reason," said Sir John.

"Someone must help her," and Auntie Sanni looked at him, the sea-green blue eyes as trustful as a trusting child's. "You will, John." It was not a question; it was a fact.

"If I can. I'll try and talk to her when she comes back from Calcutta—if she comes back."

"She owes me money, so she will." Auntie Sanni said it with certainty. "Then there's Kuku."

"She is meant to be a help not a worry."

Auntie Sanni smiled. "I know—and she *is* a help, she works hard but . . ."

"But?"

"When she left St. Perpetua's she was sweet. Now she's so knowing. We haven't done her any good, and I foresee pain. She hasn't a chance, and I can't give her one, not of the kind she would thank me for."

"I hope you're wrong. Who besides? Mary?"

"No. Mary can look after herself."

"Which is why you like her!"

"She is likable," was as far as Auntie Sanni would go. "No, John, it's the young man, Mr. Browne." Sir John noticed he was still Mr. Browne. "Oh, John, why can't we all be born with wit?" She looked far across the sea, sparkling in the morning, an increasing frown on her face. "John, I'm afraid. Mary doesn't know, doesn't dream . . . This isn't England or even Europe. It's such a violent place."

Sir John got up, went to the railing, and looked down at the out-bungalow, whistling as he pondered. Suddenly he broke off. "That young fool!"

Two men in bathing shorts were strolling along the beach. "He's talking to Menzies," said Sir John.

"No! Oh, no," said Auntie Sanni.

It was the coconut water that woke Mary out of her trance.

"Where have I been?"

"Only four hours on that damned lorry." Kuku had collapsed on the sand.

To Mary it had seemed like five minutes. Now the

lorry and its following Jeeps and cars had pulled off the
dust road into a small oasis of trees in the midst of what
had seemed to be a desert wasteland without villages.
There were no people, only birds: cranes, wading in a
stagnant pool, small wild brown birds she recognized as
partridges wandering in coteries, mynahs, and, of course,
crows. Mats were being spread. "You must rest and eat,"
Dr. Coomaraswamy told Mary. "Drink a little, not too
much," and Sharma had sent a boy shinnying up a coconut palm—there seemed to be innumerable small boys.
Some had ridden on the car roofs or hung onto their backs.
Mary tried not to think of the abominable Kanu.

The boy up the palm tree threw the nuts down to the
ground where Sharma took the tops off them with a *panga*,
splitting each so skillfully that none of the water was lost.
"Drink. You must drink." Dr. Coomaraswamy told Mary
again as she sat; she still seemed dazed.

"It has been too much for her," said Mr. Srinivasan,
but Krishnan took the nut and held it to her lips. Even
here he could not speak. "In India even the trees have
ears," Dr. Coomaraswamy would have told her but Krishnan's eyes commanded her; she felt the rough wood of the
nut edge, the coolness of the water as, obediently, she
drank.

It was Krishnan, too, who had lifted her down from
the lorry; Kuku had had to jump only helped by Sharma's
hand. Now she stood up to wring out her sari. "My God!
The sweat. You'll have to get me fresh clothes."

"They will dry in the sun," Sharma soothed her.

Mary, oddly enough, was untouched, her sari still
fresh, and, never, thought Dr. Coomaraswamy, had he
seen anything as shining as her gray eyes. He was unused
to light eyes; his ideal was for brown eyes, lustrous, deeply
lashed—Not like Uma's, he thought with a pang of guilt,
though Uma, when she was young, had been handsome.
Kuku's eyes were black, small, and, he had to admit, ma-

licious. Then why am I so much seduced? He did not know but now, "This blue-gray," he murmured to Mr. Srinivasan, "we do not have this color of eyes in India, sometimes violet or green but not this." Mary Browne's eyes today were like diamonds, he thought, brilliant in a way that alarmed him. Has she fever? and, "Eat a little," he urged her. "See, we will bring food to you. Then, on this mat, you must stretch out and sleep!"

Krishnan himself had had to be helped off the lorry; now two of the young men were pummeling him and rubbing his legs. "He has been im-mo-bile all those hours." Mr. Srinivasan hopped like an agitated bird. "How can he keep it up?"

Krishnan did say one word. *"Chūp."* Then, while Mary watched, he clasped his hands behind his neck, using his elbows to support him until he stood on the crown of his head, his feet high in the air, his powerful body erect as a pillar, "So that the blood can run the other way," Dr. Coomaraswamy explained to Mary, "which is good for the body—and the brain."

"I could not have done those hours on the lorry without yoga," Krishnan told Mary afterward as he stretched, bent, leapt, ran.

Food was brought on banana leaves for Kuku and Mary to eat in the Indian way with their fingers and apart from the men, "Usually *after* the men," Kuku said with acerbity, "with their leftovers," but Mary found it restful— no fuss with talk or plates, knives, forks, spoons. The food was hot and good; it had traveled in aluminum pans that fitted together into a carrier, the bottom pan filled with live coals. There was rice, curry, spicy little *koftas* of prawns, *puris,* vegetables, but Mary only nibbled. "I don't want to be disturbed," she could have said. Soon she lay down and was asleep.

Dr. Coomaraswamy had to wake her. It was the first time he had seen an Englishwoman asleep. He looked at the shadow her eyelashes made on her cheeks; the skin below them was . . . like petals, he thought—why did Mary Browne continually make him think of flowers? It's because she's so young, he thought—and pure. He hesitated to touch her.

Kuku laughed as she watched. "Go on, wake her with a kiss."

Dr. Coomaraswamy was shocked. To him Mary, like Krishnan, was in a different category—she was Blaise Browne's wife, but Dr. Coomaraswamy felt she belonged to Krishnan, he did not know how or why but he had seen Krishnan not only look at her and give her the especially tender smile he gave to most women and children—"and to a little goat or a squirrel," the doctor had to say—but he, Dr. Coomaraswamy, had seen that wink. The wink immediately put her on a level he could not reach.

"Go on, kiss her. You like young women."

"Kuku, you are lewd. I shall fine you fifty rupees."

"We misjudged Menzies," Blaise told the Fishers at lunchtime. "Thought he was just a journalist who likes to make a mystery. Actually, he's a sympathetic type."

"Type's the right word for him." Sir John almost said it but stopped himself, only saying, "I hope you didn't talk to him about Mary."

"Of course not." Blaise, Sir John was sure, lived by a code which laid down that one did not talk about one's wife to other men. "Of course not, at least I hope not," and Blaise defended himself. "If I did a little, what's the harm? He's on a holiday. Apparently he has a hell of a life in Delhi and in London. It seems that to write a newspaper gossip column means continual parties and pressures from people wanting to get into the news. He's here for quiet. He's taking me to Ghandara this afternoon so we can get a decent round of golf but the course wouldn't be grass, would it?"

"Sand," said Sir John. "For grass you would probably have to go to Madras . . . Pity you couldn't—out of the way," he wanted to add.

"Why should Mary Browne?" Kuku was asking. "Why should she sit when I have to stand?"

"I'll stand," said Mary. "Let Kuku sit."

"That is not the plan."

"She has stood for four hours."

"So she should at that price."

"Price?" Mary was puzzled.

"Do you think I would do this for nothing? Or do you call it love?" sneered Kuku.

"I don't call it anything. I just want to do it."

"For love?" Kuku insisted.

Dr. Coomaraswamy intervened. "It will not be long now," he soothed. "As we get toward evening it will be cooler, it will not seem so long."

"I like it long," said Mary.

"This seems a roundabout way to get to Ghandara," Blaise said in the car.

"So it is. I'm sorry. I must have taken the wrong turning. Hallo!" said Mr. Menzies. "Here they are!"

"You promised." Blaise was furious.

"I'm sorry but how was I to know where they would be?"

Mr. Menzies had to stop, the crowds around the lorry were so thick. He opened the sunroof and stood on the seat. *"Golly!"* he said. Reluctantly, Blaise stood up beside him.

Surrounded by the surging mass of people, the lorry looked small, the figures on it even smaller, but Blaise recognized Kuku, then looked from her to the smaller throne and, "Is that Mary?" he asked, dazed.

"Cleverly disguised at any rate," Mr. Menzies comforted him. "But, yes, it undoubtedly is."

Kuku, Lakshmi, in her green-and-white-patterned gold-edged sari, gold bodice, seemed to melt into the lorry's decorations as did Krishnan, though his blue-blackness could be seen, while Mary, Radha, shone in all the wheaten fairness Mr. Srinivasan had hoped.

"Couldn't be more conspicuous," Blaise agonized. "And she must be recognized as she's the only Western person there."

"She wouldn't have been the only one if you had gone with her," Mr. Menzies pointed out.

Blaise stared at him. "I? With that rabble?"

Mr. Menzies gave a soft whistle. "So you *are* at odds!" He sounded amused. "I thought you were."

"Why?" Blaise was cold, trying to fend him off.

"From what I have seen. No one can say I am not interested in my fellow men—and women," said Mr. Menzies sweetly. "Your wife is so transparently young."

"You make me sound like a child stealer. It was she who wanted us to be married."

"And now she doesn't."

"Who said so? Good God! We haven't been married a month."

"That *is* quick." Unerringly, the insidious drops of poison fell. "But India does go to people's heads and Mr. Krishnan Bhanj knows very well how to make himself— shall we say—attractive?"

"Don't!" Blaise cried out before he could stop himself, then tried to recover. "I don't think I feel like playing golf. Would you be kind enough to drive me back to the hotel?"

Kuku had seen Blaise at once and began to redrape her sari more gracefully, then waved the peacock fan Sharma had given her to help against the heat.

Dr. Coomaraswamy, for a moment released from his megaphone—the microphone had failed—followed her eyes. "Menzies, young Browne! You will not plume," he said furiously to Kuku. "You are here for the crowd. Also put that fan down or you will get nothing at all."

"It is I who have bought you for today," he wanted to cry, "so no tricks." The plain fact that Kuku liked Blaise inflamed his own longing. The bodice she wore showed the cleavage between her breasts; her sweat had stained the silk under her arms and, where the bodice ended, her midriff glistened with it; he could imagine the glistening between her thighs and delight carried him away. Besides, it was sweet to torment her. What fun, thought Dr. Coomaraswamy, if I could whip Kuku. If I could have—is it a *sjambok?*—that long whip that hisses in the air as its lash comes down. He saw himself wielding it, then had to say, as Uma would have, "And how silly you would look," and, "Stand up, girl," he shouted. "Smile!" It was no use saying, "I'll fine you," he knew he never would.

Mary had not seen Blaise, she was too interested; in contrast to the morning when she had been entranced, everything now was vivid. As the lorry drove and stopped—stopped every few minutes, it seemed to her—she had never imagined such crowds or smelled them, the peculiar smell of an Indian crowd: not dirt, Indians are personally clean, but of sweat, the *coconut* oil men and women used on their bodies and hair and an intrinsic spicy yet musty smell of clothes washed too often and seldom properly dried; of the spat phlegm, cess, and dust everywhere trodden in, and, over it in the lorry, the strong heady scent of crushed flowers and the withering leaves of garlands.

Dark hands reached out to touch her, voices and eyes pleaded; babies, their eyes rimmed with kohl, were held up to see and for her to see and bless. The voices chanted: "Jai Krishnan."

"Jai Krishnan."

"Jai Shri Krishnan."

"Jai Krishnan Hari."

Dr. Coomaraswamy's voice boomed on through the megaphone with words Mary could not understand. Mr. Srinivasan took his place but his voice was reedy after the doctor's rounded mellifluent tones. "Which could coax a bee off a flower," Krishnan used to joke but, as if the bee had stung, It can't coax Kuku, thought Dr. Coomaraswamy.

As soon as the megaphone paused, music and songs from the Jeeps and cars took over,

O Krishnakumar, the one who steals butter,
The one with red eyes,
The one who brings bliss,
O Krishna . . .

sung with drums, cymbals, and the sound of the conch, though now, Mary noticed, it was not Sharma who blew it but a disciple called Ravi.

Over it all was Krishnan enthroned, not moving, only smiling, holding up that benevolent hand. I don't care what anyone says, thought Mary, there *is* something mystical about this. Perhaps it comes from the people, their faith, yet it is through Krishnan.

One outside moment did break through: Toward late afternoon she became conscious that a red car, its sunroof open, had drawn alongside the lorry with—on its backseat—a photographer, his camera pointing through the window, first directly at her, next at Krishnan; then, as the car drew a little away, it took in both of them. The driver was Mr. Menzies and standing on the passenger seat beside him was Kanu, his eyeballs, as they rolled in excitement, showing white in his dark face as, with one hand in easy familiarity, he steadied himself on Mr. Menzies's shoulder. A moment Mary had put out of her mind came back, giving a feeling of dismay: That early morning, when she came through Patna Hall on the way to the gatehouse and had run up to the top veranda to look down on the beach to see if Blaise was still swimming, there, along the corridor, was Kanu again, sitting cross-legged on the floor outside a door. This time he was dressed in clean white shorts, a yellow shirt—silk, Mary had thought—a red flower jauntily behind his ear. As he gave her a salaam without getting up, which she knew was impertinent, she had seen on his wrist a new watch. The door was Mr. Menzies's.

Why should I have minded that? wondered Mary—and why should she, who hated telltales, have said to Samuel, who had come—solicitous as always—to see the lorry off, "Samuel, that boy Kanu is upstairs again."

"Kanu?" and, "*Ayyo,*" Samuel said with distaste. "Miss Baba, I will see to it."

Now as she saw the new watch gleam on the thin dark wrist, Mary did not like it. She did not like the camera either.

"Mrs. Browne," Dr. Coomaraswamy whispered to prompt her. With a start of guilt, Mary went back to Krishnan's afternoon.

Offerings were laid at her feet as well as his, flowers thrown in her lap: marigolds, flaunting scarlet cotton-tree flowers, white mogra buds. Coins were thrown too—they hurt like little flints: *annas, pices,* even cowries—those little shells used as the smallest possible coins; sometimes whole rupees were recklessly thrown from hard-earned savings. Kuku grew angry. "*Ari!* They hurt!" But Mary was touched almost to tears. "Scoop them up and give them back," she wanted to say but knew she must only smile and accept.

"How was it?" Sir John asked when at last the lorry drove into Patna Hall to drop off Mary, Kuku, and the disciples before taking Krishnan, Dr. Coomaraswamy, Mr. Srinivasan, and the young women back to Ghandara for Krishnan to rest before the evening *darshan* he would hold that night. Sir John came to meet them, jumping Mary down among the admiring disciples.

"How was it?"

"Exaltation!" said Mary.

"Mary," Sir John was grave, "I want to speak to you and so does Alicia."

"You're angry! You mustn't be. Oh, Sir John, not tonight. Don't be angry tonight when everything's so wonderful."

"What could I do?" he asked Lady Fisher.

"You must be tired." Lady Fisher had come into the hall.

"I'm not in the least bit tired," and suddenly Mary clasped her in a tight hug, gave her a resounding kiss, kissed Sir John, then whirled through the hall on to the veranda where she hugged Auntie Sanni, dared to kiss Colonel McIndoe and a few of Professor Aaron's ladies, Mrs. van den Mar, Professor Webster, Miss Pritt, and Dr. Lovat, who had come back from a second expedition to the Dawn Temple. She left them slightly startled, met Hannah, and threw her arms around her, darted into the dining room to shake Samuel's hands and the waiters', even the stately Ganga's. "Where's Bumble?" she called. "Oh, I expect down at the bungalow. I'll call him. It would be nice to play a silly game. Come on," she called to the disciples. "Come down to the beach. Give me ten minutes to get out of these beautiful clothes in the gatehouse and we'll show you how to play rounders. Come!"

Released, too, for the moment, the disciples came with whoops of joy. Soon the beach was full of running white figures with Mary's blue shorts and shirt flashing among them.

"She's overexcited," said Auntie Sanni, watching from the veranda, where Lady Fisher had come out to join her.

"Violently overexcited," said Lady Fisher. "Oh dear!"

"It looks rather fun," said Dr. Lovat. "Let's go down and join in."

"I'm not talking to you," Blaise had said.

"I don't want you to talk. We want you to play." Changed back into her morning clothes, her face and arms clean where Shyama had reluctantly washed off the kohl, henna, and colors—"She say you much more pretty with," Thambi had told Mary—she had run into the bungalow bedroom to fetch Blaise.

"Play?"

"Yes, with me and the young men, Dr. Cooma-raswamy's young men, and I guess some of the ladies."

"And, I suppose, Krishnan Bhanj." It was meant to be withering—Mr. Menzies's insinuations had rankled—but Mary's, "Oh, Krishnan has gone back to Ghandara," was so careless that Blaise felt slightly reassured.

"Play what?"

"Rounders." Mary had cast off her shoes.

"That's a kid's game."

"All the better." Already she was outside and show-ing the disciples how to mark out the round—"With my golf clubs!" Blaise, who had followed her, was outraged.

"It won't hurt them. They make good posts."

"You haven't a bat."

"This'll do." She had picked up a flat-faced piece of driftwood. "Anil. Ravi," she called to two of the disciples whose names she knew, "Blaise and I will go first to show you."

Blaise came portentously forward. "I'll tell you the rules—"

"We don't need rules," Mary interrupted. "We've chosen our sides. They'll pick it up as we go. You'll see. Come on. You bowl, I'll bat. See," she called to the young men and ladies—five of the cultural ladies had come—

"you have to catch the ball to get me out or catch it and throw it to hit me when I'm between posts and I'll be out. Are you ready? Blaise, throw!"

"You're not playing properly."

"Don't be such a pomp. Throw!"

They were, Blaise had to admit, quick—he had not yet met India's barefoot quicksilver hockey players—and now two more ladies came. "Can we join, Mr. Browne?"

Mollified by their presence, "Of course," said Blaise. "Join the team. I'll be umpire," and he threw the ball to Anil.

"We don't need an umpire," called Mary.

Nor did they. "Out!" shouted Blaise when Ravi fell headlong by a golf club post a moment before he was caught.

"I'm not out, my head is in," cried Ravi.

"Out."

"In," they chorused, laughing.

"Of course, if you're going to cheat . . ."

You do not, Mary sensed, even in her daredevil mood, accuse Indians of cheating: It is like holding explosives to flame and hastily she intervened. "Of course we're going to cheat. All of us will cheat. It's part of the fun. I'll cheat. You'll cheat."

"I don't call that fun and I don't cheat." Blaise stalked off into the bungalow.

Mrs. Glover went after him. "Mr. Browne, do play. You make us feel badly."

"In England we play games properly. We keep the rules."

"Well, I don't know about properly and rules but this is real fun and what we needed. We've all been at a high pitch of emotion all day." Reluctantly Blaise came out but only stood watching.

"Letters for you, Doctor."

"Not now. Not now." Dr. Coomaraswamy said it ir-

ritably. "Not when I have a thousand, thousand worries."
Then he saw that it was Kuku.

There was no one else on the veranda; except for
Auntie Sanni and Colonel McIndoe who had gone to knoll,
everyone else was in their room or on the beach. "It looks
a nice romp," said Dr. Coomaraswamy.

"I do not romp," said Kuku. "Besides I have work to
do."

"Unfortunately I, too . . . " Dr. Coomaraswamy
passed his hand over his eyes as if to shut out doings with
which he could no longer cope. Then, "Kuku, where are
you going?"

"To bathe and change."

"I myself must bathe and change."

"But first," said Kuku, "I should like my five hundred
rupees," and seeing his face grow immediately stern, came
closer with what she knew was a winning smile—the smile
he had asked for all day—as she murmured, "You are not
going to fine me, are you?"

She had never been as close; he could smell, not her
scent, that had faded in the sun, but, far more tantalizing
again, her warmth, her girl sweat. Her hair disheveled,
almost brushed his temples—she was taller than he. All
thought of Uma faded from Dr. Coomaraswamy's mind.
"Kuku, first come to my room."

"Your room?" Kuku laughed. "Don't be a silly old
man."

"You are so beautiful. I'll give"—he swallowed—"I'll
give you another five hundred rupees."

For a moment a glint came into Kuku's eyes; he
thought it a promising glint that made him quiver
but she looked down to the beach where, among the
dark figures, a blond head stood out as the last rays of
the sun going down over the sea touched the blond to
gold.

"Not for ten thousand rupees," said Kuku, her whole
face softened, illumined and, when she spoke next, her

voice was soft, "You see, Dr. Coomaraswamy, I too am in love."

It was beginning to be dusk on the beach; they could no longer see the ball; the play, the running ebbed. At the same time the flames of braziers showed on the roof of Patna Hall while lanterns shone along the parapet. Some time before Anil and Ravi had slipped away; now they came back washed and changed. They stood together and Ravi cried, "You are invited to Paradise. Auntie Sanni has agreed. Tonight is the end of our campaign so the Root and Flower Party invite you to a barbecue, Indian fashion—on the roof. Please, everyone, yes everyone, come. Sir John. Lady Fisher. Professor Aaron. Mrs. van den Mar. Professor Webster. Ladies, Mr. and Mrs. Browne—par-tic-u-lar-ly Mrs. Browne—please to accept."

"What could be better?" It was Mrs. van den Mar's voice.

"Well, I must say," said Mrs. Glover, "that was the best time I've had in months. Who would have thought my old legs could run as fast!"

"Who would have thought"—Miss Pritt was aglow—"that an archaeological tour could have ended in a children's ball game then being invited to a party by those delightful young men?"

"Charmers all of them," said Dr. Lovat.

"Julia! Beware."

"They're far too busy," Dr. Lovat said calmly, "and too committed. Later tonight we, too, shall be truly serious."

"Yes." Professor Webster spoke to Mrs. van den Mar as they walked up to Patna Hall. "We mustn't be late for the *darshan*."

"We shan't. They'll all be needed for it, the young men," said Mrs. van den Mar.

"But which *darshan*?" Professor Aaron had come to

meet them. "I've just been listening to the radio news and it seems there will be two, so where do we go?"

"To Krishnan Bhanj's *darshan.*"

"Both are Krishnan's."

"That can't be. He can't be in two places at once," Dr. Lovat objected.

"It appears he can."

It had been in that noon break in the oasis that the news had come to Dr. Coomaraswamy. One of the disciples had taken the opportunity of listening to the midday radio and had run to get the doctor to come to his Jeep in time for the repeat of the news in English. First the headlines, "Padmina Retty outwits—and outdistances—Krishnan Bhanj . . ." Then, "On this, the final day of the campaign, dismayed perhaps by Krishnan Bhanj's, shall we say, 'divine progress' through Konak's towns and villages, Mrs. Retty has gone into space. She has hired a helicopter and so today, this final day, she has covered far more of Konak than he. 'His poor little lorry is slow,' says Padmina. 'Ignorant puppy, the very crowds impede it! I shall be swift, able to appear in outlying places he cannot hope to reach . . .' "

"Damn Padmina Retty to hell!" swore Dr. Coomaraswamy. He rushed to alert Krishnan who was peacefully eating. "She will go by air. Do we now have to hire a plane?"

"Copycat," wrote Krishnan again. "Helicopter will utterly destroy image so carefully built up," he wrote, and continued eating, crunching the still crisp *dosas* between his white teeth.

"Then what to do?"

Krishnan licked his fingers and wrote, "Duplicate."

"Duplicate?"

"Yes, immediately."

As one who was now part of the campaign, though

only like Vishnu's squirrel helping to build the great bridge by bringing pebbles, Dr. Coomaraswamy told Mary about this latest move. "Fort-un-ate-ly, our benefactor Mr. Sur-ijlal Chand has an identical lorry, same make, same color. It is to be decorated i-den-tic-ally—I have detached some of our young men to see to this—same *pandal*, same garlands, colors, and posters and Sharma is so like Krishnan that, i-den-tic-al in dress and makeup, few will tell the difference."

"He's not nearly as dark," objected Mary.

"All the better. Krishnan should be fair."

"Nor as big."

"We shall seat him higher. We shall be touring until the early hours."

"What happens," asked Mary, "if they meet or the people see them both?"

"No matter." Dr. Coomaraswamy spoke almost cheerfully as he echoed what Krishnan had written, "Hindu gods can duplicate themselves, indeed multiply themselves. Did not Krishna become twenty-four Krishnas to please the *gopis*, the milkmaids?"

"My goodness," said Professor Webster on the path up from the beach. "How I'd like to go to both *darshans*."

I only want to go to one, thought Mary.

On the knoll, looking down on the empty beach, the blaze of light on the roof, "I feel there is a tide," Auntie Sanni said to Colonel McIndoe. "Listen to the drums."

When Blaise came up from the bungalow, Patna Hall's big veranda was deserted.

He had avoided Mary, going into the bathroom as she came out of it, staying there until she had gone, coming out changed into slacks, a thin jersey, then strolling along the beach until he was sure she was at the roof barbecue. He had heard the invitation; at the bar there was no one, he poured himself a drink, then another. He could hear sounds of people going up and down the outside stairs, of American voices, Indian voices, laughter; they came down too from the roof. He turned his back.

Fireflies flickered in the garden and down the path. A garden boy came out to switch on the lanterns down the path sending the bats away where before they had flown and swooped almost brushing Blaise's hair. "Yuk!" he had cried out in horror; they seemed part, to him, of this horrible night. He had another whiskey. "That girl should have been at the bar," he muttered, but Kuku, too, was up on the roof—though treating the barbecue with disdain, making a point of talking to Professor Aaron and the ladies, not to the disciples, except in their role as waiters.

"Why is the dining room closed?" Blaise had finally come in from the bar to find the dining room empty, the tables bare. Only the youngest waiter, Ahmed, was there fetching glasses from a cupboard. "Why is the dining room closed?"

"No dinner in dining room tonight." The boy picked up his tray obviously wanting to get away from this inexplicably angry sahib.

"No dinner! In Christ's name, why not? This is supposed to be a hotel."

"Plenty of dinner."

To Ahmed's relief, Samuel appeared. "Plenty but tonight served up on the roof. Miss Sanni's orders. Come, Sahib, I show you the way."

"No, thanks."

"Excellent dinner," crooned Samuel. "It is our Root and Flower Party's invitation. Miss Sanni say we all accept."

"Does she?" Blaise sounded dangerous.

"Indian-fashion barbecue. Western as well." I and Ahmed cook that. "Sahib enjoy it very much."

A voice interrupted; in the pantry Ahmed had turned

on the radio and the voice of the reader in English came through: "This is All India Radio. Here is the news. The trial of Colin Armstrong closed today. Mr. Justice Rajan . . ." A clatter of plates drowned the rest. Then, "In the state of Konak, the election has entered an impressive stage . . ."

"Turn that damn thing off!" Blaise almost screamed. Samuel was more than perturbed. That a sahib, one of Auntie Sanni's sahibs, should misbehave—Samuel could not bring himself to say "offend"—seemed unbelievable. Yet not half an hour ago he had had another such encounter, worse, a confrontation he had to admit. He had caught Mr. Menzies in the hall as he went out. Mr. Menzies had not been invited to the barbecue but did not seem to mind.

"Menzies, Sahib."

"What is it? I'm in a hurry." He had been in a hurry all day, the red car whizzing in and out. "Well?"

"Sahib, that boy Kanu, he may not come into Patna Hall," and before Mr. Menzies could object, "If Sahib is needing a body servant—"

"Body servant! That's rich." Mr. Menzies was laughing—it sounded to Samuel like demon laughter. "Ho! Ho!" He clapped Samuel on the shoulder. "You say more than you know, old man," but Samuel shook off the hand as if it had been a snake and drew himself up to look Mr. Menzies in the face.

"I am knowing"—Samuel deliberately left out the "sahib"—"I know very well, which is why I have to speak."

The laughter ceased. "And I suppose you will tell your Auntie Sanni?"

"Miss Sanni," Samuel corrected him. "I do not tell such to a lady. I am telling *my* sahib, Colonel McIndoe."

For a moment Samuel had thought he had disconcerted Mr. Menzies. Then Mr. Menzies shrugged and went off whistling to his car. Now Samuel's grave eyes took in Blaise's flushed face, overbright eyes, the smell of whiskey and, "Sahib must eat," said Samuel. "If Sahib too tired to come upstairs, I bring some good things down." He spoke a few quick words to Ahmed. "Ahmed is laying you a table."

"Don't bother. I don't want anything."

"Sahib must eat."

"Shut up, you," shouted Blaise, and went back to the bar.

"Miss Baba, come down," Samuel whispered to Mary up on the roof. "Ask Sahib to come to the barbecue. Missy, come down, please."

No, thought Mary, please no.

She had been utterly content, sitting in the firelight on a *durrie* by Auntie Sanni. The disciples had provided stools and benches for their older guests; the rest sat on mats or *durries* while a few of the young men, more adventurous, dared to sit on the parapet, their backs to the sixty-foot drop below, while they ate and dangled their legs. Samuel and his staff had carried up china, glasses, and cutlery but Mary had been delighted to see there were also banana leaves and the small metal tumblers used for drinking. The disciples, sniffing success, were overflowing with hospitality and affectionate happiness.

"Eat, please eat."

"Here is drink."

"Please, Auntie Sanni."

"Professor."

"Lady."

"Lady."

"Mrs. Browne."

"Call me Mary."

"Not Mary, Radha. We think you are true goddess, Radha."

Up on the roof is nearer to the stars, Mary had been

thinking. The sky seemed like a spangled bowl meeting the horizon far out to sea and, as she had seen when she had looked over the back parapet, was met by the tall palms and cotton trees of the village with, behind them, the hills, holders of the cave paintings that had so thrilled the ladies. To the east was Auntie Sanni's knoll, to the west, the sand dunes lit tonight by a chain of shrine lights, though the grove itself was, at the moment, dark and still. On the lit roofs plied by the disciples, she was contentedly eating the delicious food with her fingers.

"Ugh!" said Mrs. Schlumberger, and, peering, "What is it?"

"Delectable!" said Dr. Lovat.

"But I like to know what I am eating. It smells."

"Of course. It's spicy."

"Memsahib rather have Western? Hamburger? French fries?" Anil was anxious to please but when he brought them, "Not on a *leaf*, boy, I'm not a barbarian."

"I am, I'll eat them," Mary offered. "I'm ravenous," and Anil spirited up plate, knife, fork, napkin, while Ravi emptied a pyramid of saffron rice on a fresh banana leaf for Mary. Then Samuel was at her elbow.

"Missy. Miss Baba."

"Oh, all right." Like Krishnan, Mary licked her fingers, one by one, laughing. She stood up, shook out her skirt—she had changed into a dress for the *darshan*—and went downstairs.

"A pretty poor show," said Blaise, "a hotel not serving dinner."

"Blaise, don't you see, it's an exceptional night? Everyone has election fever and there's such good food. I've never tasted real Indian food before. Bumble, do come. Everyone's up there, Sir John, Lady Fisher, Professor Aaron and all the ladies. Auntie Sanni—"

"She's *not* your aunt."

Mary was too happy to quarrel. "It won't be long. We will all be going on to the *darshan*. Bumble, why won't you join in?"

"I did try to join in there, down on the beach, and a bloody fool you made me look."

"I'm sorry. I suppose I was excited."

"If anyone knows how a game should be played"—the whiskey was beginning to work on Blaise's resentment—"how it ought to be played . . ."

"It wasn't an ought sort of game."

"Then it ought to be."

"Ought! Ought!" Mary was near to losing her temper. "Ought is a bully word. Blaise, why? Why do you have to spoil everything?"

"*I* spoil?"

"Yes," but Mary felt an odd pang of pity. "Bumble, please. This is an . . . an enchanted night. Look at the fireflies, the stars. Everyone's so happy, so affectionate. Krishnan—"

"Don't talk to me about that black cheat. Don't dare to say his name. Go on," shouted Blaise, "go upstairs to him and his like," and he slapped Mary hard across her face. "And you can take that with you."

The sound of the slap seemed to reverberate through Patna Hall. In the pantry Samuel dropped a dish.

For a moment Mary stood still with shock, the red mark spreading on her cheek. Her hand came up to feel it as if she could not believe it. Then she said, in a whisper, "You won't do that again. I'm going."

It was late when Sir John went down to the bungalow. He had left Lady Fisher and Auntie Sanni on the veranda. Kuku had gone to bed. Paradise was dark now, its bonfires sunk to embers; along the beach, the noise of the surf was broken by drums beating from the grove where Sir John could see lights, flares, behind the lights of the shrines as he came down the path. The drums quickened; he could hear the high notes of a flute, then chanting, a slow rhythmic chant. Slippers, driven away by the crowd, was standing looking wistfully at the bungalow. He turned to follow Sir John. "Better not, old fellow," Sir John told him, and with a pat turned him around.

Blaise, it seemed, had had more whiskey—the room's own small bar stood open, its whiskey bottle three-quarters empty. Samuel, though his legs were tired, his feet sore from climbing up the steep stairs to Paradise, had come bringing a plate of sandwiches and a basket of fruit; they were on the table untouched while Blaise sat staring out to sea, his head on his hands. When Sir John came in he looked up, glowering, "I wanted to be left alone."

"So I gathered but I have come," said Sir John, "to take you to the *darshan.*"

"The bloody *darshan?* That's the last thing . . ." The words were slurred.

"I think you should come, for your own sake," said Sir John, and, peremptorily, "Stand *up,* boy."

At first Blaise could not walk beside Sir John but wove an unsteady way, veering down almost to the waves, back up the sand; then slowly the cooler air and the breeze revived him. Soon, too, the size of the gathering began to dawn on him; it reached far wider than the grove, overflowing through the dunes and the fluffy casuarina trees and along the beach. Blaise had seen the crowds that afternoon but here were, "A thousand? Two thousand?" he murmured, dazed.

"More," said Sir John. "Far more."

The music and chanting had stopped for a breathing space and they heard the stirrings, the undertone murmuring of a reverent multitude, men and women packed close sitting on the sand, the women with flowers in the coils of their hair; some men were bareheaded, most had small turbans—the pale cloth shone in the glow of lanterns hung in the trees and on poles, stretching away as far as they could see. Boys were everywhere, some up the trees; girls, small and older, sat with their mothers.

Among them, like vigilantes in white—again Sir John was reminded of angels—the disciples stood sentinel or moved silently offering *chattis* of hot coffee or pepper water, *biris*, fruit or *pān*—betel nut. Though the people took them, their heads never moved, their gaze was too fixed on where, in a clear space, a fire burned sending up sparks, while behind it, on a high throne heaped with flowers, sat Krishnan, blue-black as usual, his skin shining with oil, his eyes outlined with kohl, his lips vermilion, the white U mark of Vishnu on his forehead. He looked outsized as he smiled gently, tenderly, on his people. Behind was an elephant Sir John had often seen in the village; now it was unattended, content. On Krishnan's knee sat a squirrel, its gray fur ruddy in the firelight, its tail plumed up. As they watched, Krishnan absently gave it a nut; it nibbled, holding the nut in its paws, its beady eyes giving a quick look at the crowds, then trustingly up at Krishnan. "I must say he is magnificent," said Sir John.

Blaise stood staring, a little of the implications reaching him at last—until he saw Mary.

The cultural ladies were here and there among the people; most of them had brought campstools but Mary sat on a deerskin almost at Krishnan's feet. She was stringing a garland as were the boys squatting around her; as she looked down to pick up a flower her hair swung its bell around her face and fell back as she looked up again to thread the flower; her white dress seemed, like the squirrel, to be stained with red light from the fire. As Blaise looked, she held up the garland toward Krishnan.

"Lady Fisher said she was bewitched." Blaise's voice was far too loud.

"Hush!"

"She's not bewitched. She's besotted. Sotted."

"That's an ugly word." Sir John spoke quietly, firmly, hoping to calm him.

"Ugly! Look at *that!*" Blaise shouted the words out. Krishnan had smiled on the flowers. *"It's* bloody ugly."

"Chūp!" Sir John used the Hindi word and, at the same time, slapped his hand over Blaise's mouth. "How dare you disturb everyone? What is ugly in this? The fire, flowers, animals—even the monkeys behave—these children and humble people?" Then, by luck, Sir John saw Thambi standing with Moses and beckoned them with a quick jerk of his head. "Take Browne Sahib back to the bungalow. *Take* him," ordered Sir John.

"Jai Krishnan. Jai Krishnan," and as even greater reverence broke through, "Jai Shri Krishnan," then, "Jai Shri Krishnan Hari."

Chanting. Music. Silence. Silence, chanting, music; even in the silence the piercing yet sweet call of the flute seemed to go on as Krishnan now and again put it to his lips to play. "I didn't know how well Krishnan played the flute," Mary murmured to Ravi when he paused beside her.

"He has to play but, then, Krishnan can do anything," whispered ecstatic Ravi.

Can Sharma? wondered Mary.

The moon rose higher, began to go down so that it hung lower over the sea. In twos and threes, the cultural ladies began unostentatiously to leave; Professor Aaron followed them. Sir John made his way to Mary. "That's enough, young Mary. This will go on all night."

"I *should* have liked to go to the other *darshan* to see Sharma Krishnan," said Professor Webster, who had lingered.

"That will go on all night too."

"Yes." Dr. Coomaraswamy had joined them. "Also, I myself have been back and forth every hour. That *darshan* is at Mudalier, not far from Ghandara on the inland side, exactly the replica of this. The effect is ex-tra-or-din-ary!" His eyes shone. "Believe me, some of these people will walk the twelve miles to see the duplication."

"They believe im-pli-cit-ly." Mr. Srinivasan, too, was in euphoria.

"An extremely successful political trick." Mr. Menzies, in his now almost familiar way, had appeared from nowhere.

"Trick!" Mr. Srinivasan's voice was shrill from the affront. "It is to save the people. They must be saved," the little man said earnestly. "Krishnan has made no false promises—unlike other candidates—only the truth, simple truth of what he can do with this holy help, what, we pray, he will do."

"Well! Well! Well!" said Mr. Menzies. "Be that as it may, I am going to look at number two. Mrs. Browne, can I take you?"

Mr. Menzies did not ask Professor Webster, and Sir John moved closer to Mary but she had instinctively drawn back. In any case, Sharma after Krishnan, no, she thought, and aloud, "I think I'd rather not."

"Good girl," said Sir John. "I will take you back."

"Back?" Startled out of her happiness, panic set in. The slap Mary had forgotten seemed to tingle on her cheek. "I can't go back. I don't know where to go but I can't sleep in the bungalow with Blaise. I can't."

"Of course you can't." Sir John put his arm around her. "Blaise has had enough, too, for tonight. You are to sleep in our dressing room. Auntie Sanni has arranged it. Come."

Thursday

■ ■ ■ ■ ■ ■ ■ ■ ■ ■ ■ ■ ■

When the first beginnings of daylight filtered through the dressing room curtains, Mary still had not slept. Too tired? Too excited? Too dismayed? But she did not feel dismayed, even though she knew the dismay was serious, nor was she tired or excited, only awake and waiting. Waiting for what?

Then it came; the sound of a flute played softly. She flung off the sheet, went to the window, and looked behind the curtains. Yes, it was Krishnan standing under the window and with him, in the dim light, she saw the big shape of Birdie.

Krishnan wore no makeup, no garlands, only a clean white tunic and loose trousers, his hair brushed back. As he saw her, he put a finger to his lips, hushing her, then beckoned.

Mary had gone to bed in her slip; now she pulled last night's dress on, brushed her hair with one of Sir John's hairbrushes, and, taking her sandals, stole out in her bare feet and ran downstairs.

"Krishnan."

"Ssh! Mary, would you, will you, come with me?"

Krishnan seemed suddenly young and—not unhappy—troubled.

"Come where?"

"To the temple."

"The Dawn Temple?"

"No, no. There's a little temple. It's so hidden in the hills hardly anyone knows it. I call it mine. I'm going there to make my *puja*."

"*Puja?*"

"Prayer. Before the voting. I promised my mother." He took Mary's hand, twining his fingers in hers. "Perhaps, Mary, thinking of her, I find myself very lonely. Well . . ." For a moment he was proud again, "I have to be lonely but sometimes everyone needs . . ." It seemed to be difficult for eloquent Krishnan to find words. Then, "Mary, will you come with me?" and, rapidly, "Birdie will take us, it's not far into the hills, as she's always coming and going no one will notice us. I won't be long. You'll be back in bed before anyone is up to see you gone. You—"

"Ssh!" said Mary in her turn. "Of course I'll come."

Birdie knelt down to let them climb onto the pad Krishnan had fastened on her back; he swung up and reached down a hand to help Mary. "Lie down behind me," he whispered as he settled himself on the elephant's neck.

"I thought no one could drive an elephant except its *mahout*," said Mary as they went along.

"Perhaps in another time I was a *mahout*."

Mary had ridden elephants before, short rides in a *howdah* but not in this free, ordinary way; she could feel Birdie's great body through the pad, her shoulders moving, her powerful, comfortable, half-rolling half-swaying gait. Birdie had been well trained: If a branch overhung— this roundabout way to the hills led through patches of jungle—to a command from Krishnan, her trunk came up to break it off in case it hit her passengers. When they came to a swamp she tested the ground with a cautious forefoot before she would venture on it. Presently they began to climb; Mary felt a cooler air, and, as she lay, lulled by the rhythmical swaying, she went, at last, to sleep.

*   *   *

The temple was inset into the hills, higher hills fold on fold around it so that it looked out across vistas to the sea; it was walled with small bricks made of native earth turned by centuries of sun to dark gold, as was its courtyard floor of smooth, old stone. There was a stoop for water in one wall and a small pillared pavilion in which hung a bell. "What a funny smell," whispered Mary. "What is it?"

"Bats," said Krishnan, wrinkling his nose. "*Ghee* gone rancid and, I should guess, crushed marigolds." She could smell their pungency.

Krishnan set the bell lightly ringing; the sound carried over the gulf all around. Behind the pavilion Mary could see an inner temple, empty under its dome, though in the center of the floor, on a low plinth, burned a fire with a steady flame. "It never goes out," Krishnan told her.

She had woken when Birdie stopped and knelt. Krishnan had lifted her down and she had stood, rubbing her eyes awake, blinking at the sunlight while he brought down from Birdie's back the bundle of sugarcane he had brought as feed, untied it and scattered the canes. "*Kachiyundu*," he told her in Telegu as she got to her feet. The little eyes blinked as Mary's had, the mottled ears flapped, and Birdie did as she was told.

"Come."

"Why the fire?" asked Mary

"This temple belongs to another of the old, old elemental gods like Surya, the Sun God, Indra, God of Storm, Thunder, and Rain. This is for Agni, God of Fire. We all love Agni because though he is the son of heaven he lives on earth and in all our homes because he warms them and cooks our food. Perhaps that is why I love to come here when I miss home. Agni can never die because he is born each time we make a marriage by rubbing two pieces of dry wood together or strike a flint or match and he, like us, has to be fed." Krishnan laughed. "See, I have brought him an offering of *ghee*."

As Krishnan poured the butter on the fire and the flame shot up, the priest appeared: not old, a young man wearing only a *lunghi*, his hair oiled back and the Brahmin sacred thread, three-stranded across his chest from his shoulder to his waist.

"Krishna-ji," he greeted Krishnan as an old and revered friend, making *namaskar*. "*Anandum*. Peace." He gave a deep salaam to Mary, then silently opened a slit of a door behind the fire, motioning them to go in.

Mary had taken off her shoes but still she hesitated, looking up at Krishnan. "You can go in," he said, "but, Mary, it is the innermost sanctuary, infinitely holy. It is in all our temples but you have to find it. You will only find it if you come there to take *darshan* which is simply to be with, behold, God, not kneel or pray, only look . . . look . . . and not with cameras and notebooks . . . People who bring those cut themselves off, they cannot come in. We call it the womb-house because, as only God is there, in it you can, as it were, be born again."

"Even I, an outsider?" she whispered.

"There are no outsiders here. Go in."

Mary went in: The little room, windowless, smelled of incense, the oldest symbol of prayer. It was lit by the flickering of the butter-fed fire and on the wall was a painting, very old, thought Mary, painted directly onto the stone, not of a god or goddess but of a sun rising, its rays still showing traces of pigment, red and yellow; below it, storm clouds were dark and swollen with rain falling. At the base, rising to meet them, as if challenging the storm, rose Agni's flames, colored red with deep yellow. "Sun—Storm—Fire—Surya—Indra—Agni," whispered Mary, and, as if he would say that too, Krishnan took her hand again. They stood together, looking as he had said she should look, only looking while, behind them, the young priest took a shallow brass bowl with, in it, five *dipas* burning in oil and, quietly chanting his mantra, waved it before the fire, walking around it.

As they came out, he handed the bowl to Krishnan who waved it too, his lips moving, as the light of the small flames shot high up into the dome. Krishnan handed the bowl to Mary and, as she waved the flames, "O God, Gods, please, for Krishnan," she urged in a mantra of her own. "For Krishnan, please."

It was late when she woke in the dressing room. "I shan't go to sleep," she had told Krishnan. "I can't after this."

"At least lie down," he had said, and yawned himself. "I shall sleep now. I haven't for two nights, it hasn't been possible but, you see, for twenty-four hours before voting all parties have to stop campaigning, not a move, not a step, not a speech. Of course, we are all busy behind the scenes getting ready for tomorrow but dear Coomaraswamy will do that. I shall sleep, sleep, sleep and I am not homesick anymore. Thank you, Mary."

Though Patna Hall had been stirring, no one had seen her go and come; undisturbed, she had slipped into bed, and before she could tell it all over again in her mind as she had meant to, she was asleep.

Now as she lay in bright sunlight, for a moment she wondered where she was until she saw Sir John's hairbrushes, ivory-backed and crested, on the dressing table, his ties hanging over the looking glass. Someone had hung her dress over a chair, put the shoes she had cast off neatly together; they were a reminder that "People expect me to do everyday things . . . I shall have to do them," she told herself. "To begin with, go down to the bungalow, wash, and get into clean clothes." She could have asked Hannah to bring her things but, "You'll have to go sometime," she told herself. "With luck, Blaise will be asleep."

"I'm afraid Blaise will have a massive hangover," Sir John had said, but, of course, sometime he'll have to wake. What then? thought Mary. The mark of the slap was still on her cheek, and it had stung more deeply. "I'll never speak to him again!" she had vowed. Now, "Don't be childish," said what seemed to be an older, steadier Mary. Then, "What am I to do?" she asked, and, as if Krishnan had answered, "You can try being kind."

Two days ago, she would have been in revolt against that. Why should I be kind when Blaise . . . ? But now she seemed to see, in the temple, the little flames in the bowl as Krishnan waved it, sending the light high into the dome. "I couldn't send it as high as that," she whispered. "But, yes, I can try."

Slowly, she got out of bed.

"Hannah," said Auntie Sanni when, on the upper veranda, Hannah brought her morning tea. "I should like you to go down to the bungalow this morning and see if Manning Memsahib's things are ready to be packed."

"Packed?" Kuku looked up from where, at Auntie Sanni's dictation, she had been writing out the day's menus. "You think she won't come back?"

"She may not be able to," and Auntie Sanni went on to Hannah, "Do any washing that is needed and Kuku, in any case, put flowers in her room."

"She owes you so much money, she will probably stay away," said Kuku.

"That is the one thing that may bring her back," said Auntie Sanni.

"I'll go to the bungalow," Kuku offered.

"I asked Hannah," said Auntie Sanni.

Blaise, a long mound in the wide bed, stayed inert while Mary washed and dressed. He was breathing heavily and, He reeks! she wrinkled up her nose in disgust, then, unexpectedly, Poor Blaise! She left the shutters wide open for the sea breeze to blow in, salty, cleansing, and went up the path for breakfast; again, she was ravenously hungry.

After it she lingered on Patna Hall's veranda, trying to

will herself to go down to the bungalow. If I want to swim, and I do, I must get my things. She had some sugar lumps for Slippers. He's waiting for me, but I'll walk along the beach first, she decided, putting off the moment of going back to Blaise.

As, carrying her shoes, she walked, in and out of the ripples of the waves, the water cold on her feet, the sun warm on her neck, How I love this place, thought Mary. It isn't only Krishnan. She lifted her face to the sun, the breeze, and shut her eyes, standing to feel the sun through her eyelids, but, "You can't stay here all day with your eyes shut," she told herself. "You have to go back. But what can I say?" she asked. "What can either of us say after that slap?" Then, "Be patient. Something will come," and suddenly, That might be a little splinter of Auntie Sanni's wisdom, she conceded smiling.

The fishing boats were coming in; it must have been a good morning because they had been out twice. Mary could hear the men chanting as they pulled in the heavy nets, long lines of them along the beach. As usual, the best of the catch was being taken either to the refrigerated lorry vans drawn up ready or to the drying sheds; the rest was spilled out on the sand for the fisherwomen to take, either to use or to sell in the villages. A little group was standing looking at something on the sand, something boys were racing up to see.

Mary went closer.

"Bumble! Bumble! Wake up. *Please.*"

Mary was calling that from the veranda but Blaise was already awake, sitting up in bed holding his throbbing head as she came hurtling in. All Mary's serenity was gone: Half sobbing, her eyes wide with horror, she begged, "Blaise, don't ever, *ever* even think of going swimming farther along the beach away from our own. Don't, *please.*"

"What *are* you talking about?"

"You've said you would from the beginning. Remember how cross you were with Thambi and Moses, but, Blaise, don't. Don't."

He saw her shorts were soaked and stained red, her legs too, her arms and hands. "Is that blood?"

"Yes . . . Yes."

"Come here," said Blaise. He was still wearing the shirt of the night before, his hair rumpled; he still stank but Mary came. Gently he pulled her nearer, she was shaking. He put his arm around her and took her to the bathroom.

"Please . . . get the blood off my hands." Her lips were trembling.

He washed her hands over a *gharra*, washed her face, too, and gave her a glass of water. "Rinse and spit it out," then he brought her back to the bed. "What is all this about? Tell me."

"The catch was on the beach, the part left for the people to take, fish, flapping and slipping, starfish, crabs. There was a baby shark." Mary began to tremble again. "Not longer than three, four feet. They had turned it on its back; it was white and hard though it was a baby. When its tail flailed it knocked over a small boy. Its mouth came down almost to its middle, hideous"—she shuddered—"almost a half hoop with teeth. Cruel teeth. An old woman bent down to look and touched it and it snapped . . . took . . . took off her hand." Blaise held Mary fast. "The other women made a great noise but kept back. Thambi came and clubbed it. I had to help him hold the stump in the sea until the men came and took the old woman away. Blaise, promise me you won't swim anywhere, *anywhere* outside our nets."

"I thought you didn't care what I did."

"Of course I care." How could I help caring about that for anyone? but this different Mary did not say that. A new thought had struck her. That night when I swam with Krishnan, there weren't any sharks—or were there?

But Blaise was speaking urgently. "Mary, let's go away. There's a midday train. Let's go now."

"Now?" She pulled away from him. Sat up. "Before the election?"

"Damn the election. It's nothing to do with us."

"It is. It is to do with me," she said the words slowly. "I'm bound up in it," and, more quickly, "I couldn't possibly go now."

"Mary, please. Since we came here everything's been wrong."

She looked at him in amazement. "For me everything's been right."

"It's this Krishnan. You're under a spell." Blaise was choosing his words carefully. "Mary, you don't realize it but you are. I'm not going to blame you," he said magnanimously. "Lots of girls go in at the deep end when they first meet Indians."

"In at the deep end?" Mary looked at him, incredulous. "I'm up. Up where I have never been before."

"He's using you—"

"That's what's so wonderful and I never dreamed until this morning he could need . . ." again she did not say it as, "Tell me something," Blaise went on, "did you go to him or he to you?"

"I didn't go. I . . . came across him. In the grove our first night. The night you drove me out over Slippers. I sat by Krishnan's fire. We talked," said Mary, half dreaming.

"Was that all?"

"That was all." All! It was everything.

"Did he ask you to come back?"

"No."

"Who asked you to go on the lorry?"

"Dr. Coomaraswamy."

"Not Krishnan?"

"Krishnan told him to. I asked the young men to play rounders."

"You went to the *darshan*."

"We all went."

"Did he ask you to?"

"He never asks." That had been true—until this morning—and Mary had to pause.

Blaise noticed that and, at once, "Mary, I want a straight answer to a straight question. Tell me the truth."

"Krishnan doesn't need to ask." It was the best evasion she could think of. "People come to him. They give."

"More fools they."

"Don't be horrid."

"I'm not horrid. I'm worried." Blaise took her firmly by the shoulders and swung her around to look at him. "Mary, I have to ask you, have you done anything wrong?"

"Wrong?" She was startled. *"Wrong?"* How could it be wrong? Then she looked at Blaise's face, perplexed as it was honest and miserable. "You mean . . ."

"Yes. You wouldn't be afraid to tell me, would you?" He was still gentle. "I'd rather know."

At that moment Mary liked Blaise more than she had liked him since Bombay and, "If I haven't told you everything," she said, "it's only because you wouldn't have understood but I know I haven't done anything—wrong."

"I believe you," said Blaise. "But promise me one thing."

"What?"

"That you won't go to the grove or near any of them, unless you are asked."

Mary thought she owed Blaise that and, "I won't go unless I am asked," she said resolutely, at once, perversely remembering under her window at dawn the sound of the flute.

There were footsteps on the veranda. Hannah had come to look after Mrs. Manning's things.

"Ayah," called Blaise. "Ayah."

Hannah was not used to being called "ayah" but came. "Will you help the little memsahib? She has had a shock."

"Thambi told me." Hannah clicked her tongue when she saw the blood on Mary. "Come, Baba."

"If you don't mind I'll sleep some more," Blaise said when Hannah had gone. "Mary, I'm sorry about last night." He had realized his state. "Then I'll have a swim, from our beach." He smiled at her but, It won't do, thought Mary as, leaving him, she went up to the house. "I want a straight answer to a straight question. Tell me the truth." That rang in her ears but, "How can you answer when you are only just finding out?" asked Mary. No one had told her of the Indian concept of truth, that it is like water poured into your hand but you can only catch a few drops.

Professor Aaron and the cultural ladies were leaving.

Their coach was drawn up under the portico which was crowded with luggage while they gathered in the hall; all had their raincoats, cameras, binoculars, shooting sticks, campstools, and satchels of notebooks. "Far more full than when we came," they said in satisfaction. Last snapshots were being taken of Auntie Sanni, Kuku, Samuel, Hannah, Thambi; Professor Aaron was counting heads and trying to placate Mrs. Schlumberger. "We should have had a discount for sharing a room and you should tell Mrs. McIndoe about the disgrace of the bathrooms," but, from the others, "We've had a wonderful, wonderful time," was said over and over again. "We never expected anything like this."

Miss Pritt was almost in tears. Mrs. van den Mar had the recipe for mulligatawny soup, Mrs. Glover a collection of flowers Hannah had helped her to press. Professor Webster declared she was coming back next year, "If you will have me, dear Auntie Sanni."

"And me," cried Dr. Lovat.

Kuku was dazzled, though at first she had been offended, by large tips. "No. No, nothing. I cannot take this. I cannot possibly take this."

"Of course you can, my dear, you deserve it."

Mary appeared panting. In her distress over the shark she had forgotten the ladies were leaving until Hannah reminded her; she had had to run up the path.

A chorus broke out. "We thought you weren't coming to say good-bye."

"Of course I was."

"I should have hated to go without seeing you."

They gathered around her, gave her their addresses. "If you come to the States again be sure to let us know," and, "We'd love you to stay awhile with us."

"My apartment's so small," Mrs. Schlumberger hastened to say, "I can't offer a guest room."

"I can offer you three," Mrs. Glover laughed, "any time." They thanked her for last night. "It was real fun," and, "You're no ordinary girl," they told her. "We didn't know English girls could be like you," and Ms. van den Mar called, "Say good-bye for us to that lord of creation of yours."

"Lord of creation?"

"More than a mite dictatorial," said Mrs. van den Mar. "My dear, you shouldn't let him."

"And don't *you* get dictatorial," said Dr. Lovat.

When the coach had gone, Patna Hall was extraordinarily quiet. Are the disciples all asleep? wondered Mary. Or are they away working behind the scenes as Krishnan had said? Dr. Coomaraswamy and Mr. Srinivasan had breakfasted in the bridal suite, though Mr. Srinivasan had been out early to Ghandara. He had come back disturbed. "Hari, do you know who made all the arrangements for Padmina Retty's helicopter?"

"Who? Not Surijlal?"

"Surijlal is most loyal adherent. It was that Menzies."

"Mr. Menzies! I thought he was on our side."

"I think he is playing loose and fast. Hari, I fear trouble."

"There can't be trouble now," said Dr. Coomaraswamy.

Mary did not want to go back to the bungalow and Blaise. Anyway, he's sleeping it off. Then, Shall I swim? But a shudder came. I'd rather swim with him. Sleep in the sun? She had had little sleep yet was filled with a curious energy. What can I do?

"Mary."

"It is strange," Auntie Sanni had said to Colonel McIndoe. "This girl I have never set eyes on before, nor she on me, seems to feel much as I do about Patna Hall," and did not all the servants call her Missy, Miss Baba? While Christabel, the pet mynah bird, had begun to call "Mary" in Auntie Sanni's voice.

Colonel McIndoe had patted Auntie Sanni's hand.

Now Auntie Sanni, wearing a huge white apron and drying her hands on a towel came to call Mary. "Thursday is the day," said Auntie Sanni, "when we make what Hannah calls 'dainties'—desserts and sweets for the week. These cannot be trusted to Alfredo. Always I make them myself."

"Yourself! Only Hannah, me, two boys, and a washer-up woman to wait on her," Kuku was to say in an aside to Mary.

"Also, today, we are crystallizing cherries. They have been flown in from Kulu in the north where it is almost the cherry season. These are early. I thought you might like to come and help. Would you?"

"Would I!" If a life belt had been thrown to Mary in a choppy sea she could not have caught it more thankfully.

*   *   *

It was, Mary saw at once, a ritual, "Every Thursday," as Auntie Sanni had told her. The confectionery pantry, as it was known at Patna Hall, was separate from the kitchen, in fact in the courtyard annex, next to the linen room, storerooms, and near Auntie Sanni's office. The same flowers were there but no cats, goat, or kids were allowed; no birds could fly in; doors and windows were screened with fine mesh.

The room had a tiled floor and walls that could be washed; counters were fitted with surfaces of wood that could be scrubbed and on them were slabs of marble of different sizes. Shelves of copper saucepans, molds— "Best French ones," said Auntie Sanni—were in easy reach, all sparklingly clean and polished with ashes, "Our washer-up women earn their pay." The Calor gas cooker was large, the refrigerator larger, a vast old-fashioned one run on kerosene; its whirring filled the room, punctuated by the cooing of Auntie Sanni's doves outside, the only birds bold enough to come near. Monkeys had thieved some handfuls of cherries as they had been carried in but Hannah had scolded them back into the trees.

The cherries from Kulu, in finely woven traveling baskets, were on the floor; two boys, well scrubbed, wearing white shorts and tunics, were carefully destalking them under Hannah's watchful eyes. "To stay fresh, cherries must be picked on their stalks," Auntie Sanni told Mary. They were carefully destoned, too, the boys using small silver picks, the stones thrown into a bucket, while the cherries were put, carefully again in case they bruised, into large bowls. When enough were ready they were taken to Hannah who was stirring hot syrup, heavy with sugar and tinged with rosewater. "They must not boil or they won't stay firm," said Auntie Sanni. "Then, when they're cooled they will be rolled in fine sugar."

As Hannah worked her bangles clinked. "It's not hygienic. You ought to take them off," Kuku told her.

"They will not come off," said Hannah serenely. "My hands are grown too big."

The crystallized cherries were not only for the week but to last the whole year. "These are the second batch. Hannah is just finishing off the first—it has taken twelve days."

"Twelve days!" Mary looked with awe at the racks of cherries drying, plump and tender.

"Fresh syrup has to be boiled every day, then poured over the fruit, then they are drained. On the sixth day the fruit is simmered for three or four minutes—this helps to keep the cherries plump; they are left to soak for four more days. Then you carefully take the cherries out, put them on racks to drain, next in a cool oven to dry until they are no longer sticky to handle. Now Hannah will give them the crystallized finish."

Kuku gave a yawn but Mary, enchanted by this minutiae, watched how skillfully Hannah dipped each cherry in a pan of boiling water, then rolled it in sugar that had been spread on clean paper.

"Come," said Auntie Sanni, "I will teach you to make *rasgula*, a Bengali recipe. See, we take two pints of milk, lemons, semolina . . ."

"Semolina?" Mary was surprised.

"Here it is called *sooji* and we shall need green cardamom seeds for spice." The spices, dozens of them, were in a special glass-fronted cabinet.

"They are very costly," said Kuku. Hot and cross, she pushed her hair back with sticky fingers. "We could buy these sweetmeats far more cheaply in Ghandara. There are good Bengali sweetmeat sellers there."

"It wouldn't be the same."

Of course it wouldn't be the same, Mary felt, almost fiercely. This—this is home, what makes a home, which is why I love Patna Hall so much. She remembered what Krishnan had told her that very morning—her secret morning—of Agni who warms our homes and cooks our food and, "How can you say it would be the same?" she upbraided Kuku.

"Besides, they haven't the good milk," said more practical Auntie Sanni. Her desserts were made with rich milk from the Jersey cows she had imported. Their faces look like Krishnan's wise cows, Mary had thought. They were kept in Patna Hall's small homestead behind the knoll where, too, was the poultry yard so that eggs were fresh every day, chickens and ducks provided plump for the table instead of the usual Indian scrawny ones. "Besides," Auntie Sanni went on, "bought Indian sweetmeats are too sweet for Western tastes. But don't think we do all Indian," she said to Mary. "We have *hereditary* recipes, some, I think, unique. There is a velvet cream that came from my English grandmother, perhaps from her grandmother, rich cream, lemon, a little leaf gelatine, wine . . ."

"In the recipe it should be raisin wine. We have to use Golconda"—Kuku was spiteful—"and the cream can curdle as you put it in."

"Only if you are impatient," said Auntie Sanni.

"Costs a fortune but that doesn't matter," said Kuku, but Auntie Sanni only said, "Put on this apron, Mary, and I'll show you."

The time went more quickly than Mary could have believed, they were so busy. Samuel brought cold cucumber soup—"Delicious," she said—rolls and butter, fruit.

Later, "Why don't you take this into the dining room," Auntie Sanni said of the latest confection, "and let them taste what you have made?"

Only Sir John, Lady Fisher, and Blaise were in the dining room, sitting together. Blaise had swum, then sluiced himself in the bathroom, put on fresh clothes, but his face was pinker than usual. His eyes look as if they had been boiled, thought Mary, which was not kind, I must have cooking on the brain, but how can you help what leaps into your mind?

"This is Mrs. Beeton's 'Pretty Orange Pudding,' " she

said, putting the dish down in front of them. "Auntie Sanni has one of the earliest editions of the cookbook, eighteen sixty-one. It says, 'Take six oranges,' though we took sixty to make ten puddings, for dinner tonight. Mrs. Beeton calls it 'a pretty dish of oranges, exceedingly ornamental,' and isn't it? I made it."

She was wearing one of Auntie Sanni's capacious aprons, wrapped and kilted around her; her cheeks were flushed, her hair dark with sweat; her spectacles were askew—"It's too hot for contact lenses," she had said—she had a dab of powdered sugar on her nose but to Sir John she looked almost pretty; the gray of her eyes lit almost to blue. "Thank you, hussy," he said.

"It is a pretty pudding," said Lady Fisher.

"Mary seems to have been adopted as the child of the house," said Lady Fisher.

"She isn't a child. She happens to be a married woman." Blaise was stiff again. "Something Mrs. McIndoe chooses to forget."

"Auntie Sanni?"

"I prefer to call her Mrs. McIndoe. I'm afraid I don't share your high opinion of her."

"It's not only high," said Lady Fisher, "it's loving. We've been coming here for years, haven't we, John, and we know how wise she is."

"I don't subscribe to that either. In any case, I am taking Mary away tomorrow, a day early."

"Will she go?" asked Lady Fisher, which Blaise ignored.

"When she is through with this nonsensical cooking, I'll tell her *and* she has promised me not to go near this Krishnan creature again."

They looked at him, both incredulous. "Mary promised that?"

"I'm glad to say she did."

"I'm not glad," said Lady Fisher, and, "Blaise," began Sir John, "Mary is having an experience—"

"Which I don't choose to let her have—"

"You have just said she isn't a child. Don't you see," Lady Fisher pleaded, "how Mary longs to be part of something, to be needed, be of help . . . ?"

"She can help me. That's what she married me for, didn't she?" He got up, leaving the pudding. "If you'll excuse me, I'll go and get some more sleep. I still have a bit of a head and, of course, I apologize about last night."

When he had gone, "Insufferable young dolt," said Sir John, but Lady Fisher only said, "Poor silly boy."

The confectionery was over by two o'clock. Hot, sticky all over even to her hair, but happy, Mary ran down the path to the bungalow and came quietly into the bedroom, thinking Blaise might be asleep. He was not; looking considerably ruffled, he was writing a letter.

"Who is that to?"

"Mrs. McIndoe."

"Auntie Sanni. Why?"

Instead of answering he looked at her. "God, you look a mess. You'd better go and wash."

"Not before you've told me why you are writing to Auntie Sanni."

"To tell her we are leaving tomorrow."

"No!"

"Yes." Blaise held up a hand. "Please, I don't want a fuss. Besides, what is there to stay for? You've promised to have no more to do with the election."

"I didn't say that."

But Blaise had risen. "I'm taking this up to the house now."

How dared he? Left in the bedroom, Mary felt choked. Without asking or consulting! She walked up and down in helpless anger, then, I'll go for a swim. It was either that or tears.

Thambi came to help her. Somu too but Thambi, as if he sensed something was more than wrong, took Mary himself, Somu swimming alongside, but there was none of the exhilaration and joy of riding in on the waves. Afterward they brought a beach umbrella as Mary spread her towel and lay down; only then could she give way.

No tears came though, only indignation. Without even consulting. I can't go now, not before the election, yet how can I stay? Blaise has all our money. She could not be sure where Rory was. Peru—or it could be Washington or London.

Then, suddenly, I know, thought Mary, I'll go to Auntie Sanni. She'll find a way. I'll talk to her tonight after she has seen Alfredo.

It was a comfortable thought; the anger ebbed. Mary gave a great yawn and was soon asleep.

When Mary had gone to sleep, the sun had been hot on her legs so that she had been careful to keep her head in the shade of the umbrella. When she woke she was chilly.

As she sat up, rubbing her eyes, she saw that the men had left; the foreshore was empty and the sun was going down, its rays sending a path almost to her feet. She could still feel the battering of the waves on her body; they still crashed down but beyond their white crests the sea was calm, deep blue. Then the sun went behind the horizon, the gold lingered and was gone. The heat haze from the water rose in a mist over the waves; by contrast, a chill little wind blew over the sand.

It was twilight, the Indian short twilight, "cow-dust time" Krishnan had called it, and Mary remembered what she had seen from the train, cattle being driven home, dust rising from their hooves, patient cows, lumbering oxen and buffalo while smoke rose from the cooking fires among the huts of the villages. As she looked now at the bungalow, lights were up on the veranda: Thambi must have switched them on as he went to his gatehouse, as he had the lanterns along the path.

Why is twilight always a melancholy time? wondered Mary. She listened, there was no sound of a drum. Along the beach no small lamps burned before the shrines. Paradise was dark, everything was in abeyance, though probably the disciples were in Ghandara or in other countless voting places getting ready for tomorrow. Probably Krishnan too. That's why the grove is dark and the thought dawned poignantly, I shan't see Krishnan again and, in desolation, I suppose I must—*must* go in and dress, have some dinner—though she wanted neither. She got up and picked up her towel. Thambi or Moses would put down the umbrella when they drew out the fencing along the foreshore. As, reluctantly, she walked toward the bungalow, more lights came on in the other half and she saw Thambi putting down luggage, Hannah drawing the curtains. Olga Manning was there.

"You *have* come back," Mary said in the doorway, and before she could stop herself, "Auntie Sanni and Hannah thought you mightn't."

"There was nowhere else to go."

At once Mary's own unhappiness dwindled into an ordinary everyday trouble, this was tragic. Olga's usually erect figure was bowed. Still in her traveling clothes she was making no effort to unpack or change but sat at the room's solitary table looking out at the darkening sea. Under the electric light her skin looked bruised; her hair had come undone, its coil was tumbling down her back; her hands were dirty.

"Olga, is there anything I can do?"

"Please, Mary, I can't talk to you now." The deep voice was a hoarse whisper.

Mary went next door. Blaise was in the bathroom. Fresh whiskey had been put in their bar. She measured a large one, added more, took the tumbler around the partition, and put it quietly on the table.

"Bless you."

"Would you like . . ." Mary ventured, "like me to get Samuel to send your dinner down here?"

"My dinner!" Olga laughed. "I don't think I can say 'my dinner' any longer but I suppose one must eat while one can," and seeing Mary's concern, "No, Mary darling. I shall change and come up as usual."

For dinner the dining room was full. Dr. Coomaraswamy and Mr. Srinivasan were eating less hurriedly than usual. "I have only two speeches to write," Dr. Coomaraswamy had said, and Mr. Srinivasan, "A success speech and a loss speech—just in case." "Victory! Victory!" Dr. Coomaraswamy had let himself write but, "Victory is not yet," said cautious Mr. Srinivasan.

Auntie Sanni and the colonel and Mr. Menzies were at their accustomed tables. Olga Manning had appeared, groomed, clean, changed, to Mary's relief, and had gone unobtrusively to hers, only nodding to Auntie Sanni; Blaise and Mary were dining with the Fishers, "As it's our last night." Mary did not contradict him. At least it means I needn't talk to him.

The diners were augmented by a dinner party of men. "From Ghandara," Sir John told them. "Here for some kind of conference." It seemed to be a festive meeting; there was laughter, even cheers as Kuku, in the beautiful violet-colored silk sari Lady Fisher had given her, flitted around them. Dr. Coomaraswamy kept his eye on his plate as the banter filled the room.

Suddenly it ceased. "This is All India Radio. Here is the news." There was absolute attention. "I expect there'll be something about their meeting," whispered Blaise as the news began, but first was the election.

"In Konak, expectancy is tense on this day before voting as interest mounts in the struggle between the long-established Mrs. Padmina Retty and Krishnan Bhanj's new Root and Flower Party. In spite of Mrs. Retty's helicopter, all yesterday it was Krishnan Bhanj who drew the crowds. In fact today he has had to hide himself to avoid the charge of illegally campaigning. 'He campaigns in spite of himself,' said Dr. Coomaraswamy, leader of this brilliant concept. Here are a few words from Dr. Coomaraswamy himself . . ."

As his words boomed out, Dr. Coomaraswamy kept his head bowed while the whole room listened. Samuel had interrupted the serving; he and the waiters stood respectfully still. Only Kuku moved and flaunted. When the voice finished everybody clapped.

The news, though, was not finished: "Today in Calcutta, Mr. Justice Rajan sentenced the Englishman, Colin Armstrong, to twelve years' imprisonment. Mr. Armstrong was convicted of fraud, embezzlement, and trafficking in drugs."

At an imperative nod from Colonel McIndoe, Samuel switched off the radio. At the same moment Mr. Menzies got up and crossed the dining room to Olga Manning's table. "Good evening, Mrs. Armstrong," he said.

A gasp went from table to table. The whole dinner party had turned to look. Mary sprang up but Blaise pulled her down as Auntie Sanni rose to her massive height. Her dress billowing, she, too, crossed the room. "Mr. Menzies," she said, "you will leave my hotel, *now*."

"Of course you knew he was Ajax?"

"I'm afraid I didn't." Blaise blushed.

"No? I should have thought those recordings, those articles were unmistakable."

"Auntie Sanni knew from the beginning," Lady Fisher had pleasure in saying.

"Then why didn't she turn him out before?"

"He was being very useful," said Sir John, "bolstering our election. Auntie Sanni, remember, is a dear friend of the Bhanj family and Menzies could hardly have been more helpful but tonight . . . Swine!" said Sir John.

"After all this distress and unpleasantness," Blaise said a little later, "what I feel like is a game of bridge."

"Sensible idea." Sir John stopped walking up and down. "But we haven't a four."

"Mary," said Blaise, "it's time you learned to play."

"You know I hate cards." She was seething with—she sensed unreasonable—anger and indignation. "If you're uncomfortable about anything, play cards!"

"There is nothing we can do for Mrs. Manning," Sir John told her gently. "She has gone with Auntie Sanni, so she's in good hands."

That was part of the dismay. There would be no chance now of talking to Auntie Sanni. So I'm trapped, thought Mary, trapped.

"McIndoe might play," Sir John was saying. "He sometimes does. I'll ask him."

The colonel got up, willingly Mary thought. I expect he, too, wants to put this out of his mind. Kuku brought the card table, fresh packs of cards, scorepads, and stood by while they sat down, her eyes fixed on Blaise as Lady Fisher dealt.

Mary had thought of asking Sir John to intercede with Blaise; now she remembered vividly how once Lady Fisher had—gently, it was true—remonstrated with her when she, Mary, had gone to the bazaar instead of the Dawn Temple, "As Blaise so wanted you to do," and she had retorted, "I've been doing what Blaise wanted for three whole weeks. Can't I have anything for myself?"

No sympathy, instead, "Diplomats have to keep a certain position," Lady Fisher had not said "prestige." "Their wives, in a way, have to be diplomats too, even if it means tremendous self-sacrifice. I did it, your mother did it, so why not you?"

It would be no use talking to either Fisher—and a surge of frustration filled Mary, made worse when, "Mary," said Lady Fisher, "come and talk to us when one of us is dummy." "Good God, *no!*" Mary wanted to scream but succeeded in only shaking her head. She stood up and put on Blaise's jacket. "I think I'll go to bed. I'm chilly and tired." Yes, go to bed, put her head under the sheet, and shut out everything, everyone and never care about anything ever again.

As she stood up on the path, the shadowed garden seemed dark and empty, the lanterns on the path dim. Only the lights on Patna Hall's veranda were bright, shining down on the four heads bent over the green table. Bridge! thought Mary furiously.

A waft of sweetness came to her. Who was it who had once told her that flowers can send you a message? The scent was queen of the night, with its small scented flowers. Carnations? Roses? I know what I can do, thought Mary. I'll pick a bunch of flowers to put in Olga's room, with some more whiskey. That will show her at least *someone* cares about her. In the pocket of Blaise's jacket was a small mother-of-pearl-handled penknife; she took it out. Cutting stems along the borders was soothing, laying one flower against another, sniffing the fragrance; the storm in her mind began to lull, and, though she could not exactly remember the words, she began to hum that Hindi lullaby . . .

> *A cradle of . . .*
> *A cord of silk . . .*
> *Come, little moonbird . . .*

When she had cut enough she went, softly singing, down the path. "All right, Slippers," she called, "I'm coming." She had his sugar and carrots in her handkerchief.

He whickered back.

"Tsst."

A small boy stepped out of the shadows. Mary knew him; he was one of the boys she had made garlands with. True, he had tormented the squirrel but he was smaller than the others and had attached himself to her, hanging all day yesterday around the lorry. Now he held out a paper to her, thin Indian paper folded. She recognized Krishnan's writing and her heart began to beat quickly as she took the paper to the nearest lantern to read.

"Mary, can you come and help me? I am alone."

"Krishnan Sahib. Where is Krishnan Sahib?"

The boy pointed along the beach.

He's here! In the grove! A surge of happiness rose in Mary but she looked toward the veranda.

"Kachiyundu," she said to the boy as Krishnan had said at the temple to Birdie, *"kachiyundu*. Wait," and gestured that she would give him money.

Forsaking Slippers, she ran to the bungalow, left his sugar on the chest of drawers, quickly arranged the flowers in a vase, carried them and a glass of whiskey to Olga's room, then wrote on the back of the paper "For Blaise. You see I *have* been asked!" In the pocket of his jacket she found some change, and taking a rupee, she hung the jacket on the back of a chair—she was no longer chilly. Tingling with warmth, she ran back to the boy. "Take this." She gave him the paper. "Take." She pointed to the lit veranda. "For Sahib." She held up the rupee.

The boy's eyes gleamed as he saw it. He nodded, took the rupee and the note, and set off up the path. Mary watched him then, "Stay," she said to the disappointed Slippers, "I can't stop now," and ran to the beach.

She did not see a bigger boy, wearing a yellow shirt, leap out of the bushes and jump on the smaller one, screwing the rupee out of his hand and beating him until he fled.

For a moment the boy in the yellow shirt scrutinized the note, crumpled it, and let it drop as he set off after Mary.

The note lay on the side of the path.

Mary did not have to go as far as the grove. From a distance, across the stretch of moonlit sand, she saw what first seemed to be a dark rock in the froth and whiteness of the waves' edges. It can't be a rock, she thought, this beach doesn't have rocks. Then, as she came nearer, she could see a figure standing on it, a dark-skinned figure wearing only a loincloth. As she looked, something like a thick snake came up—A sea monster, thought Mary for a horrified moment, or no, a hose, as a spray of water was sent up into the air then fell, deluging the figure. *"Ayyo!"* came a furious voice. *"Mŏsāgadu! Pishācha mu!* Bad girl! Devil!"

It was Krishnan. He saw Mary and came to meet her, streaming with water, his hair in wet streaks.

"I thought you were hidden at Ghandara, or are you your double?"

"In a way, yes. Sharma is there. But come, we are wasting time."

As he spoke the rock stood up—an elephant, Birdie. Mary stared. "What *has* happened to her?"

"You may well ask. Idiots! Idiots!" It was the first time Mary had seen Krishnan angry.

Birdie had been painted—Decorated? thought Mary— her forehead and trunk, her sides and legs bedizened with patterns in yellow, vermilion, indigo, black, and white; her ears were patterned as was the length of her trunk. "Idiots!" cried Krishnan again. "They have spoiled everything."

"Spoiled what?" Mary had to ask.

"Tomorrow, election day is crucial—you know that."
She nodded. "All parties will go each in their procession
through Ghandara ending at the town hall; the candidate
from Madras, Gopal Rau, of whom no one seems to have
heard, Mrs. Retty, and us. Gopal Rau will not have much,
Padmina will have everything, a great *tamasha*—razz-
matazz, bands, military, maybe even a tank, loudspeakers. She has a white Jeep but probably she'll arrive in her
helicopter."

"And you?"

"We shall have nothing."

"Nothing?"

"Let Padmina have the blare, we shall be dulcet."
Krishnan lingered on the word; he had recovered himself.
"Fortunately, she has chosen to go first, then poor Rau, so
we shall be last which is propitious. The last will be first."
He laughed. "In front will walk our young men and
women, the men all in white, feet bare—they will be making *namaskar*—the girls in our colors, muslin saris, simple,
hair coiled with flowers, they will be leading garlanded
cows—"

"The *gopis*," said Mary.

"Exactly. For weeks we have been fattening them and
grooming them—the cows not the girls. Then will come
children; we have chosen the healthiest, again a little
plump. The boys will have garlands and carry paper kites,
again in our colors; the little girls will have baskets of
flowers to scatter, constantly replenished." He sounded as
if he were Dr. Coomaraswamy. "They will sing. For other
music there will be only the conch, drums, a single flute.
I think there will be silence to hear it. We must leave room
for reverence.

"Then will come my friend the priest from Agni's
temple, wearing a saffron robe with his beads, his staff—
he is of height but not the height of me. He will lead a
sacred bull. Then I shall come, not in regalia or paint as the

god Krishna but as I, myself"—and he said, "I sound like Coomaraswamy—not wearing a best English suit but, like my people, a loincloth, walking in the dust . . . little Udata on my shoulder."

"If she'll stay."

"She'll stay. I, not riding on an elephant but humbly leading her, she to be carrying her fodder on her own back." The fury returned. "To decorate an elephant takes two, three days and we must wash it off tonight—the *mahout* is too drunk to help. To call the village or fishermen would be publicity, take away surprise. Look, I am scrubbing Birdie's sides, legs, and feet with sand and a brick. That is too heavy work for you but could you do her face and ears? I went to the Hall and borrowed scrubbing brushes—but be careful, her ears may flap you."

"Won't Birdie mind?"

"She adores it, all elephants love their bath and she is accustomed. She does, though, get playful—watch her trunk. When you come to do her trunk stand astride it so that if she lifts it you will only tumble into the wash of the sea, but you will be soaked as I am. Better take off your dress," and, suddenly formal, he said, "Mrs. Browne, it is most good of you to come."

"Browne with an *e*." Mary felt suddenly impish.

"Browne with an *e*," said Krishnan, and laughed again. "Oh, how I like you, Mary. I like you very much. See, my temper has gone." Suddenly, too, he leapt and danced across the beach, did handstands, then, "That's enough. Come to work."

"Is Mary with you?" Blaise was standing at Olga Manning's door.

The game of bridge had petered out as soon as Auntie Sanni came out alone on the veranda. Colonel McIndoe immediately laid down his cards with an apology, got up, went with her to the swing couch, and sat down beside

her. Sir John and Lady Fisher followed them, leaving
Blaise at the table; he shuffled the cards, put them into
neat packs, stood a moment looking over to the now
moonlit beach. Then, "I had better go down to Mary," he
said, and to Auntie Sanni, he began, "I know I booked for
a week but . . ."

"You will not be charged for the extra day." Auntie
Sanni cut him short.

"Well, goodnight."

Talking in low tones, their faces grave, they hardly
noticed him go.

At the bungalow steps Slippers was patiently waiting,
he was missing Mary and, "Where is my ritual of carrots
and sugar?" he was patently saying. He whickered at
Blaise who only said, "Shoo," then waved his arms, ad-
vancing so threateningly that the little donkey shied away.

"Merry, where are you?"

No answer.

"Mary."

The room was empty, the shutters wide open, the
bathroom empty too; the bed sheets were folded back, his
lunghi and Mary's short nightdress laid out in Hannah's
way.

"Is Mary with you?"

Olga Manning came to her door. She was wearing a
faded kimono, her hair hanging down her back; even
Blaise noticed the tiredness of her face and was moved to
say, "Rotten about your husband."

She flared. "It isn't rotten. It never was. Colin did not
do that. He was framed." She put her hand to her throat
as if it choked her to speak. "Better not talk about it. No,
I haven't seen Mary."

"Didn't she come to the bungalow?"

"Not that I know of," and Olga offered, "She goes to
the grove."

"I know but they're all at Ghandara."

"Krishnan Bhanj isn't. I met him in the hotel garden as I came down."

"Krishnan Bhanj?"

"Yes," and innocently Olga said, "Perhaps she has gone to see him."

It was Blaise's turn to flare. "Then she has broken her promise." He stopped and his own innate honesty made him say, "Yet I'm sure Mary wouldn't do that." Then the seeds Mr. Menzies had sown began to grow. "Or would she? It seems she will do anything," and bitterness burst out. "We haven't been married a month. You'd think she could be faithful for just a month, and with an *Indian*. All right," he shouted. "All right!"

He strode across the veranda on to the beach.

"Phew!" Krishnan stood up, wiping the sweat and salt water off his face with his hand. "There seems to be a mighty lot of elephant."

The paint had lodged in the cracks of the coarse-grained scaly skin. "They must have put oil in the tempera," said Krishnan. Both he and Mary were stained with yellow, vermilion, and blue; the black had got under Mary's nails; only the white came off in flakes.

"I should have thought the fisherboys would have loved to help." She rested: After a fierce bout of scrubbing her arms ached.

"They would but they would have talked."

"How did you get rid of them?"

"Told them to go." His look seemed to say, "How else?"

"It's odd"—Mary put back a wet strand of her hair, staining it red—"when you tell someone to do something, they obey and want to do it." She was thinking aloud. "When Blaise tells them, they don't—and won't. Why?"

"Because Blaise Sahib is Blaise Sahib and Krishnan is

Krishnan. There is no other explanation. There never is," said Krishnan.

A voice came from the beach. "Mary. Mary. Where are you? Come back at once."

Blaise!

He came bearing down on them, with a splat of wood—the piece of flotsam they had used in rounders last night—in his hand. "Mary!" The shout was so loud that Birdie surged to her feet. Blaise stopped and gaped. "What in hell are you doing?"

"As you see, giving an elephant a bath," Krishnan said equably.

"Giving an elephant a bath? What tomfoolery is this?"

"It is anything but tomfoolery. For reasons I have no time to explain, it is imperative she is bathed," and, "*Ūrakundu,*" Krishnan ordered Birdie, "*ūrakundu*—lie down."

"In any case I was not speaking to you," said angry Blaise. "I have come to fetch my wife. Do you hear?"

"Then you are speaking to me."

"Yes."

"Ask her if she wants to go," Krishnan said between scouring—Birdie was recumbent again. "Better stand back if you, too, don't want to be soaked."

"Mary, *will* you come?"

"I can't. An elephant has two ears, and I have only finished one."

Blaise turned on Krishnan. "I also came to have this out with you. Come on." He brandished the splat of wood.

"My dear man, I'm far too busy to fight with you just now," said Krishnan. "Why not forget it, get a brick—there's a pile over there—and help us?"

The hand holding the wood dropped as if Blaise were bemused. Mary again felt that pang of pity. "Yes, Bumble, be a sport"—she knew that word would appeal to him. "Join in. There's nothing to be cross about."

"Nothing to be cross about! I'm not a fool. Do you think I don't know what's been going on?" Astonished they stood up though Krishnan kept a quiescent hand on Birdie. "Look at you," screamed Blaise, "both half naked and soon you'll be more naked from what I hear. I'm not going to have it," and he advanced on Mary with his splat.

"Don't do that," Krishnan warned him. "You won't want to have done that."

"Out of my way," and Blaise came on.

With one leap Krishnan was off Birdie, caught Blaise, and, with a twist, sent him spinning down on to his back on the sand; next moment Krishnan had lifted him and set him on his feet. "Go back to the Hall," Krishnan said sternly. "Mary will doubtless come when we are finished."

"*We!* You impertinent bastard."

"I am not impertinent and I am not a bastard and I don't want to have to knock you down again," said Krishnan. "Please go so that we can get on with the work—the little elephant is getting tired and hungry."

"I'm not one of your sycophants," ranted Blaise, "to do what I'm told. Do you think I don't know all about you pseudo Krishnas? We have them in England too. You with your young girls and boys, your slaves."

Krishnan took no notice but worked on with his brick.

"Mary!" It was a bellow now. "I'll give you one more chance. Come now or don't come at all. Which? *Which?*" Mary did not answer; she, too, went on scrubbing, this time on Birdie's second ear.

For a moment Blaise stood irresolute in his anger, then before turning, he spat.

"*Blaise* spat!" Mary sat back on her heels amazed.

"Being an Indian I can spit farther than you," Krishnan called after him. "Naturally. We have had centuries of practice."

*　　*　　*

Even Krishnan did not see a small yellow-clad figure come out from behind the nearest casuarina tree and take itself quickly to the road where a red car was waiting.

Blaise heard the noise before he came into the bedroom, heavy hooves clopping about on stone. Seeing him gone, Slippers had dared to come into the bedroom, seeking the sugar he thought was his due. He had knocked over the photograph of Blaise's mother that stood on the dressing table, breaking the glass; nuzzled brushes, combs, creams, and lotions off onto the floor, and now, having found on the chest of drawers the sugar Mary had left, was munching contentedly when Blaise switched on the light. At the sight of him, Slippers gave the equivalent of a donkey scream, a bray.

"What are you doing here, you little brute?" and, seeing the devastation, all Blaise's thwarted anger broke. "Take that and that," the splat of wood came down again and again. *"Chelo. Jao.* Go. Go. *Hut jao.* Go at once. *Chelo. Chelo.* Hurry up." But Slippers could not go. In panic, slithering on the floor, trying to get away, he had pinned himself behind the bed. The little donkey's ears were laid back, his eyes rolled but he could not move. *"Hut jao!"* There was a sudden stench: A flux of liquid dung spattered onto the floor. "Christ! Phewgh!" screamed Blaise.

"He couldn't help it." Olga Manning had come in. "You drove him behind the bed. Here, help me push it and let him out," and, to the miserable donkey, "Here, boy, gently, boy. Come. Come." Trembling, guided by her hand, Slippers back-clopped out and fled. They heard him slipping on the veranda then crash down the steps.

"You deserved that," Olga said to Blaise. "I'm glad he did it. Just because you can't juggernaut over your very nice wife, you take it out on an animal. You big bully."

"Go away and mind your own business!" Blaise exploded. "A dirty business it is from what I hear, dirty, no matter what you say. Go!"

"With pleasure," said Olga. "You can clear up the mess."

Kuku answered the house telephone—she had an extension in her room. "What? *What?* My God, how disgusting! I am coming down. Go on to the veranda and we shall come. I am bringing the sweeper women, hot water, disinfectants."

The explosions had done good and Blaise was calmer now. "I'm sorry to have disturbed you."

"You didn't disturb me in the least," but Kuku was in a thin wrapper dressing gown; the two sweepers, roused from sleep for the second time that day, were grumbling under their breaths.

"I'm afraid I did disturb you but donkey shit is no joke."

"Certainly it is not. I shall speak firmly to Miss Sanni in the morning. As for disturbing, that is what I am here for. Now, while the women are finishing, let me straighten the bed."

As she bent forward, the dark hair brushed the side of the bed where Blaise's *lunghi* was laid; as she carefully smoothed it, her wrapper swung open showing the rounded brown body, the perfect small breasts, rose-tipped nipples. Modestly Kuku caught the wrapper together, glanced up at Blaise, and laughed.

Blaise had not looked, really looked, at Kuku before, taking her almost as part of the hotel furniture and not far removed from Samuel and Hannah, though he had thought her saris a little flaunting. "Showing off," he would have said.

Now he was struck with her beauty, provocative beauty: the small roguish face set in the mane of black hair, eyes brilliant—and knowing—below expressive eye-brows and, when she looked down, as she met his gaze, he saw the long lashes that had so entranced Dr. Cooma-raswamy. Kuku's mouth was slightly pouted, she had a small tip-tilted nose, small pretty teeth. When she stood up, supple in every movement, and tightened the wrap-per around her, Blaise could see through it even to the fuzz of hair between her thighs; it was dark brown not black; at once he felt an answering movement in himself. "I suppose I've been starved," he almost said aloud, pity-ing himself.

"Now that the sweepers have gone, let me get you a drink." With her gliding undulating walk, Kuku went to the small bar. "You were so-o distressed," she crooned.

"Well, donkey shit on your bedroom floor." Blaise tried to be normal.

"Disgusting!" She brought him the glass. "I have put ice in it."

"You deserve one."

Kuku's eyes shone but, "Auntie Sanni doesn't let me drink."

"Just for me," said Blaise, and she poured a small one.

"And give me another," he said.

She brought it. Now she was so close he could smell her scent and sweat, as the doctor had done; as he took the glass her fingers touched his; he let them tighten.

"Kuku is a beautiful name."

She shrugged. "One gets tired of it. 'Kuku, do this. Kuku, do that.' Day in, day out. I am an orphan, you know. I cannot do what I want."

"What do you want, Kuku?"

She looked up at him. "You," breathed Kuku. The worship in her eyes was balm to his soreness. "I have loved you from the first moment I saw you," she whis-pered. "These people are all blind. They do not know what you are." This was balm too. "Your little silly Mary thinks she has found a god in that Krishnan. I know when I have found mine."

The two heads, black and gold were together on one pillow; the sheet, thrown back, showed brown and pale legs closely entwined. Kuku's hand again and again caressed while his played with a strand of her hair. "Kiss me, a long, long kiss," and, "Love me again," pleaded Kuku.

"No more." Blaise was sleepy.

"One more." She bit him on the ear, raising a spot of blood. "I'm a tiger." A shrill squeal of laughter.

"You're a mosquito." Another shriek as he rolled over on her again.

"No! No!" squealed Kuku.

"You asked for it . . ."

"Well. Well. Well." Once again it was Olga Manning. "You'd think," she mocked, "he could be faithful for one month—and with an Indian."

An outraged shriek came from Kuku as, startled, she snatched her wrapper and ran to the bathroom. Blaise, caught midway in the act, looked up as dampness spread around him.

"I'm sorry I interrupted you"—Olga was contemptuous—"but I couldn't think what the noise was. Well," she said again, "you've done it now."

"Have I? Did I?" He sounded dazed. Then, as he looked around the room, the floor still wet where the sweepers had washed it, his clothes flung down on it, and smelled disinfectant mingled with the jasmine scent on his pillow, realization came back, realization and disgust. "To hell with all women," shouted Blaise. He caught up a towel, pushed past Olga in the doorway and out on to the beach.

"That was the last I saw of him," Olga Armstrong was to say.

*　　*　　*

It was beginning to be dawn, the sky paling over the sea as Krishnan at last led a clean and shining Birdie out of the waves; not a speck of paint was left on her as she stood, flapping her ears to dry them, lifting her trunk in happiness to spray herself again. "She did not like the paint either," said Krishnan as he took her up the beach. "Now she must have a good feed. I have sugarcane, *gram* and *jaggery* balls which she loves." Mary followed them wringing the water out of her slip. She was so tired she staggered.

"For us I will make some tea. You must take off your wet things. Here, dry yourself with this." He threw her a towel.

As Birdie contentedly ate, breaking up the cane with her foot and trunk, picking up the balls and stuffing them into her mouth, Krishnan put the remains of the fire together, poking it with a stick, throwing on pieces of wood. He had lit a small methylated stove, incongruous in that setting, but soon a pan of water was boiling and he threw in tea leaves. Mary, unaccountably shivering, was glad of the fire, even more glad when Krishnan handed her a bowl of strong sweet tea. She had pulled on her dress, hung her slip and briefs on a bush to dry.

"A little rice?"

She shook her head. "I had dinner."

"More than I had." The rice had been left cold. Krishnan warmed it, mixed it with dried fish, and soon was scooping it up with his fingers. Again she saw how white and even his teeth were.

"I think," he said, "it would be better if you did not go back to your husband tonight."

"I don't think I could."

"The question is, what to do with you? All Patna Hall will be asleep and we don't want to cause a stir. If I made you comfortable, here in the grove, would you be afraid?"

"I'm too tired to be afraid."

"True. You're half asleep," but, "Where will you be?" she asked, all at once awake.

"Udata and I have to ride Birdie to Ghandara. I dare not trust Birdie to her *mahout* and his people. They might try to paint her all over again." He laughed.

"Krishnan, are you ever tired?"

"Not when I cannot be." He got up. "Here is a clean *lunghi*. Sleep in that."

He arranged a bed for her on the deerskins, taking quilts and pillows from the throne. Mary lay down, the *lunghi* around her. Krishnan tucked its end in, Indian fashion. "Your hair will dry. Sleep."

But, "Krishnan, what about Blaise?" she asked. "Is it my fault? Why is there all this trouble?" and Krishnan answered as he had answered before, "Because you are you and Blaise is Blaise. The two don't mix."

"Then what am I to do? How can we live together?"

"You will get older," said Krishnan. "So will he. I don't think he can change but you will learn how to live with him—and not mix—as many wives do, the wise ones. Indian women, I think, are particularly wise in this: They know how not to mix yet never let their husbands guess it."

"Must I?" asked Mary.

His hand closed over hers; she could have stayed with that warm clasp forever.

"There are destinies," Krishnan said. "Yours and mine. But don't think of that tonight. Go to sleep."

He took his hand away, touched her hair, and left. She heard him call to Birdie, then a rustling as they went through the trees.

Friday

■ ■ ■ ■ ■ ■ ■ ■ ■ ■ ■ ■ ■ ■

Mary was woken by the parakeets. A pair was quarreling in a tree overhead, their bright green flashing between the dark-leaved mango branches, their red beaks chattering as they made their raucous cries. Perhaps they're husband and wife, thought Mary smiling—Blaise and me—then ceased to smile as she remembered the angry words on the beach. Krishnan did his best, even when he had to interfere. Mary thought Blaise would really have hit her; He slapped me before. She shut her eyes trying to keep thoughts of Blaise out of the way. This is Krishnan's day, his vital day. She thought of him riding Birdie away last night, through the dark—with Udata, of course; Birdie would be docile. Docile, dulcet, there was a sweetness about those words; with Krishnan everything, everyone became docile—even me, thought Mary and, Yes, I must go back.

When she sat up she found she had been showered with scarlet petals, the *simile* trees were dropping their cotton flowers. In one week they are going over, thought Mary and realization came to her—Today we go away too. She could not believe it, the very thought brought such a feeling of emptiness that she hurriedly put it out of her mind. "Don't think about it yet," she told herself. Instead, "Today is the election."

Krishnan will win, thought Mary. He couldn't not, yet the skeptical voices intervened: "Of all the way-out notions." "The man's mad!" "Masquerading as a god."

Krishnan himself had told her, "It will be tricky." Mary picked up a cotton flower that had fallen without breaking and began to pick off the petals. "He will win. He won't. He will. He won't." Yet knowing, as the scarlet petals fell over her feet, they would end, "He will."

"But I," she whispered, "have to go back to Blaise."

"Must I?" she had asked Krishnan.

"I think you must."

If I can, thought Mary. I . . . I have to get over myself first. I can. She picked up another flower. "You can. You can't. You can." Mary sat looking at the sepals of the flower, bare now that the brilliantly colored petals had gone all but one. She pulled it. "You can't," it said.

"The elephant was decorated especially and at great cost for the pomp," pleaded Dr. Coomaraswamy.

"I had told you, *ordered* you." The campaign was over. Krishnan could speak. "There will be no pomp."

A bitter scene was going on in the Ghandara headquarters between Krishnan and Dr. Coomaraswamy.

"You have undone the elephant," the doctor almost screamed. "After such work! Such cost!"

"Against express orders." When Krishnan was cool, it meant he was angry.

"*I* am the director of this campaign," Dr. Coomaraswamy blustered.

"He is the director," Mr. Srinivasan echoed.

"And I am the campaign."

"True. True," said Mr. Srinivasan, "but—"

"There is no 'but.' Everything is to be carried out exactly as I said."

"Krishnan, think. I beg you to think. This is *the* day. The crucial day."

"Then this is all the more crucial."

"Surely it is time for a little display? True, you have brought the people out marvelously . . ."

"Most marvelously," piped faithful Srinivasan.

"They will be disappointed."

"Far more disappointed if I renege."

"Renege?"

"Destroy my image, which is what you would have me do. *Stupidity!*" cried Krishnan

"I do not like stupidity." Dr. Coomaraswamy drew himself up.

"Then don't be it. Can't you *see?*" asked Krishnan.

"I see that Padmina Retty will come with a great splash, helicopter, bands, decorations—maybe *decorated* elephants—horses, parade."

"Yes, and you will ask her, demand of her, to tell you, in public, then and there, what it cost. You will say to the crowd, 'Ask your Mother Padmina what it cost'—'Mother' will be mockery. 'Ask her what it cost and who will pay.' " Krishnan stood up, his eyes flashing. " 'Who pays? Not your mother. Not any Retty. Oh, no! Then who? You,' " stormed Krishnan. " 'You, the people. Ask her how many of the *pice* you have been allowed to earn with your toil, your poor tools, have gone into her pocket. Or the pockets of her aides who talk to you so sweetly. Oh, yes! They hold out a hand to you, sweetly, sweetly, while the other hand is robbing you.'

"Then ask, 'What is the cost of Krishnan Bhanj? Nothing. He asks nothing. Not one *pice* do you have to pay. He himself takes nothing. His followers take nothing. He gives and so people give gladly to him. Brothers and sisters, give him your votes.' That is what you will say," said Krishnan.

"But . . . I have already ordered two bands."

"Then you can pay them yourself or tell them to go away."

"I have hired horses. Already they are caparisoned."

"Then uncaparison them."

"Boy and girl scouts."

"Boy and girl scouts I don't mind."

"He doesn't mind boy and girl scouts." Mr. Srinivasan was thankful.

"Yes, that is a good idea—but—scouts? *Are* there any in Konak?"

"In truth, no," and Dr. Coomaraswamy had to admit, "I have had to buy uniforms."

"The children can keep the uniforms. They will be delighted but wear them they will not, *will not*," repeated Krishnan severely, "for the procession. If anything is not in truth, then no. This political campaign, unlike all other political campaigns, must be in truth. Absolute truth. Nothing else will I have."

"Then it will be disaster."

"Then it will be success."

Mary sang as she went along the shore. Singing! I oughtn't to be singing. I have to make peace, at least a sort of peace, with Blaise. I'll try—though it seems unlikely, thought Mary. Yet still she sang:

> *Early one morning,*
> *Just as the sun was rising,*
> *I heard a pretty maiden in the valley below:*
> *Oh, never leave me,*
> *Oh, don't deceive me.*
> *How could you use a poor maiden so?*

She laughed as she picked up a piece of seaweed with her toes and cast it back into the sea.

There were no boats on the shore; the fishermen must have gone out early; it was, as well, too early for people to come down to the beach. The dawn was rosy—she thought of Usas the Dawn Goddess, daughter of the sky, sister of night. There was a pink light over the sea, pale tender pink, giving no inkling of the heat that was to come. Yes, it will be hot, thought Mary, hard for the people who have to walk in the processions.

She would have liked to have gone up to the Hall to see if she could find Hannah and ask her for some earlier-than-normal early tea but first she had to make herself respectable. I need a bath. The stains of color would be difficult to wash off. I wonder if it's too early to ring the house for hot water. I could telephone quietly so as not to wake Blaise. I must look an apparition. I need to wash my hair too.

Her bare feet made no sound on the veranda; the shutters were open; a half door swung in the sea breeze. Mary stepped inside and stood puzzled.

There was no one in the room; the bed was oddly rumpled, its pillows cast aside. There was, too, an odd smell; strong disinfectant but with it, or under it, a stink, thought Mary, wrinkling up her nose . . . something that reminded her of the smell that hung about stables.

Coming farther in, she saw Blaise's clothes lying in a crumpled heap at the foot of the bed. Perhaps he had wanted to swim to cool himself off after the quarrel . . . but his bathing trunks, put to dry, still hung on the veranda rail.

Did he change to go up to the Hall? But why change? He didn't get wet. Was he so angry that he had determined to leave Patna Hall at once and gone up to order a taxi? She looked through his clothes; they were all there. He wouldn't have gone up to the Hall naked. Besides, wouldn't he have packed? She couldn't imagine Blaise leaving his possessions behind. Then where is he? wondered Mary.

She looked at the partition. Shall I ask Olga? But there was no sound from her rooms. She looked so tired and unhappy last night she should sleep, and Mary quietly went out. "Blaise, Blaise," she called along the beach. "Blaise." The sound came back to her from emptiness.

It was then that she heard a whickering, not a pleased sound but a whickering of distress: Slippers came out of the bushes and with him the stench she had smelled in the bedroom but stronger. He was limping, worse than limping, lurching as he tried to move; one foot was dragging and Mary saw the fetlock was swollen, the pitiable hoof was on its side. Slippers was shaking in violent spasms. His sides were smeared with dung and there were marks on his neck—Blaise with the heel of his shoe again! Mary, too, was shaking but with fury. He had hit Slippers on the eyes as well: one was swollen and bleeding; there was blood on his nose. "Horrible," cried Mary aloud. "Horrible! Blaise must have found you in the bedroom again," she cried to Slippers. "Oh, why did you go in?" and then she knew. "You were looking for your sugar because I forgot to give it to you. It's *I* who am horrible." She buried her face in Slippers's furry neck. "He drove you off the veranda too quickly and you have broken your poor foot. Stay there," Mary ordered him. "Don't try to move. Stay."

She tore up the path; the house was silent, shuttered. How odd! People come for the sea breezes and sleep with their shutters closed, but at the gatehouse she found Thambi, squatting on his haunches, beginning to blow up a small fire for the lazy Shyama.

"Thambi! Thambi!"

Thambi rose to his feet at this frantic apparition.

"Thambi—Slippers—donkey—hurt, very hurt. Get vet. Vet-er-in-a-rian animal doctor. Animal hurt. Doctor. Quick."

Thambi, always intelligent, understood "Animal hurt," but doctor seemed to him strange. Donkeys, to Thambi, were neither here nor there, a means of transport, bearers of burdens. He, Samuel, and Hannah had often deplored Auntie Sanni's keeping of Slippers. The donkey did not matter but Mary's distress did. "I come," said Thambi. "First I call Miss Sanni."

"The vet. The vet," Mary was still saying it hysterically as she stood by Slippers.

"There is no use for the vet," and Auntie Sanni said words in Telegu to Thambi who ran to the house.

Auntie Sanni's nightclothes looked no different from her dresses; she had come down the path billowing and calm. Gently she spoke to Slippers, touching the bloody marks on his head and eye, only her mouth had tightened, the sea-green of her eyes grown dark. Gently she had felt down his leg to the broken fetlock and had shaken her head. "The bone is fragmented. See, bits are through the skin. He has made it worse by dragging it. Besides the hoof is too heavy for it to mend. Poor donkey," she said. "Why wouldn't you let us . . . ?" Then to Mary, "Colonel McIndoe will come."

"Colonel McIndoe!"

"He is firm and quick," said Auntie Sanni. "Mary, go inside."

White to the lips, Mary said, "I'm not a child, Auntie Sanni, I'll stay."

The shot rang out to the hills and echoed back. "Better go to Mr. Browne," Auntie Sanni told Mary. "This will startle him."

Mary stood up from where she had knelt by Slippers, stretched prone now on the sand. Her tears had fallen on his fur.

"No more pain," said Auntie Sanni. "No more blows. Poor little donkey."

"Just because I forgot his sugar." Then, "Blaise!" Recollection came flooding back. "Auntie Sanni, Blaise isn't there. He isn't—anywhere."

Quietly, methodically, Auntie Sanni went through the room, questioning Mary as quietly. "If he had come up to the Hall, I should have known—our night watchman would have called me and"—Auntie Sanni sniffed—"Mary, someone else has been in this room."

"Who?"

Auntie Sanni did not answer that. Instead, "You are sure he has taken nothing?"

"Nothing," and, out on the beach again, Mary said, "He must have gone swimming but what—" she felt as if she asked the sky, the sea itself, "what's the harm in that? Blaise is a strong, strong swimmer."

"Miss Baba, look," and Mary saw what she had not noticed before, the long mesh screen with its barbed top and hinges was still stretched between its iron posts across the Patna Hall beach. "Is not open," said Thambi—he had not unlocked it. "Ten foot high," said Thambi. "No sahib, even athlete, get over that."

"Then . . . ?" Mary looked with rising horror along the beach. "No. Oh, no!"

"I think yes," said Thambi. Scanning the wash of the waves, he saw something, darted along the sand, lifted a small object, white, limp, and brought it to them. It was a hotel towel.

"*Ayyo!*"

"*Ayyo! Ay-ayyo!*" Thambi cried in horror. "*Ay-yo-ma!*"

Up in their room, the Fishers heard the shot. Sir John put on his dressing gown and went out on the upper veranda to look. "As far as I can see," he called back to Lady Fisher, "something has happened to the donkey. Colonel McIndoe is there."

"The colonel? Then it's serious."

"Yes. The poor beast is down."

"Mary will be upset. Poor child."

Then came running footsteps, a voice, "Sir John! Sir John!"

It was a Mary they had not seen before, her dress limp, stained with odd colors as was she, color-stains from Birdie's paint and blood—that had been from Slippers's eye. Her feet were bare, her hair stiff with dried salt, her face tear-stained, the eyes wide with panic.

"The poor donkey's been put down," Sir John began,

but, "Worse—than Slippers." Mary was out of breath. "Worse."

"What is worse?"

"Blaise," stammered Mary. "Blaise. He went for a swim."

"Is that all?" their looks seemed to say when a sound like another shot but a muffled shot came from over their heads. The next moment, across the veranda, they saw a shower of colored stars descending over the sea. "A rocket," said Sir John.

Next moment came another, then another. "It's Patna Hall's own alarm signal," said Sir John. "Thambi is letting rockets off from the roof to alert the fishing boats, maybe the coastguards."

"Great God in heaven!" said Lady Fisher.

Out on the veranda, carrying the Fishers' morning tea tray, Hannah heard the rockets. As if in echo of Lady Fisher, putting the tray carefully down on a table, Hannah knelt, made the sign of the cross, and she, too, whispered, "God in heaven. Merciful God. Mother of God. Blessed Virgin."

Kuku was woken by the shot.

From the window she saw the gathering on the beach and drew a sharp breath. Like Sir John, "Colonel McIndoe is there," she whispered. "My God!"

She dressed as fast as she could but her fingers were trembling so much that she could hardly knot her sari; when she tried to brush out her hair, she dropped the brush. Managing to slip through the house without being seen by any of the servants, she ran, not down the path but by a side track through the bushes to the bungalow, coming around its far end. No one was near as she knocked on Olga Manning's door.

"Olga. Olga. Please may I come in? It's Kuku."

There was no answer.

"Olga, I *must* come in." The door was not locked. Kuku pushed it open.

Drugged by tiredness and the whiskey Mary and Auntie Sanni had given her, Olga had slept through the shot, the voices, the rockets. Now Kuku shook her awake. "Olga, *please*. Try and wake. It is *urgent*. Olga."

Slowly, struggling through waves of weariness and heaviness, Olga sat up. "It's morning." She blinked at the light.

"Of course it's morning. Olga."

"Who . . . who is it?"

"Kuku. Kuku."

"What d'you want?"

"Promise," cried Kuku, "promise you won't tell."

"Tell what?"

"What you saw last night."

"Last night?"

"Yes. Blaise—Mr. Browne—and me. Please, Olga. They're all out there now. They can't find Blaise and Mary is making a great fuss. Nobody knows but you. It all depends on you. Auntie Sanni would send me away."

"I don't think she would." Olga Manning was struggling to be aware, to remember. "Not Auntie Sanni."

"She might. Hannah, Samuel, they'll sneer. Always they have hated me. Olga, I was virgin. I am not a girl like that. Blaise was the first and I love him. Olga, don't injure him or me. Give me your word. Promise you won't tell."

"I promise I won't tell. In any case, it's not my concern, nothing to do with me. Now go away and let me sleep."

"I can't drink brandy before breakfast." Mary said it with a tremulous laugh. "I can't."

"You are going to," said Lady Fisher.

"I not understand English memsahibs," Thambi had told Auntie Sanni. "Miss Baba, she cry for donkey, no tear for husband."

Mary was too appalled to cry. "I told Blaise about the baby shark," she had said that over and over again. "I told him. I thought he had listened but he was so angry. Why was he so angry? I don't understand. I don't. I don't. I don't."

"Mary, tell me something," said Lady Fisher. She had not attempted to hold Mary close as she would have liked to do or try to comfort her. "She would have cast me off," she told Sir John.

"Tell me something," she said again to Mary, "did you promise Blaise you would not see Krishnan Bhanj again? Did you?"

That arrested the frenzy. Mary looked at Lady Fisher in astonishment. "I didn't. I wouldn't have. I promised Blaise I wouldn't go near any of them—unless I was asked."

"You were asked?"

"Of course. Krishnan asked me. I left you playing bridge. I hated you for playing bridge when poor Olga . . ."

"Yes, yes, but go on," said Lady Fisher.

"There was a boy waiting on the path. He had a note, a piece of paper really, from Krishnan." Mary's voice trembled. "It asked me to come and help him in the grove."

"But he was at Ghandara."

"He wasn't. He was with the elephant."

"Elephant?"

"Yes. We had to wash the paint off Birdie. It was *imperative.*" In her distraction Mary quoted Krishnan to Lady Fisher's bewilderment.

"I don't understand a word you are saying."

"No I don't suppose you do, nobody does but it's true. There's to be no grand decorations in Krishnan's procession, so we had to wash the paint off the elephant. Krishnan couldn't do it all, so he asked me to help him and I went. I don't care if you don't believe me, but first I made the boy wait and wrote a note on the back of the paper—so Blaise knew where I was. The boy took it."

"No note came."

"I gave the boy a rupee."

"No note came . . ." but light broke on Mary. "I see! Blaise thought I had broken my word. *That's* why he was so angry but I did send the note, I did."

"Yes, you did."

Sir John had come on to the veranda. "I found this on the path." He had undone the crumpled ball of paper, wet and limp but decipherable. "For Blaise," read out Sir John, and, " 'You see, I have been asked.' "

"Yes." There was a slithering sound. To her surprise Mary slumped to the floor.

"But what are they *doing?*" That was Mary's first frantic question.

She had come around to find herself lying on her dressing room bed with Hannah mopping her face with cold water, pouring more over her hands while Lady Fisher held her. Impatiently Mary shook her head but Hannah persisted. "Baba, lie still. In a moment better," and, strangely, Mary let her. Hannah dried her face and hands, sat her up, and Sir John held the glass of brandy to her lips. "Not a word until you've drunk this . . ."

Then, "Something. We must do *something*—at least *try*," begged Mary.

"Look," said Sir John, and took her to the veranda rail.

The fishing boats had come back but not to the beach. Thambi and Moses had taken Patna Hall's own motorboat out, ". . . and a battering they got as they went through the waves," said Sir John. Now the other boats had closed in to make a flotilla; through Sir John's binoculars Mary could see Thambi conferring. Then, as the gazers on the veranda watched, the flotilla broke up, the boats going in different directions.

A few minutes later, a speedboat from the coastguard stations came into sight and soon was circling around them. "I should be on that," Mary cried. "Sir John, I ought to be looking. I must go out. I will."

"You would only be a hindrance," said Sir John. "You must trust them, Mary. No one knows this coast better than these men. If anyone can find Blaise they will."

"And if they can't?" Mary stared across the sea. "Give him back. Oh, please, give him back," she was pleading.

"Mary, *baba*. Come with Hannah. You must change that dress, wash, eat. Many sahibs will be needing you," but, "Leave me alone," cried Mary. "Just for one minute, leave me alone." She tore herself from Hannah and ran down into the Hall.

"Let her go," said Sir John. "Samuel and I will see she doesn't go down to the beach. Let her go." He followed her downstairs.

"Sanni, is there any chance?" Sir John asked as Auntie Sanni came to join him.

"If there were, the fishing boats would have picked him up long ago—they went out first at midnight. The coastguards say there has been no other boat near." Auntie Sanni seemed heavier than ever.

"Blaise was a strong swimmer."

"Even so, our strongest young men don't go out alone into this sea, John, it is infested. If they find him," said Auntie Sanni, "God knows what they will find."

"Mrs. Browne."

Mary spun around. She had gone into the Hall. No one was there and holding onto the reception desk she had been trying to still her turmoil. Now she saw that a familiar small red car was drawn up under the portico.

"Mr. Menzies!" Mary recoiled. "I don't want to talk to you."

"But you will." Mr. Menzies smiled. "I have come to bring you good news of your friend Krishnan Bhanj. He is your friend, isn't he?"

"I . . . I have been working for his party." Mary's instinct told her to be cautious.

"Very laudable," said Mr. Menzies. "So you will be very glad. Voting began at dawn this morning. Konak is usually politically apathetic. Krishnan has roused it. I have never seen such a turnout. In my opinion Padmina Retty might as well pack up and go home."

"You mean Krishnan might win?" Mary, off her guard, came nearer. "He will win?"

"I believe overwhelmingly. There! At least that has made you happy," and Mary felt she had to say, "Thank you for coming to tell me."

"And now you tell me," said Mr. Menzies. "Mrs. Browne, when did you last see your husband?"

Mary flinched but firmly shut her lips and turned to go.

"You won't tell me? I have just been to see Mrs. Armstrong. She won't tell me either. Pity. You ladies are making a mistake. If you won't tell me, I shall have to make it up or rely on other people—as perhaps I have done already—perhaps someone who doesn't like you so well. They are apt to distort. So am I." Mr. Menzies laughed but he was serious. "Of course, this *isn't* gossip, in which I specialize, yet it soon could be. You wouldn't want this catastrophe—"

"It isn't catastrophe—"

"Yet," he finished for her. "You wouldn't want it turned into sensationalism, would you? Wouldn't it be better to talk to me? When did you last see your husband?"

"He was—playing bridge."

"And where were you? That is the question, isn't it?"

Mary, unfailingly transparent, was looking around the Hall this way and that, trying to escape but Mr. Menzies came nearer.

"Mrs. Browne, tell me. I think your father is a well-to-do man, isn't he? Very well to do."

"Rory?" Mary could not think what Rory had to do with this. "I . . . suppose so."

"And the parents of poor Blaise . . . more than well to do. Wealthy?"

"Why are you asking me these questions?"

"Well, you see," said Mr. Menzies, "I know what happened later that night on the beach."

For a moment Mary looked at him wide-eyed, then she followed his glance to the portico and the red car and saw the now familiar curly black head, though the yellow shirt had been changed for a red one and, "I see," said Mary. "Kanu!"

"Kanu is an excellent small informer—and helps me in more ways than one."

You really are repulsive, thought Mary, with your horrible ribbon scruff hair and crab pink face and horrid plumpness.

"Still there are ways," he was saying, "of keeping things out of the papers."

"Certainly there are." Sir John had appeared in the Hall. "Ways and means you probably have not taken into account, but, Menzies," said Sir John, "Miss Sanni ordered you out of her hotel. Will you go or shall I have you put out?"

"I have a reason to be here, Sir John."

"I am sure you have. In fact, I know you had a hand in this mischief, if tragedy or near tragedy can be called that. I hope it will rest on your conscience."

"My conscience is perfectly at ease, thank you, Sir John. I am a newsman and news is news."

"Not all news. We have a police injunction."

"Injunction!"

"The police insist that nothing is released until the full facts are known. They are thinking of our Office and of Mr. Browne's family—which is more than you have done—also of Patna Hall which you will leave at once and take your scurrility with you."

*   *   *

"Sir John, did you say, 'the police'?"

He had brought Mary back to the veranda, holding her, trying to stop her quivering. "You and Hannah are the only people she would let touch her," Lady Fisher was to say, and soon, "Sir John," Mary managed to whisper, "did you say the police?"

"It has to be the police, Mary. Chief Inspector Anand has sent a message—he cannot leave Ghandara while the voting is on, he hasn't that many men, though he has sent to Madras. He asks that you, Mrs. Manning—I mean Mrs. Armstrong—and Kuku will come to him."

"Olga and Kuku?" Mary was puzzled.

"Also Thambi and the sweeper women who cleaned up the mess in the bungalow last night."

"Slippers's mess?"

"Yes, he fouled the floor."

"*That* was the smell and Blaise hit him, hit him with the heel of his shoe like he did before and it's all my fault. Oh, I can't bear it. I can't bear it." She was shuddering from head to foot.

Sir John held her but Auntie Sanni had come out. "Stand up," said Auntie Sanni to Mary. "We have Kuku in hysterics. That's enough. Go and get yourself ready and be of help."

"Oh, Auntie Sanni," Lady Fisher demurred, but it acted like a charm. Mary stood erect, tossed back her hair, tried to give them a smile, and obeyed.

"That is my girl," said Auntie Sanni.

Krishnan had told Mary that election days in India were joyous events but she had not known it would be like this. "It's a *mela*—a fair," said Sir John. All along the roads on the way to Ghandara, men, women, and children, in what they had as best clothes, had come on foot, singing. "All over Konak they have been out since dawn," said Sir John. They came, too, in bullock carts, the bullocks garlanded, the carts decorated with flowers and scraps of bright cloth. Lorries wearing jewelry and tassels swept by, while cars and Jeeps, sent by the parties to ferry voters, had drapes in party colors, the blue of Padmina Retty, red for Gopal Rau, green, yellow, and white for Krishnan Bhanj. Bicycles were decorated too, as were the rickshaws; some of the rickshaws had loudspeakers.

The square by Ghandara's town hall was packed, and as in every town in the state, entertainers had come: men who danced on stilts, conjurors, puppet theaters—those whose puppets told the story of the God Krishna were especially popular, as were his storytellers. There were sweetmeat sellers; rival teahouses were free, paid for by their parties. "One bowl of tea or coffee with one biscuit only," Dr. Coomaraswamy had specified, "and that will cost me a *lakh* of rupees." Toy sellers came through the crowds carrying poles wound in straw, stuck with paper windmills in bright colors, paper dolls, long paper whistles which made piercing squeals.

Coming from a side road, hooting as they inched through the crammed roads, the Patna Hall cars had to wait while the processions passed. Gopal Rau had decided not to process at all which, under the circumstances, was wise but they saw the tail end of Padmina Retty's display: mounted soldiers in full dress, their lances fluttering pennants; foot soldiers wearing the dress of the Maharajah's late army. Behind them Padmina rode, not in her famous white Jeep but in the blue *howdah* of a decorated elephant much larger than Birdie. "They must have had to send away for that one," said Sir John. All around her marched her men in brocaded *achkans*, gauze turbans, or English suits; her women helpers in glittering saris carried peacock feather fans. Behind them came brass bands blaring Indian and English music, new tunes and old favorites, the "Dambuster's March" and "Colonel Bogey," while overhead circled her helicopter, pulling a banner, bright blue with a star. The rear was brought up by horsemen and boys running almost between their hooves.

It was impressive. "Very well done," said Sir John. "Horrendously well done," Dr. Coomaraswamy had said.

Then came a silence, all the more striking after the fanfare and tantara that had gone before, until an old and reverend priest with a white beard and saffron robe appeared on a white horse without saddle or bridle. The priest held up his hand for quiet. Even the rickshaws hushed as the ululation of a conch sounded and Krishnan's procession came into sight.

It was exactly as he had said with, after the deafening bands, that soft undulating ululation introducing the drums beating to keep time with the seductive melody of a flute piercing through the crowds—"Yes, dulcet," murmured Mary. Then came the disciples, young vigorous men barefoot in spotless white, their hair flowing, their hands held in *namaskar*.

Behind them, on a lorry, bare and plain, Dr. Coomaraswamy spoke through a microphone. "I cannot walk and speak," he had told Krishnan. "I am too aged. Besides, on the ground no one will hear me."

"All the better," said Sharma, the irrepressible.

When the doctor paused to draw breath, the young men sang.

Then came a space in which another priest, young—"From Agni's temple," Mary whispered—dressed in saffron, led a huge sacred bull, the cap on its hump worked in beads, its neck garlanded. It placidly chewed its cud as it walked, veering from side to side when the crowd offered it tidbits.

Next walked the children, healthy pretty boys and girls. They drew "ahs" and "aies" from the people as the little girls scattered flower petals while the boys carried their kites and garlands. They too sang, their voices shrill:

Lord Krishna, Lord of All,
We put you in your cradle.
We bind you with a chain of gold,
Your hands are red with henna.
We gave you milk, we gave you kisses.
Little Lord Krishna.

Last came Krishnan, magnificently tall, his skin oiled so that once again it shone but with its own darkness, still almost blue-black—Perhaps Krishna blue is intrinsic, thought Mary, and even in her misery that strange happiness swelled. He wore only a loincloth; the squirrel was on his shoulder as he led Birdie on a saffron-colored rope, the elephant shining too with cleanliness, her trunk every now and then touching Krishnan. He did not look at the crowd, only straight forward as waves of reverence and, yes, love, thought Mary, came on all sides and a murmured, "Jai Krishnan. Jai Krishnan," then "Jai Shri Krishnan. Jai Shri Krishnan Hari." It swelled louder and louder as the crowd took it up. Behind him, which drew delighted laughter, three of the most good-looking girl disciples led the three cows of the Root and Flower symbol.

For a moment Mary forgot the terrible present. "Jai Krishnan," she breathed. "Jai Shri Krishnan."

The crowds had surged around the bull so that the procession had to halt while the young men ran to persuade the people to move back. "No police. No force," Krishnan had laid down so that it took a little time. Meanwhile, the lorry was on a level with the first Patna Hall car which held Sir John and, in the backseat, Mary, Olga, and Kuku—Thambi and the sweepers were behind. Dr. Coomaraswamy, who was not sweltering in a suit—he had to wear national dress: "Though I am not habituated"—saw that Kuku, nearest the window, was weeping.

Weeping! Immediately Dr. Coomaraswamy was

transported into a dream . . . "Uma, here is a girl in trouble"—he did not know what trouble but never mind—"Let us take her into our home and befriend her. Always she has been treated as a nobody—we will set her on her feet. You, Uma, will teach her in your wonderful ways. I . . ." He did not know quite what he would do but he saw a grateful Kuku, sweet, emollient, "I am so grateful, *so* grateful," and he would say, paternalistically, of course, "Kuku, come here." At that the dream broke. "For what," Uma would, of course, ask, "are you befriending this girl? Tell me the truth." Dr. Coomaraswamy had to admit he knew another truth. "I too am in love." He saw Kuku's face illumined, softened as she had said that and he knew, no matter what her grief, there was no place in it for him. It was as well that the lorry was able to move a few paces. The cars succeeded in getting by and Kuku was borne away, as far as Dr. Coomaraswamy was concerned, forever.

The police station, undecorated, was a sturdier building than the town hall, made, too, of stucco. "It will be cool," Olga said thankfully.

Two policemen stood on the steps in regulation khaki shorts, tunics, puttees, boots, and red-banded turbans; brass shone on their belt buckles and shoulder straps. "Chief Inspector Anand keeps his men in trim," Sir John approved.

The chief inspector came out to meet them: A plump, dapper little man, his uniform, too, was impeccable. He had a mustache so fine it looked as if it had been penciled in dandy fashion but his eyes were kind as he took them into a waiting room, apologizing for bringing them out in the heat.

"May I see you first, Mrs. Armstrong, since you were the last person to see Mr. Browne . . ." He did not add "alive."

Olga Manning Armstrong did not lie; she simply told the truth but not the whole truth, giving her testimony with a quiet steadfastness that impressed the chief inspector.

"Well, I am used to courts," she told Mary afterward.

"Mr. Browne came to your door."

"Yes, to ask if I had seen Mary, his wife."

"And you had not?"

"No. I was going to bed."

"It must be painful for you," said sympathetic Chief Inspector Anand, "to have me question you just now when there is so much tragedy but you can be of utmost help. What made you, Mrs. Armstrong, go in later?"

"He, Mr. Browne, was hurting the donkey—of course, I didn't know then how badly it was hurt but I heard the blows. I couldn't stand that."

"He was angry?"

"Very. Then I heard Kuku—Miss Vikram. She had come down with the sweepers."

"And later?"

"I thought I had better look in to see if there was anything I could do—really for Mary's sake."

"She was not there?"

"No. I didn't do any good. Mr. Browne pushed past me and rushed out."

"Why do you think he rushed out?"

"He did not like what I said."

"About the donkey?"

Olga bowed her head.

"You did not see him again?"

"How could I? I went back to bed."

"Thank you, Mrs. Armstrong."

To Kuku lies were second nature but she did not dare to tell them now. "Mr. Browne telephoned the house. You answered?"

"Nat-u-rally. I am hotel manager." Kuku did not say it with pride, she was terrified. "I called two of our women sweepers. We cleaned up the room. It was—disgusting. Blaise—Mr. Browne—was right to be angry. He was right," pleaded Kuku.

"When the sweepers had gone?"

"I tidied the room. The donkey had smashed a photograph—glass . . ."

"Then?"

"I went back." There had been only an infinitesimal pause.

"You did not see Mr. Browne go out?"

"No. I had gone myself," said Kuku with truth.

"Thank you, Miss Vikram."

"Do I have to tell the inspector everything?" Mary asked Sir John, still shuddering.

"Strictly speaking, you don't have to tell him anything. It is simply that we and they are trying to find out what has happened to Blaise. We must find out so that it will help if you tell them what is relevant."

"That I was with Krishnan?"

"It is relevant. I'll be with you, Mary. Tell the chief inspector openly how you helped Krishnan with the elephant, how, from the time you came to Konak, you have helped with the party's plans, made friends with all of them, believed in them," but the chief inspector was to ask, "Your husband, did he share in this belief?"

"No."

"Do you know why?"

Mary was too honest to prevaricate. "He did not like me having anything away from him."

"Ah!" said the chief inspector. "Perhaps last night he came after you?"

"Yes."

"Has he done that before?"

"Yes," and, "I know what you mean," flashed Mary, "but he saw nothing because there was nothing to see."

"Last night? To be fair, Mrs. Browne, most men would not be pleased to find their wife, a newly married wife, Mrs. Browne, out on the beach at night with someone who was to him . . ." the chief inspector did not say "outsider," instead he said, "a stranger," and he asked, "Was there a quarrel?"

"Not a quarrel. We were only teasing him. I wish we hadn't."

Chief Inspector Anand was acute. "Because your husband did not understand you were only teasing?"

"Yes," and Mary had to say, "I'm afraid he took it seriously."

"Seriously enough to make him take his own life?"

"Take his own life?" The aghast astonishment was genuine. *"Blaise,"* and involuntarily it came out, "Blaise would never have done that. I was the one who was always wrong."

"Yet he must have gone deliberately into that dangerous sea."

"He was angry, too angry to think what he was doing. Oh, don't you see?" cried Mary. "He was angry with us. He went back to the bungalow and found Slippers—the donkey. That was my fault. I had forgotten the sugar." Tears came into her eyes. "Slippers made that mess. It must have made Blaise furious. I'm sure he didn't know what he was doing. He probably felt filthied. He was always very particular. I'm sure he just wanted to get clean." Into her mind came Krishnan saying, "The sea washes everything away," and suddenly, "Don't. Don't," cried Mary. "Don't ask me any more."

There was the sound of a motor scooter, the Indian put-putti. A policeman came into the room and whispered to the chief inspector. "Excuse me for a moment, Mrs. Browne, Sir John."

They heard a murmured colloquy but not the words. Then quick orders. Sir John got up. The chief inspector came back and with him a middle-aged policewoman, the first Mary had seen. I didn't know India had them, she thought. This one wore, Mary was always to remember, khaki trousers, tunic, and cap like the chief inspector's, with a red border. She moved quietly to stand behind Mary's chair.

Chief Inspector Anand cleared his throat. "A messenger has just come from the beach at Shantipur. Mrs. Browne, I do not want to distress you but I must ask you, do you recognize this ring?"

A heavy gold ring with a crest, a stag's head and a motto Loyauté et vérité. "Yes," Mary said with stiff lips. "It's his. It is—his signet ring. He always wears it on his left hand."

"Mrs. Browne, a fisherman found it. Diving, he saw on the seabed a small shine of gold. It was on . . . on . . ." The inspector hesitated to go on. The policewoman moved to Mary. "On—a finger, Mrs. Browne."

"Only a finger?" Mary whispered.

"I'm afraid it is only a finger. The—the shark must have dropped it. Maybe there were two sharks and they had a fight. That can happen . . ."

"I told him about the baby shark!" Mary screamed it so loudly that the policewoman put her hands on the quivering shoulders. Mary shook her off. "I told him. I begged him. He wouldn't listen. I told him." She suddenly stood up. "I think I'm going to be sick."

They had been a long time at the police station. Mary had vomited until she thought she had brought up the dregs of her being. The chief inspector had wanted to call a doctor but, "She'll be better after this," said Olga, whom Sir John had called in; strong and capable, she had held Mary steadily, not sympathizing but encouraging her. When at last they drove back through the town it was in the afternoon sun; the processions had long ended, the crowd was milling around the town hall, though voting was still going on, the queues, seemingly endless, moving step-by-step toward the polling booths.

Voters made their cross or mark opposite the symbol, many of the women holding a baby on their hip while a toddler clutched their sari, but all eyes were alight with interest and awe.

Krishnan, though, was standing alone on the town hall steps. "Good!" Sir John could not help saying, "Good!"

Mary opened her eyes and looked.

Krishnan was no longer wearing his loincloth; he was dressed like the disciples, all in white, but stood head and shoulders above them as they gathered jubilantly around him. He stood making *namaskar* over and over again to the crowd. There was no sign of Padmina Retty.

"Is he winning?" asked Mary.

"Counting will go on all through the night," said Sir John, "but it looks as if he has already won."

Of course he doesn't know, thought Mary. How could he? As she thought that, Krishnan looked up.

He saw the car, the police—Chief Inspector Anand had given them outriders. Krishnan looked, a long look. Then he bent and whispered to Sharma who ran down the steps, wriggled and squeezed his way through the mass of people. He could not get to the cars but reached a police outrider.

"Get me a car," ordered Krishnan.

"A car? Why a car? You can't go anywhere now," cried Dr. Coomaraswamy.

"I must. I shall be back as soon as I can."

"But, *Krishnan!* How can you go? Look at the multitude. You cannot leave them."

"I must. You must talk to them until I come back."

"That will not satisfy them. Krishnan, wouldn't someone else do? Sharma . . ."

"No one else will do." Krishnan was violent. "I have a debt to pay. Sharma, get me a car—or better, a motorbike and a helmet and gloves to disguise me."

As evening came on a hush lay over Patna Hall, a tense hush. Hannah, Samuel, and the servants did their work quietly with shocked faces, Hannah's lips moving constantly in prayer. Kuku was prostrate in her room. "Why should she take on so?" Hannah said to Samuel. "We go on with our work, why cannot she? What was Browne Sahib to her?" asked Hannah indignantly. "While little Memsahib, poor little Memsahib . . ."

For the second time Hannah had helped Mary to clean herself. Auntie Sanni had moved her out of the bungalow into the room next to the Fishers. There Hannah had put her almost bodily to bed. Mary had gone into a deep sleep with Lady Fisher watchful in the next room. "Eighteen and a widow," she had said in grief.

Olga Manning—it was still difficult for Patna Hall to think of her as Olga Armstrong—had tactfully gone down to the bungalow. "Do you mind being there alone?" asked Sir John.

"I think I am past minding anything."

Now Sir John was on the telephone trying to get calls through to England and New York. "Mary," he had said, "you must tell Rory."

"Rory? What is this to do with Rory?" her look seemed to say. "Rory may be in New York, Washington, Peru."

"It's quite easy to telephone any of them."

"I know. At school I used to have to call all kinds of places but if I did, what could he do?"

"Look after you," but Sir John refrained from saying it. "And Blaise's people. His poor mother . . ."

"Mrs. Browne? Yes," said Mary. "I know I must speak to Mrs. Browne."

"Perhaps tomorrow," said Sir John. "For now, better let me."

"If you would."

The telephone system at Konak was antiquated. "It takes time to get through," Auntie Sanni always told her guests. "You need to have patience," and now, "Kuku should have got through for you." For the first time that day Auntie Sanni was exasperated.

The beach was empty now. All the fishing boats had come back, the coastguard speedboat had gone. There was no more they could do. Thambi had let them go and sorrowfully made his way back to the gatehouse, where, for once, Shyama had made him an evening meal. "Is my fault," he had said miserably again and again. "I am guard."

"Not all night as well as all day." Auntie Sanni had tried to comfort him. "Besides, Browne Sahib was headstrong."

The villagers, too, had gone back to the village—those who had not gone to Ghandara to vote or had come back. A drum was beating but mournfully, though, as usual, smoke from the cooking fires had begun to go up. "Life has to go on," said Auntie Sanni.

At Patna Hall the cookhouse was already lit; Samuel, in the dining room, was beginning his ritual. "They must have dinner," though who would come he did not know. Not, of course, Dr. Coomaraswamy or Mr. Srinivasan— Samuel had not thought it respectful to switch on the news. Not, he was glad to think, Mr. Menzies. Mrs. Manning, perhaps. Sir John and Lady Fisher, Miss Sanni, Colonel Sahib—that evening the Hall was closed to outsiders. "Attend to the bar," he told Ganga, "that good-for-nothing will not come down."

Auntie Sanni herself had bathed and changed; Colonel McIndoe had dressed, and as usual walking together, they went up to the knoll where they sat on the bench. Every now and then Colonel McIndoe's hand patted Auntie Sanni's knee.

"It looks all just the same," she said at last. Patna Hall and its domain, its private beach where the net was up and locked; today no one had wanted to go swimming. The palm trees in the village stirred quietly in the breeze, the hills behind were darkening; the grove was still darker. "But I think they will light the lamps at the shrines tonight," said Auntie Sanni. There was a little break in her voice: Colonel McIndoe patted her knee.

Suddenly she stiffened, stood up, shading her eyes from the rays of the setting sun as she looked.

"Aie!" said Auntie Sanni. "Aie! Look, Colonel. Look."

A lone figure was coming down the beach. Straining her eyes, Auntie Sanni saw the height and size, its blue-blackness.

"Krishnan," she whispered. "It's Krishnan."

As they watched he dived into the sea.

"Mary. Mary dear. You must wake up." Lady Fisher, usually so gentle, was shaking her firmly. Mary sat up, dazed. "Here, put on your dress." Hannah had put one ready and Lady Fisher brought it. "Wash your face." She led Mary to the washbasin, splashed cold water, dried her, brushed her hair. "You're needed downstairs."

Lady Fisher was grave, portentous. She took Mary's hand. "You know, dear, that Blaise is dead."

"Worse than dead." The shudder came back.

"No," said Lady Fisher, "Krishnan has brought him."

"*Krishnan?*"

"Yes, brought his body," and, as Mary did not move, "It's not frightening, Mary. It's touching. Come and see."

It was in the courtyard. There was no sign of Krishnan—Of course, he has to be at Ghandara, thought

Mary. The servants had respectfully kept out of the way but Samuel and Hannah, as privileged, moved to stand protectively by her.

Thambi, Moses, and Somu were with a circle of fishermen and villagers. They had made a bier. "It was the only way they could carry him," said Sir John, who stood beside it as it lay where they had put it down on the courtyard ground. It was a simple Indian bier of bamboo poles, laced together like a hammock with coconut fiber string, a bier the fishermen would have used for themselves though—as probably they would not have done for themselves—it was garlanded with leaves and flowers, hibiscus, marigolds, a tribute to Auntie Sanni: Blaise had been her guest.

His body was covered with a clean white sheet but Indian fashion his head, left bare, rested on the flowers. His hair had dried and looked strangely fair against their brilliance; his eyes were shut as if he were asleep. The healthy sunburn of his skin had gone: It had a blue tinge as did the lips; there were dark bruises, too, but the face was peaceful. Blaise was handsome even in death.

"He was a wonderful swimmer," said Sir John. "Instinctively he must have dived deep down and the currents wedged him between two rocks. There are caves down there but it's a miracle the sharks left him and that Krishnan found him."

"Krishnan is his father and mother's son," said Lady Fisher. "He risked his life going into that sea."

"He always does," Mary said it almost absently. "He and Thambi have been swimming there since they were little boys. I've been in that sea with him."

"With Krishnan?" Sir John and Lady Fisher looked at one another.

"With him it was quite safe," explained Mary. "He knows the currents and crevices and the sharks don't touch him, but Blaise . . ." Shudders shook her again.

"He went in without a helmet," said Sir John. "They were all locked up. Thambi thinks he would have been at least half stunned by the waves—mercifully."

There was the sound of frantic cries. Kuku rushed into the courtyard, her sari dragging, her hair half over her eyes. She cast herself down by the bier, tears flooding as she pulled the cloth back to kiss Blaise's feet. When she saw them mangled, her shrieks filled the courtyard.

"Kuku! Stop that."

"What are you doing here?"

"How dare you interfere?"

"You should show more respect."

Hannah, Samuel, even Sir John were trying to drag her away. "Come away at once," Lady Fisher commanded, but Kuku took no notice, only clung.

"I loved him. You never did," she flung at Mary. "I loved him."

"Mary, don't speak to her."

Kuku crouched over the bier, her sobbing went on. "I loved him."

"I'm glad you did," said Mary, and put her hand on Kuku's shoulder. "I'm glad." She looked at the others. "Help her, please, please," and Auntie Sanni came, lifted Kuku gently, and led her away.

Mary bent down, touched the flowers, not Blaise. She stood up and, "Thank you," she said to the men. "It's beautiful." As Thambi translated, she made them a *namaskar*.

They, too, turned away.

"Bumble," Mary whispered as she stood looking down at the bier. "Blaise. The sad thing is," she whispered, "that you would so much rather have had a proper coffin. I'm sorry. I'm sorry."

Saturday

■ ■ ■ ■ ■ ■ ■ ■ ■ ■ ■ ■ ■ ■ ■

Blaise was buried early in the morning next day. "There is nothing else to be done in this heat," Sir John had said on the telephone to Mr. and Mrs. Browne. "Even if you flew out tonight, you couldn't be in time."

It was so early that, as Mary had seen the morning before—Only yesterday, she thought—the waves breaking on the beach were pink, the sands rosy, too, in the first light. Auntie Sanni had suggested that the burial should be in Patna Hall's own small cemetery set behind the knoll and securely walled against jackals and roving animals. In its center was a gulmohar tree, now in blossom, a riot of orange and yellow. "My grandfather, grandmother, father, and mother are all buried, here," said Auntie Sanni, "as Colonel McIndoe and I shall be in our turn." She did not mention a little grave, with an even smaller cross that had only a name. "Mary McIndoe," the daughter who had lived only one day. "We will put Blaise here," Auntie Sanni had said to this second Mary. "They can move him later if they like."

Auntie Sanni did not say "you." It was as if she knew that, in her mind, Mary had handed Blaise back to the Brownes.

Overnight he had lain in the chapel Samuel and Hannah had hastily improvised. They knew what had to be done. A coffin was produced—"It was to have been mine," said Auntie Sanni. "The Colonel and I have always kept ours handy. Coffins do not exist in Shantipur, not even in Ghandara."

It was put on trestles in the center of the room, a wreath laid on it—Hannah would have liked a cross; candles in tall candlesticks were lit on each side to burn all night; there were cushions to kneel on and, "I'll watch with you," Hannah told Mary.

"Watch whom?" said Mary's puzzled look.

"I shall watch," said Kuku, who had stolen in to look.

"That Miss Sanni will never allow."

"Kuku shall do as she likes"—Mary was firm—"but if it had been me . . ." she looked at the candles, the shut room, "I should have liked to be burned on my bier on the beach."

Kuku was shocked. "English people do not do such things."

"Shelley did," said Mary.

"Shelley?"

"But he was a poet," Mary went on, "Blaise wasn't."

No Episcopalian priest was near enough. "He would have had to come from Madras." There was a priest at Ghandara, Father Sebastian Gonzalives was chaplain at the convent but, "Roman Catholic," said Sir John. "Better not. The Brownes might not like it."

"Why do religions have to have edges?" asked Mary.

Surprisingly, Colonel McIndoe, not Sir John, read the burial service and led the prayers. All Patna Hall's staff was there except Kuku: "I couldn't bear it. I couldn't," she had wept. Olga Armstrong, as she was beginning to be called, was beside the Fishers. The servants stood in a circle, Christian, Muslim, Hindu, every one of them from Samuel down to the sweepers including the two women who had cleaned up Slippers's ordure, but as untouchables, they had to stand apart, especially from the gardeners who were Brahmins—More edges, thought Mary.

I suppose Slippers has been taken away. Do they have

knackers in India? She shivered. I wonder, she thought
dizzily, if he and Blaise will ever meet—would it be in
heaven? The next world? Another world? Or would it be
in what, I think, they call limbo? And what would they say
to one another? You're supposed to forgive and the
thought struck her, How surprised Blaise will be to find a
donkey in heaven. To me, it wouldn't be heaven without
them. She came back to the funeral and listened as Colonel McIndoe's voice, modulated and clear, went on, ". . .
We therefore commit his body to the ground, dust to dust
. . ." But here it shouldn't be dust, she thought, it should
be sand. If it had been the sea—this time she did not
shudder.

> *Of his bones are coral made,*
> *Those are pearls which were his eyes . . .*

That would be right for Krishnan. Krishnan had had
to go back, after all, thought Mary, there is still an election. She looked up at the spreading gulmohar tree; Blaise
would have liked an apple tree or a rosebush. The sound
of the waves was too loud now. He was stunned by the
waves—mercifully. "Oh, God, stun me," prayed Mary.

"Mary. Mary dear. They want you to sprinkle a little
earth on the coffin. You have to be the first." All of them
sprinkled, the servants salaaming when they had done it.
Samuel and Hannah made the sign of the cross. Then the
grave was closed.

"Kuku, you will get up im-me-di-ate-ly." It was after the
funeral breakfast which Samuel, to fit the occasion, had
served at one large table, a breakfast even more lavish
than usual though nobody ate more than a little. Kuku
had still not appeared. "Now, get up. Dress yourself properly and come and do what you are here to do." Auntie
Sanni was stern

"I can't."

"There is much work. Everyone is leaving after lunch. Sir John will want his account, also Dr. Coomaraswamy. That will be large because of all the young people in Paradise. Let the Brownes' bill rest. I expect Mr. Browne Senior will settle that."

"The Brownes' bill? Blaise's! How can you be so heartless?"

"We are running a hotel. The accounts must be done. We must go through the register and allot rooms. Other guests will be arriving."

"Other guests." Kuku sat up. "Haven't you any *feeling*?" she demanded. "If not any respect? Out of respect, surely, we should close for tonight."

"And inconvenience and disappoint several people who are coming, maybe have already left home, hoping for a little rest and peace? I will give you half an hour," but in the doorway Auntie Sanni stopped and said more kindly, "It is time to stop crying, Kuku. I have been running this hotel for fifty years. In that time, of course, all kinds of things have happened, small things, big ones, bad and good, happy and tragic, but Patna Hall has never closed," said Auntie Sanni.

"Mary, would you like me to help you pack?" asked Olga.

"Pack?" It had obviously not occurred to Mary.

"Yes. Say if you would rather I didn't but today is Saturday, changeover day. Hannah is too busy to do it for you. I don't know if your room in the bungalow is let or not but in any case I thought packing might be painful for you, especially Blaise's things, and being in the bungalow alone."

"I don't want to be in the bungalow at all."

"These things have to be done." Olga was kind. "If you let me help you, it can be very quick." As Mary still did not answer, "I assume you will be going away like the rest of us."

"You?" asked Mary.

"Yes, I can't trespass on Auntie Sanni's kindness any longer."

"Where will you go?"

Olga shrugged. "Somewhere, probably in Calcutta. I have been offered work—of a sort."

"I was going to tell Blaise I would stay on here with Auntie Sanni without him," said Mary. "Now that I'm without him, I can't stay."

Samuel had not thought it respectful to put on the radio during the funeral breakfast so that Dr. Coomaraswamy and Mr. Srinivasan had to follow the news in the papers.

"Krishnan Bhanj triumphs in Konak." "A landslide victory for Krishnan Bhanj." "Though counting is still going on, Krishnan Bhanj and the Root and Flower Party already have a majority of some hundred and forty thousand votes over the other candidates, a near record for any candidate in elections anywhere in India." Dr. Coomaraswamy marveled, "A hundred and forty thousand plus! Even the great Aditya family landowners have forsaken Gopal Rau and come over to Krishnan."

"Mrs. Padmina Retty, eighty-nine thousand."

"Gopal Rau, fifty."

Every fresh paragraph was balm to Dr. Coomaraswamy—Uma cannot say now I should not meddle in politics.

There were, of course, other headlines. "Young English diplomat drowned . . ."

Dr. Coomaraswamy hastily folded the papers.

Though he and Mr. Srinivasan had been up all night they had come from Ghandara for the funeral. "When we have so much to do," complained Mr. Srinivasan.

"It is only seemly. We have been, after all, staying in the same hotel, Mrs. Browne has taken part in the campaign. Above all, Sir John Fisher would expect it. In any case we have to leave. There is packing up, accounts to settle—I must leave you to do that and we must prepare for this afternoon. We are holding a victory celebration," he had told Sir John. "But before anything else," he said to Mr. Srinivasan now, "we must pay condolence respects to Mrs. Browne."

"Is she able?" asked Mr. Srinivasan.

"Probably she will be lying down but still . . ."

"When my daughter had the measles"—Mr. Srinivasan was filled with concern—"we caused her to lie on a mat on the floor, a mat woven of grasses and dampened for coolness—to cool the fever," he explained. "Also, we surrounded her with fresh neem leaves. Neem is so very soothing."

"Mrs. Browne has no fever." But Dr. Coomaraswamy was distressed. "She is so young to be widowed. I do not know what to say."

To put off the moment, they lingered on the veranda and leafed through the papers again until, at last, "Speak from the heart," suggested Mr. Srinivasan, "then you cannot be wrong," but Dr. Coomaraswamy's heart was elsewhere.

He had not lingered only from embarrassment; in spite of all resolutions he had been waiting, hoping—A last glimpse, he told himself, though to Sir John, "I, myself, must go straight to Delhi and make my report," he had said, "also see Krishnan's father. I expect he and Mrs. Bhanj will come here. Then I must return to my neglected work and, of course, to my beloved wife, Uma," but, as he said it, the heart Mr. Srinivasan had spoken of felt like lead. He saw his clinic—he had been so proud of it—with its spacious grounds, its chalets, communal lounges and dining room, the big medical building, and it all seemed sterile; even the corridors were sterile, everything arranged according to Uma. Outside the clinic windows would be neat gravel walks, no vista of green lawns, white sands, blue sea, colors of flowers; no blooms of jasmine to put in someone's hair. There would not be the teasing voice, the laughter, even if the laughter, the teasing were not for him.

"It's getting late," Mr. Srinivasan reminded him, and Dr. Coomaraswamy was forced to ask Samuel, "Where is the little memsahib?"

"She helping Miss Sanni with the accountings."

That shocked both the doctor and Mr. Srinivasan.

"Surely she should be weeping?"

"A widow should weep."

"She is in the office," Samuel assured them.

Mary had never seen Auntie Sanni as pressed—Come to that, I have never seen her pressed at all. Now she was busy in her office, busy at reception, in the linen and storerooms.

Olga had been right: The packing had not taken long, the luggage was soon ready, Mary's separate from Blaise's, ". . . which will go to England if his father and mother want it." Mary looked at the golf clubs in their heavy bag, the tennis rackets in their presses, the camera, and turned away. His watch had gone; the signet ring she had put in the pocket of her shorts. Then, going to find Auntie Sanni in the office, seeing her desk littered with papers, account sheets, stacks of small signed chits on different spikes, "Can I help?" asked Mary. "I'm quite good at accounts."

"That's more than I am." Auntie Sanni laid down her pen. "Kuku says we should have a computer but who of us knows how to work one? There is a calculator but I don't know how to use that either"—she sounded in near despair—"and there are all the flowers to do. I can*not* arrange flowers."

"Where is Kuku?"

"Lachrymosing." Mary had not heard Auntie Sanni be as cross.

"If that one takes on so much over what is nothing to do with her"—Hannah with two houseboys, their arms full of folded sheets, pillowcases, and towels, had brought the key of the linen room to Auntie Sanni—"what she do," demanded Hannah, "when she have real sorrow?"

"Perhaps it is real sorrow," said Mary.

"Pah!" Hannah sounded as if she spat.

"If you really could do these accounts," Auntie Sanni wavered, "but it doesn't seem fitting."

"It is. It is," urged Mary. "I should be better with something to do. *Please.*"

"Well, then. Here are the account forms. You see they are divided—hotel accommodation and board, telephone, laundry, drinks—each room has its chits. You check them and enclose them with the account. For Dr. Coomaraswamy there is another account for the young people in Paradise, they only had half board and then," Auntie Sanni said of what evidently defeated her, "you have to add them all up to a total."

"I think I can do that."

"You enclose them neatly in an envelope, *sealed*," Auntie Sanni specified. "Kuku wanted to add ten percent for service charge but no, we would not do that. Guests give or not give as they choose."

It was peaceful working in the office; the doves' cooing seemed gently healing. The stack of envelopes—sealed, thought Mary with a smile for Auntie Sanni—grew steadily. By noon she had almost finished. "Perhaps I can do the flowers as well?"

When Sir John had seen Mary come up to the Hall and go in to Auntie Sanni, he went down to the bungalow. Olga, dressed to travel, was sitting on the little veranda. "May I join you for a moment?"

"Of course."

"Mrs. Armstrong, Olga, would it be an intrusion if I asked you what you are planning to do?"

"I must do what I can."

"Alone in Calcutta?"

"Well, I don't see people now or expect them to see me. I shall have to earn, of course, some kind of living. Colin, naturally, has had no salary these past two years. There is a clinic I worked for in Calcutta, a poor one, not like Dr. Coomaraswamy's"—she smiled—"in the slums. They will take me back and provide a room but, at the moment, we're penniless."

"Then I suggest you let me give you this."

Startled, she said, "Oh, no!"

"Oh, yes! Alicia and I have worried about you."

"Worried about *me?*"

"Is that so unusual?"

"Most unusual, I have found . . ." She could not go on.

"Then . . ." and Sir John put a folder on the table.

"What is it?"

"An air ticket to London—London's a good starting ground—and a little wherewithal to help while you find your feet. We, Alicia and I, want you to take it. Will you?"

She was silent, looking at the folder, struggling, then, "I can't find any words," she said.

"It doesn't need words. Take it."

"Colin would tell me to accept."

"Well, then?"

"I can't, Sir John." The eyes lifted to his were full of tears. "There are no thanks good enough, grateful enough to you and Lady Fisher but I can't. I must stay as close to him as I can."

"For twelve years?"

"It may not be twelve years. He may get remission but, if need be, forever."

"They will only let you see him once a month."

"I shall still see him once a month."

Sir John put his hand on hers. "And I thought . . ." he said, "I thought I knew something about loyalty and love."

"It makes one do silly things, doesn't it? Like staying in abominable Calcutta. Never mind." With a smile, she gave the folder back to him. He had not seen her smile before; it transformed the ravaged face and lit her eyes to a luminous brown. "Please don't feel badly. One day, even if it's not for twelve years, I may come and ask you for other air tickets—for two."

"I go to my beloved wife." Dr. Coomaraswamy had repeated that when he had made his farewell speeches, flowery to Auntie Sanni, more flowery to Mary, "My beloved wife," but could not stop himself saying, "Miss Kuku, I think, is not appearing . . . No?" asked wistful Dr. Coomaraswamy.

"Our doctor," said Auntie Sanni when Mr. Srinivasan had escorted him away, "our dear doctor, fancies Kuku. I say 'fancies' because he will never get as much as a glance from her, poor man. His wife is a gorgon. Yes. Poor man." Auntie Sanni sighed.

Poor Kuku, Mary wanted to say, but instead, "Auntie Sanni, may I go up and see her?"

Auntie Sanni gave Mary a long and penetrating look. "I'm sure you will be kind," she said.

"Kuku?" Mary knocked again.

"Kuku?"

"Go away. I don't want any of you to come in," cried a hysterical voice.

"I'm not 'any of you,' " said Mary and pushed—the door had no lock.

Kuku was lying on the bed as disheveled as when Mary had last seen her at the foot of the bier. Her sari was half off and rumpled, her face so swollen with tiredness and crying that she looked almost ugly. Has she watched all night? wondered Mary, who had not gone near the chapel but stayed, watching, in her room.

"And of them all," snarled Kuku, "the last person I want is you."

"I know."

"Then why force yourself on me? What do you want?"

"To give you this."

Mary took the signet ring out of her pocket and held it out. "It was his."

"His?"

"Yes. Didn't you notice. He always wore it on the little finger of his left hand."

"The finger that the shark . . ."

"Yes." Mary hurried on. "Look. This is his crest, a stag's head. He was proud of that."

"Most people not having a crest?" Kuku whispered.

"Exactly."

Kuku seemed stunned by wonder. She held the ring close, turning it, turning it; her own little finger traced the stag's head. "He should have been proud. His ring—and you want me to have it."

"Yes. I think you should."

"What do the words mean?"

"They're French. Loyalty and truth. You should have it. You were more loyal than I and you loved him."

Kuku was driven to be honest. "Mary, he didn't love me. He . . ." she brought herself to say it, "for him, I didn't exist . . . until the end."

"That doesn't matter. You loved him." Mary closed Kuku's fingers over the ring.

"Mees." As Mary came out of Kuku's room, an apparition startled her, as did the urgent voice. "Mees."

Kanu, in his haste to reach her, was scrambling on all fours to the door opening on to what had been Mr. Menzies's room. His red shirt was as rumpled as Kuku's sari had been; his face, too, was swollen with tears. He has been hiding under the bed, thought Mary. Behind him, the room was empty, clean, swept, dusted, the bed freshly made up; towels, drinking water, flowers, ready for an incoming guest.

"Kanu. If Hannah—"

"Hannah!" He spat, got up on his knees, entreating Mary.

"Menzies, Menzies Sahib. Mees. Please."

"Menzies Sahib has left hotel. Gone." Mary tried to free herself but the small black hands held her.

"Gone car," sobbed Kanu, "no take Kanu. 'Get out car. Get *out!*' " he mimicked Mr. Menzies. " 'Out!' " Then sobs overtook him. "No take Kanu. No take." Terrible sobs. Kanu was suddenly a small boy woefully bereft. A gabble of Telegu followed—Mary guessed he was saying, "Where is he?" and, "I don't know where. Not know." She shook her head. "Ghandara? Madras? I don't know."

"Kanu go too. Please. Mees."

Mary shook her head again. "Kanu, I can't help."

They heard Hannah's bangles, her tread: With a cry of despair, Kanu vanished down the stairs.

Chota Memsahib." Mary had been promoted: "Little Memsahib." It was Samuel. "The telephone. Master's father and mother. They wish speak with you."

"Oh, no." Mary visibly shrank.

"They waiting," Samuel said severely.

The line was not good but Mary could hear the grief and concern in their voices—they were speaking on party lines—"Dear, dear Mary. Are you better? Sir John said . . ."

"Much better now."

"He says you are being very brave. Poor little girl."

Mary winced. "Not brave. Not little girl."

"Can't hear. Never mind. Just to tell you we are bring-ing darling Blaise home from that horrible place."

"*Horrible* place?" From the open telephone kiosk Mary could catch a glimpse of the garden, gulmohar trees and pink and white acacias, parakeets flying in them. She could hear Auntie Sanni's doves and, distantly, the sound of the waves, feel the sea breeze, warm, scented. She tried to come back to the telephone. "Take Blaise?"

The voices seemed to go on in a meaningless babble. "I don't understand," said Mary.

"Never mind. We don't want to distress you, dear child, Sir John will explain," and, "Mary, darling," came Mrs. Browne's voice, "the moment you are home, you must come straight to us."

"Home?" asked Mary, bewildered.

"Yes, Archie has been trying to get in touch with Rory."

"I don't know exactly where Rory is," said Mary.

"Your own father?"—faint disapproval.

"I often don't know where he is."

"Can't hear. Never mind, get Sir John. Don't worry. We'll take care of you."

I can take care of myself—but this new and learning-to-be-more-gracious Mary did not say it, only, "Thank you . . . thank . . ." Unexpected sobs overtook her. Sir John quietly put her out of the way.

"They said, 'Bring Blaise home.' "

"They mean back to England."

"How?" The telephone call, its jerk into reality, had amazed Mary.

"A special coffin is made, then they fly him home by air."

"You mean dig him up and bury him again?"

"Dear Mary! I hope you didn't say that to his mother?"

"That's what it is, isn't it?"

Like Mrs. Browne, Lady Fisher wanted to be tender. "Don't distress yourself," she said. "It will all be seen to. You needn't know anything about it," but, "I think it's the best thing," said Mary, "Blaise never liked it here. I think it's what he would have wanted." Her face lit. "And it means I can come back here to Auntie Sanni. She says I can come whenever I like."

"Mary,"—Lady Fisher knew she had to be practical—"you're leaving here with us, of course, coming to Delhi?"

"Delhi?"

"John," called Lady Fisher, "John."

"You'll stay with us in Delhi, won't you?" Sir John used tact. "At least until we get in touch with Rory. If he's in New York I'm sure he'll fly over to fetch you."

Come straight to us. You're leaving here with us. Fly over to fetch you. "No," said Mary. "Thank you both and everyone, especially you," she said to Lady Fisher, "and Sir John for all you've done but I'm going by myself."

"Where?"

"To Calcutta. That's the worst place, isn't it? I want the worst. To Calcutta like Olga."

"To do what?"

"To try and do what Krishnan has taught me."

There was a silence then, "Mary," said Lady Fisher, "you seem to have known Krishnan Bhanj well, far more well than we thought."

"It *was* well." Mary smiled, a happy confident smile. "Dear Lady Fisher, don't worry. I'll find work in a hostel, a poor people's or children's home."

"Mary, you don't have to. There'll be plenty of money."

"I do have to. I need to do something difficult, dreadful. Don't you see I have to try and . . . and make up."

"Expiate," said Sir John, and touched her cheek but, "Isn't that a little exaggerated?" asked Lady Fisher.

"No it's *not*. Olga understands. She'll help me."

"How can she, in her situation?"

"That makes her the very person."

"At least try and tell us this: What did Krishnan teach you?"

"To love," said Mary simply.

Again the Fishers looked at one another in some consternation.

"Mary, do you know what you are saying?"

"For the first time I do."

"You and Krishnan Bhanj!"

"Not just Krishnan." Mary's eyes were dreamy. "Everyone. Anyone."

"Mary!" For a moment they were shocked, but afterward, "We ought to have trusted her," Lady Fisher said to Sir John. "Besides, we knew that Krishnan as a true Hindu would not in any way traduce another man's wife. While Mary . . ."

"It's not what you think." Mary had said that at once. "It's . . . it's that . . ." she had picked up a shell from one of the bowls of shells kept on the veranda tables. And suddenly she found words—I only had thoughts, could never say them—but now, "Most of us, almost all of us," said this newly eloquent Mary, "are shut in a shell and because it's so filled with ourselves, there's no room to let anyone or anything in, nothing outside ourselves when, if we only knew, there's the whole of . . . well everything . . ."

"Creation?" suggested Sir John.

"Yes. We don't know it but we are part of everyone, everything." Mary saw Krishnan's hand stroking Udata's gray squirrel back, saw her stripes from Vishnu's hand. "It's all there only we're too small in our shell to see it or feel it. Krishnan opened my shell and let me out. It's perfectly logical because"—she held the shell to her ear and listened—"it's only in an empty shell," said Mary, "that you hear the sound of the sea."

"All the same," Lady Fisher told Sir John with certainty when Mary had gone, "it's Krishnan that girl really loves."

"Mrs. Browne, please to excuse me"—it was a flustered Mr. Srinivasan—"but I have looked in Reception and there is no one there. Not Miss Kuku. Not Miss Sanni. It is the last thing I had to do and urgent as I have to go to Ghandara for the parade. You were in the office, Mrs. Browne. Can you help me?"

"If I can," and, "If you will come to Reception." Mary followed him and, "What is it you have to do?"

"Book a room, a permanent room, for Mr. Krishnan Bhanj."

"Here? At Patna Hall?"

"Where else?" asked Mr. Srinivasan. "He will have to come so often to his constituency. Not like other members, he will be continually among his people, working with them," and seeing her startled face, he said again, "Where else? Always he has been coming here, first as a little boy with father and mother."

"Of course," said Mary slowly, "that's when he made friends with Thambi."

"He will need to be much at Konak. He must be with his constituents."

The words were like small hammers driving reality in. "Here, not in the grove?"

"The grove, I think, is over."

When Mr. Srinivasan had gone and she had made a note for Auntie Sanni and entered the booking in the register, "Mr. Krishnan Bhanj, MP," which looked strange, almost foreign, Mary put her elbows on the cool teak wood of the reception counter, her hands over her ears to shut out the sound of the sea, her eyes closed to keep out the sunshine outside. "Understand," said Mary to Mary, "Krishnan will come and you will not be here. It is probable you will never see Krishnan again."

"Then you are not looking," said a voice.

Mary's eyes seemed to fly open, her hands to fall. It was Krishnan's uncanny way of knowing her thoughts but who was this elegant young man standing in the hall, tall, exceedingly good-looking, exceedingly dark? He wore a well-cut European suit of fine linen, a shirt of palest blue that set off his good looks, a public school tie—Harrow? wondered Mary—pale socks, and polished shoes; his hair was cut and brushed back. "Ready for the victory parade," said Krishnan.

Then he came closer, "Mary, I am sorry. Deeply, deeply sorry. I wish I hadn't taunted Blaise," said Krishnan.

"So do I. We both did."

"We are birds of one feather."

"We have always been," said Mary, and, unsteadily, "Except . . . Krishnan, I can't forgive Blaise for Slippers. The rest I can manage but that . . ."

"It is still raw," said Krishnan. "Still sore."

"But for us, it's over." "Over" seemed a desolate word.

"Not at all," said Krishnan. "When something is over, something else begins. Therefore"—Krishnan still kept some tags of old-fashioned English—"we shall see one another again."

"I don't think so. I shall be, I hope, working in a slum in Calcutta. You will be in Delhi in Parliament. Don't they call it the Round House?"

"The Monkey House," said Krishnan. "I am still not there yet. Also, I may not stay there just as you may not stay in your slum. Perhaps one day, when we are old, Auntie Sanni might ask us to run Patna Hall for her. That would be fun."

"Yes," said Mary fervently.

"And, Mary, I should very much like you to meet my father and mother. And now," said Krishnan, "let's go and have a drink."

Mary came around the reception desk counter. "I have never known you to drink anything but coconut water and that out of a coconut shell."

"Monkeys can change their ways," said Krishnan.

"Krishnan. Sir John. Krishnan. Sir John." The frantic voice reached the drawing room where they were all gathered; a sudden squall of rain had driven them from the veranda where Kuku, dressed and groomed, only her face still marked with tearstains, her eyelids red, had been serving coffee after luncheon—a special luncheon that Samuel had been allowed to plan as if to show that Patna Hall was still Patna Hall, "no matter what," as Auntie Sanni said. The luncheon had included mulligatawny soup.

It was also a farewell to which the drawing room lent a certain stateliness. Everyone was ready to go; the luggage was in the cars. When Kuku finished serving, she began taking around the visitors' book for signing when Dr. Coomaraswamy, his bald head and coat shoulders wet with rain, came in panting, Mr. Srinivasan at his heels. "Sir John! Sir John!"

"Doctor! What is it?"

"It is that"—Dr. Coomaraswamy almost choked—"it is that in two hours we should be holding the victory parade, ju-bi-lant-ly. We were—" Dr. Coomaraswamy really did choke.

"We were dry and home," Mr. Srinivasan helped him. "Krishnan has won by a hundred and sixty-nine thousand votes, far over Padmina Retty. A record! A hundred and sixty-nine thousand."

"I myself was so jubilant. Now look at this. *Look* at this!" Dr. Coomaraswamy had a typewritten sheet in his hand. "Scandal!" cried Dr. Coomaraswamy in an extreme of horror. "We cannot have scandal now."

"But we have," cried Mr. Srinivasan.

"No Member of Parliament can afford scandal. Oh, why didn't you tell me, Krishnan? You could have confided. We could have prevented. Sir John, you have influence in London, more influence here but even you, I think, cannot avert this."

"But it must be stopped." Mr. Srinivasan was wringing his hands.

"Stopped! It must be blown sky-high but who is to blow it? How can we block this?"

"You can't."

Mr. Menzies, as cool as Dr. Coomaraswamy was hot, sauntered into the room. "Coomaraswamy is right," he said, "not even you, Sir John, can stop it. The injunction is over. This is public news now. News."

"What news?" Krishnan stood up.

"Ah! The successful candidate, God Krishnan!" Mr. Menzies made a mock bow.

"Tell us what news." Krishnan was unperturbed.

"I suggest you read it," said Mr. Menzies. "Read it aloud. As the doctor seems upset, for which he has every reason as you shall hear—perhaps you, Sir John?"

Sir John took the sheets with disdain. " 'The gods amuse themselves,' " he read aloud. " 'Indeed they do! Who was the dressed-up girl who traveled Konak with Krishnan Bhanj on his lorry? Was she Radha the goddess, conveniently come to life, or was she, in fact, the young bride of Mr. Blaise Browne who has so mysteriously drowned? What was Mrs. Browne doing alone with Krishnan in the grove at Shantipur where he had made his ashram? An ashram for two?

" 'Is it surprising that there was a midnight quarrel on the sands? A quarrel that ended in Mr. Browne's being knocked down after which a certain lady did not come back to her hotel all night, the night on which Mr. Browne took an unaccountable swim in a sea he knew to be dangerous, so dangerous he might not come back. One has to ask, "Did he want to come back?"

" 'Krishnan Bhanj has won his election in a landslide of triumph. Could it not turn into an avalanche to bury him?

" 'Krishnan Bhanj took the vow of silence we have heard so much about; it would seem he took no vow of anything else. How ironic if his—shall we call it appetite?—and his temper, will silence him forever.' "

The appalled stillness was broken by a shriek of joy. "Menzies Sahib! Menzies Sahib!" A scurry of small feet and into the drawing room hurtled Kanu in his red shirt, his face bright with happiness as he flung himself on Mr. Menzies. "Sahib back. Come back for Kanu. Sahib! Sahib!"

"Well," said Krishnan, "your little spy."

Kanu clung to Mr. Menzies, the curly head rubbing against him, his face upturned in rapture. "Sahib. Kanu's Sahib."

"*Chūp!* Get out!" Mr. Menzies wrenched the thin arms away. There was a slap, a piteous cry. "Haven't I told you? Go!"

He was holding Kanu by the back of his shirt, shaking him, when Auntie Sanni spoke, "Let that boy go. How dare you hurt a child in my drawing room?" She said a few words in Telegu to Kanu as he stood whimpering and cowering, then clapped her hands.

Samuel appeared as if by magic—"Or not magic," Krishnan murmured to Mary, "he has been listening."

"Samuel take Kanu away," Auntie Sanni said in English. "Keep him. Don't let him out of your sight and send for his father and mother. We shall be needing them."

When Samuel had taken Kanu, "That boy," said Mr. Menzies in bravado, "has been pestering me all this week."

"So you pestered him with silk shirts, a watch, car rides, sweets," said Krishnan. "Or should we say paid him?"

"Krishnan, please," Dr. Coomaraswamy interrupted in misery, "the boy is not important—"

"He is very important," said Auntie Sanni.

"But, Miss Sanni, time is running fast. Can we not return to our business?"

"Certainly," said Mr. Menzies.

Sir John came back to the paper. "I take it," he said with disdain, "this will go out tonight?"

"To every Indian newspaper. It is my own, shall we say, scoop? It will be on the evening news, radio and television. It may make the evening papers. London will follow suit, press and all the media, unless . . ." said Mr. Menzies.

"Unless?"

"It is always possible to buy things," said Mr. Menzies to the air.

"He is asking"—Dr. Coomaraswamy could hardly bring himself to say it—"asking eighty *lakhs* of rupees."

"Five hundred thousand pounds," moaned Mr. Srinivasan.

"Almost a *crore*."

"You are lucky it isn't a *crore*," said Mr. Menzies.

"Eighty *lakhs* is not possible. I have not got it. The party has not got it. All that I have is already staked in this election."

"Pity," said Mr. Menzies. "Would the Brownes not help since they would be, shall we say, distressed?" Mr. Menzies was smooth. "They, I think, have plenty stashed away—or your father, Mrs. Browne? The redoubtable Rory, Roderick Frobisher Sinclair Scott," he mocked.

"Blackmail is, may I remind you"—Sir John had even more disdain—"a criminal offense."

"So it is. The trouble with blackmail"—Mr. Menzies

seated himself on the arm of one of Auntie Sanni's sofas and lit a cigarette—"is that to prove it all the allegations have to come out, be made public, and you wouldn't want that, would you?" He turned to Krishnan. "Or you, Mr. Bhanj. Your parents are very wealthy. What is this worth to them and you?"

"Nothing," said Krishnan. "To them or to me. Publish your filth." He looked at his watch. "In precisely one hour I shall be facing my people. I shall face them and—Sir John, would you give me that paper—I shall read to them, but in their own language, yes, over the loudspeakers, what Sir John has just read to us here. Every word," said Krishnan. "Then I shall ask them what I am to do with my victory—forfeit it or use it to serve them: The Root and Flower Party is founded on the people, for the people. It is for them to decide but not one *anna* will you get from any Bhanj."

"And Delhi?" asked Mr. Menzies. "What will they think in Delhi?"

"What they think in Konak." Krishnan was steady. "My father is there."

"And London? I think I can say I am certain of London. They will be extremely interested in . . . shall we call it the personal side?"

"London is very far away," quavered Mr. Srinivasan.

"Not for the Brownes," said Lady Fisher.

"Not for Blaise." Mary, who had sat proudly up after Krishnan's words, hid her face in her hands.

There was a movement. Auntie Sanni, majestically massive among them, held up her hand, then said what they had all heard her say many times, "That is enough."

"You must all have wondered," said Auntie Sanni, "what Mr. Menzies was doing here at Patna Hall. Now we know—almost in full. As Ajax, a clever journalist, it seemed he was attracted to Konak by the scent of an unusual story, Krishnan's vow of silence, but he found more.

In elections there is usually something more, which can be very rewarding in a different way. That is perhaps why Mr. Menzies is so assiduous in attending them.

"I am not concerned with politics," said Auntie Sanni. "They pass but some things do not pass. Though I wish Krishnan Bhanj's party well, this attempted blackmail is not so important." Dr. Coomaraswamy gave an indignant gasp. "What is of utmost concern is the damage you, Mr. Menzies, have done or are trying to do to other people's lives: to a rising politician who has dedicated his life to his cause; to a young woman who, no matter how you make it seem, is innocent. Worse, a young man on whom your insinuations worked to such a pitch that it ended in his death."

"You can't accuse me of that."

"In part." Auntie Sanni did not falter. "And, perhaps worst of all, a child. Kanu may not seem of much importance to any of you as Dr. Coomaraswamy has said, but he is significant, very significant.

"I must remind you, Mr. Menzies, that under Indian law, homosexuality, even with consenting adults, is a criminal offense. Seduction of a child is an even worse offense and Kanu is only ten."

"What has he been telling you?" Mr. Menzies's tongue came out to moisten his lips which seemed to have gone dry; his pink was now a curious gray. "What?"

"Nothing as yet but he will. As you heard, Samuel has sent for his father and mother. Also we can tell Chief Inspector Anand."

"The police!"

"Yes." Colonel McIndoe got up and stood by Auntie Sanni's chair. "We shall give you one chance, Menzies. You will not only leave this hotel, you will leave the state of Konak today. I and two of Dr. Coomaraswamy's aides—if you will allow them, Doctor—will have much pleasure in escorting you to Madras, Delhi, Calcutta, wherever you prefer to go, but the moment you publish one word of your allegations we shall inform the police—as you said of London, they will be much interested in the personal side."

Mr. Menzies looked at him with hate.

"Well?" said Colonel McIndoe. "Yes or no?"

"Why do you ask me? You know I have to say yes."

"Very well, we'll go now. We'll arrange about your car. My wife will take care of Kanu. Doctor, please call your young men."

"Not yet." Krishnan, too, was up. "I have a few things to settle with Mr. Menzies." He took Mr. Menzies by the coat collar almost lifting him off his feet, and as Mr. Menzies cried out, "I'm not going to hit you," said Krishnan. "Unfortunately, you are as much protected by the law as we innocents are. I shall not leave a mark on you, I promise. It will be a little wrestling match, except that I do not think you are a match for me."

"No. No." Mr. Menzies's cry was almost a shriek but Krishnan only said, "Come outside."

"Congratulations on your victory, Doctor, and to you, Mr. Srinivasan," Auntie Sanni was saying as she stood making farewells. "I don't suppose we shall see you again for a time. Let us hope Konak will not need another election for some years."

"Miss Sanni, madam, Colonel McIndoe," Dr. Coomaraswamy cleared his throat, "we can never express our gratitude. This momentous victory . . ."

"Most momentous," said Mr. Srinivasan.

". . . is entirely owing . . ."

"Don't let him make a speech," Sir John whispered in her ear. "We shall miss our train," and, "Good-bye, dear Doctor," Auntie Sanni said firmly, "Good-bye, Mr. Srinivasan. You must leave, I know, for Ghandara. Your victory parade," and she went on to the Fishers. "John. Alicia. Next year and I hope more peacefully."

Kuku had drawn Mary aside. "Will you tell Miss Sanni you have given me the ring? They will think I stole it else."

"Kuku, they would never—"

"Hannah and Samuel would," and Mary had to admit she could hear their voices, "Give poor young master's ring to that good-for-nothing girl."

"I'll tell her."

Kuku gave Mary a kiss.

"Mary, come to us and Patna Hall whenever you can and bring Olga."

"I shall. I . . . can't begin to say thank you."

"Then don't. You will be my girl always."

"Always."

Mary had been down to the beach to say good-bye to Thambi, Moses, and especially Somu. They were gathering up the helmets to clean them, shaking out the umbrellas, raking over the sand, getting ready for the incoming guests. The umbrellas, like the sand, were wet from the rain.

They came to greet her. Mary had brought Blaise's splendid pair of binoculars to give to Thambi who took them with deep respect. "Memsahib come back soon," said Thambi. "Memsahib not be afraid. Sahib, he rest now."

"They are taking him to England"—Thambi inclined his dignified head—the ways of Westerners were unfathomable to him—"but Memsahib stay India."

"I hope so." Yet Mary could not help a sense of a knell sounding in her: The scarlet cotton flowers are dropping. Well, all flowers lose their petals, the brilliance fades. Slippers has gone. Udata and Birdie will come looking for Krishnan. It is over, thought Mary, then stopped. Hadn't Krishnan said, "When something is over, something else begins?"

At the same moment, "Look," said Thambi.

Over the sea, still dark from the storm, far out away from waves made angry by wind and rain, their crests a strange gray as they crashed on the shore, was a rainbow, a perfect rainbow, its arc in all its colors, meeting the sea on either side, "*Indradhanassu.*" Thambi gave its Telegu name. "Is bow of Indra." Indra, God of Storm, and Mary remembered the painting in the hill temple: He sets his bow to show that every storm has an end.

"Mr. and Mrs. Prendergast," Kuku read from the register.

"Number one," said Hannah.

"They are old friends," explained Auntie Sanni.

"The Right Honorable Viscount Normington and Viscountess Normington," Kuku read with relish.

"They have booked the bridal suite. Their servant can go in Paradise."

"Mr. and Mrs. Arjit Roy and three children."

"They will have the whole bungalow." Kuku gave a little gasp; if Auntie Sanni and Hannah heard they made no sign.

"Mr. and Mrs. Banerjee . . ."

"Two hundred *and fifty* sheets this week. Five hundred pillowcases," shouted the *vanna* in the linen room. "Worse than last week. It is *too* much."

"It was because of the election." Hannah tried to soothe him. "The election is over. This week will be more peaceful. There will not be so many. Come, brother," she crooned. "Take them and wash them."

"Wash them yourself." The *vanna* left them on the floor.

All the clamor had died away. Everything was . . . "normal," said Auntie Sanni. The fishing boats had gone out, come back; the catch was on the shore. The grove was silent, the village went about its daily chores. The *mahout* had taken Birdie back to the palace. A small gray squirrel, plump now and agile, played in the trees. "I wish you could have had a more peaceful time," she had told the Fishers as they said good-bye.

"Oddly enough, no matter what happens, here there is peace," said Lady Fisher.

"Yes," said Auntie Sanni. "Sometimes there is upset, this week a deep upset, but slowly . . ." she dropped into her singsong voice, "it is like the sea, the waves—they beat in such thunder, the wash surges up the beach but cannot help spreading into ripples. Then they ebb. Everything goes with them, in a short while there is not even a mark left on the sand. No. There may be a little mark," conceded Auntie Sanni.

Epilogue

■ ■ ■ ■ ■ ■ ■ ■ ■ ■ ■ ■ ■

January

Dear Mr. and Mrs. Browne,

[wrote Auntie Sanni who still kept her careful schoolgirl script—she remembered the e.]

I am writing to you at the request of Miss Kuku Vikram recently in my employ. She has gone now to better herself at a hotel in Bombay. She wishes me to tell you that a little boy was born to her here at Patna Hall on Christmas Eve, the son of your late son, Mr. Blaise Browne. There is no mistaking; the resemblance is extraordinary. The child is fair, with his father's blue eyes and shows promise of the same . . . [Auntie Sanni was not sure how to spell "physique" so wrote] physic. *A lovely healthy child. He has been baptized as Blaise.*

Kuku, who is now only twenty-one, is unable to support him, she is an orphan and has to make her way. She will make no claim on him if you will take him as your own. He is presently at Patna Hall with me.

I await your instructions.

Yours truly,

Sanita McIndoe
Proprietress

Underneath she wrote "Auntie Sanni."

Glossary

■ ■ ■ ■ ■ ■ ■ ■ ■ ■ ■ ■ ■ ■

N.B. Telegu words are spelled phonetically

achkan	tunic coat, high-collared and buttoned, as worn by Nehru
almirah	wardrobe
anna	small coinage equivalent to a penny; 16 to the rupee
apsara	celestial dancing girls dedicated to the gods
ari!	"oh!" but stronger; frequently a remonstrance
atcha	agreed, good
ayah	children's nurse or female servant in the service of women
ayyo!	as for *ari!* (Telegu)
bania	merchant, moneylender, shopkeeper
biri	type of cigarette made from raw dried leaves
brinjals	eggplant/aubergine
charpoy	simple Indian bed with wooden frame and legs laced across with string, usually coconut string
chatti	earthenware bowl; for a tea *chatti*, small, and smashed when it has been drunk from

chelo	get going, go!
choli	tight-fitting bodice
chūp	hush, shut up
crore	a million rupees, 10 *lakhs*
darshan	an audience, as for a king or holy man, but also, for the person attending, gaining grace by the single act of "beholding," looking without speaking or trying to make any sort of contact—certainly not photographers
dipa	small earthenware lamp, heart-shaped with a little wick floating in oil
dosa	pancake, sometimes stuffed, made from slightly fermented *gram* flour
durbar	state or court formal reception
durrie	cotton, woven, striped rug or carpet
gharra	large earthenware vessel
ghee	clarified butter
gopi	milkmaid
gram	grain
hut jao	go at once, swiftly
jaggery	a kind of molasses but thicker, almost like fudge
jai!	(pronounced "Jy") hail!
jao!	go!
kachiyundu	wait (Telegu)
kofta	ball of fish or meat
lakh	100,000 rupees
lota	small pot
lunghi	sarong
mali	gardener
namaskar	a greeting made with the hands held together as in prayer
pandal	a form of awning, usually connected with a religious feast day or a wedding; can be made of silk or cotton, brightly colored,

	or leaves, such as banana leaves on their stems
panga	a long blunt-ended blade with one sharp side
pice	a quarter of an *anna*
punkah	overhead fan, now usually electric-bladed
puri	deep-fried small round of puffy flat bread, sometimes stuffed
shabash	fine, good; well done
shaitan	devil
simile	cotton tree
tamasha	a great show; something done lavishly
vanna	washerman (Telegu)